S HOBHA DÉ'S SHARP eye for detail, her piercingly accurate characterisation, her perceptive probing of the secret depths of the human psyche are all evident in this volume. Godbolé with his fantasies about his neighbour. The pathetic cravings of Dheeraj, the highly successful advertising executive. Ageing Simran's obsession with beauty. Kalindi's discovery of herself. Ritika's wild and uncontrollable longings. Amla, the recluse born of a desolate, despair-filled childhood. Sushma and Asif—the newly married couple trying desperately to prevent the strained threads of their inter-caste marriage from snapping. Easily recognisable everyday people, their lives and souls laid bare, the subtle nuances in their characters brought out in stunning detail. Each story encompasses its own exquisite world of passion, romance, fantasy and, inevitably, hard reality. The author's lucy, racy and captivating style invokes vivid images, which compel the reader to identify himself or herself with the characters and situations of each story. The sensitive, introspective stories in this volume will linger to haunt you long after you have finished reading them.

O NE OF THE HIGHEST selling Indian authors, Shobha Dé is the Queen of Indian fiction. Born in 1948, she graduated from St. Xavier's College, Bombay, and began her career in journalism in 1970. She became the dreaded editor of the Bollywood magazine *Stardust* and later founded *Society* and *Celebrity*. At present, she is a free-lance writer and columnist, whose writing has cut across caste, class, age, sex, race and religion, and captivated the entire nation.

Shobha Dé lives in Bombay.

REVIEWERS' COMMENTS
on *Shooting from the Hip*

Staggeringly beautiful, she's also touchingly humble about her work. Looking into her eyes, I saw loneliness, passion, fear, humour, uncertainty, anger, sorrow, and enormous strength. Not at once, but in succession, a reaction to circumstance – like a chameleon. Rarely have I encountered such windows into a soul opened so freely. What emerges is what one reads in her work: enigmatic, straightforward, crude, erudite, girlish, wise, and, ultimately, uncontrived truth. She doesn't know how good a writer she is – which is *why* she is so good a writer.

Paul W. Roberts
– The Toronto Review

A mélange of themes, personalities, random thoughts, all forcefully even colourfully expressed – there is much that is amusing, outrageous, throught-provoking, even shocking. But above all, it is the transparent honesty and the facile prose that impresses... Dé is immensely readable. And whether it inspires derision or admiration, *Shooting from the Hip* is impossible to ignore.

– The Hindustan Times

Dé retains the reader's attention whether she writes on or about Bombay or godless persons. The authoress has the courage of her convictions and the ability to express them in punchy journalese. The prurient would be best aware *Shooting from the Hip* is also bereft of pornographic ingredients.

– The Telegraph

Rarely does one see an Indian author writing with such frankness and obvious feeling...

– Business Standard

She slaughters macho males with vengeance, and rattle-poisons her gender with disdain and disregard. She is Shobha Dé, and she is scintillating and straight. She is a ruthless writer with a ramrod of a pen, and a raging urge to kill somebody. She demolishes reputations and civilisations with effortless grace, and one thing she does not stomach is hypocrisy of any kind. She wields a powerful camera, and she needs to keep shooting that way, whether anyone likes to photoframe or not.

— The Tribune

It covers the versatility of Dé's writing, be it on politics, media, food, festivals, films, books, people, travelogues or articles pertaining to her city of joy and pain (Bombay) and much more.

— Free Press Journal

Those who have enjoyed reading Dé are certain to go for this book, and this is as good a collection as any.

— Newstime

SHOBHA DÉ

SMALL BETRAYALS

UBSPD
UBS Publishers' Distributors Ltd.

UBS Publishers' Distributors Ltd.
5 Ansari Road, New Delhi-110 002
Bombay Bangalore Madras Calcutta Patna Kanpur London

First Published 1995

Cover design : UBS Art Studio
Cover transparency : Gautam Rajadhyaksha
Cover model : Avantika Kilachand

Lasertypeset in 11 pt. Times Roman at Alphabets, New Delhi
Printed at Surya Print Process Pvt. Ltd., New Delhi

To My Critics ....
So There

CONTENTS

One

VOICES

IT WAS said that Sumantai made the best puran-polis in Girgaum. The funny thing was that nobody expected someone like Sumantai to be a good cook. Her younger sister Manik, yes, for Manik was "only a housewife". But Sumantai was a star — an outstanding classical singer with a vast and loyal following. Friends would say in wonderment, "But when does she find time to cook? Puran-polis at that?" Which, in a way, was true. Puran-polis were not something anybody could just knock off during a slow afternoon. They required planning, skill, expertise and a great deal of patience. And Sumantai's puran-polis were perfect, starting with their appearance — a light, golden brown. They were paper-thin as well. This was a remarkable feat in itself, given that a poli had a ball of sweet filling stuffed inside it. In order to get it even and flat, the consistency of the filling had to be just right — without a single lump. If it was even slightly sticky the outer covering tore on the rolling board itself. If it was too dry, the poli presented a shrivelled up, unhappy picture. Rolling out a good-looking specimen wasn't an easy job — any Maharashtrian would tell you that. And a woman — particularly an accomplished, talented woman like Sumantai, for instance, who could stun her family and friends with a neat pile of round, symmetrical puran-polis minus any dark spots, was obviously specially blessed.

Blessed, Sumantai most certainly was. First, there was the gift of her voice to be considered. Perfectly pitched, wonderfully modulated, with a range that astounded her critics. Manik sang too. But "only at home", as she mentioned apologetically whenever anybody asked. There were startling physical differences between the sisters as well. Sumantai was tall, statuesque, with a commanding personality. There was a certain restrained glamour in her appearance — nothing too obvious or dramatic, but evident enough in those special touches her fans associated with her — the fresh flowers tucked into her dark hair, the large, light eyes carefully outlined with kohl, pale lipstick gleaming over a generous mouth, and the trademark saree blouses — never matched with her finely-picked one-of-a-kind sarees, but imaginatively contrasted and embellished with tiny gold motifs, or narrow borders

"Queen of Melody. Queen of Beauty", they said about her as she swept into large auditoria, making sure she kept the crowd waiting for at least twenty minutes. Occasionally, Manik accompanied her on stage, sitting behind her famous sister, eyes downcast, concentrating on providing the right sur for her raag on the gleaming tanpura resting reverentially against her left shoulder. She rarely made eye-contact with the audience and seemed content enough to remain in the background, observing her sister minutely so as not to miss even the subtlest switch in tempo or pitch.

Their mother, the legendary Mangalabai, was still alive — a singer without parallel in her particular style. Mangalabai was in her seventies — a strong, powerful matriarch who oversaw the lives and careers of her two daughters. Manik would laugh when asked about her relationship with her mother. "What can I tell you? She is a goddess." Sumantai would be less exuberant but invariably respectful.

Mangalabai had retired from the concert circuit nearly two decades earlier after doctors had diagnosed non-malignant nodes on her vocal chords. She lived at Thakurdwar, not too far from her daughters. Each evening, the heavy wooden doors of her dilapidated old bungalow were thrown open and admirers from far and near flocked to meet her, to gossip about the music world, perhaps even to persuade her to sing — just for them. She rarely did, waving them off imperiously and pointing to some other young singer in her coterie. This was considered a singular honour for the chosen one. Nobody dared to refuse once Mangalabai had issued a command.

Her daughters met her regularly on Sunday afternoons, often bringing something they'd cooked themselves for her to sample. It was understood that on the day Sumantai made puran-polis Manik would bring vangi-bhaat. The two dishes complemented each other perfectly. The rice, richly flavoured and aromatic with diced egg-plant and subtle masalas, had a texture that was velvety without being mushy, the long basmati grains still moist but well-separated. It was always left to Sumantai to pick the day this would happen. The question of consulting her sister had never arisen, because, as Mangalabai said in her characteristic off-hand manner, "Manik will manage. After all, she isn't doing anything else. Poor Suman, she has so many commitments — all that and the puran-polis too." If Manik resented the arbitrariness of this arrangement she didn't show it. Not even when she'd already cooked the regular rice on Sunday and Sumantai called to say, "All right, I'm half-way through my puran-polis. Will you bring the vangi-bhaat as usual?"

Manik's husband did mind however. And so did her children. "This is just not fair, aie," they'd grumble, "What does she mean by ordering you around like this?"

Manik would smile and say mildly, "It's all right. After all, "tai" has such a hectic schedule. It's not fair to complain. She does what she can, whenever she can. Besides...she is older than me."

Manik's young daughter, Anisha, would snort, "Older, huh! She's just a bully. And you put up with all her nonsense, that's all. She takes advantage of you. And aji too."

Manik would cheerfully begin roasting and grinding all the fresh masalas for the bhaat as she waved her family's objections away.

Sumantai was childless. Her husband, Shrikant, worked as a middle level manager in an oil company. He was away on tour

3

most of the year, leaving Sumantai to run the house her way, rarely interfering in her concert schedules. Whenever he was around, they had an easy relationship, with a democratic sharing of domestic chores. Visitors to their home would be shocked at the sight of Shrikant walking out of the kitchen with a hot cup of tea for his exhausted wife. They'd mistakenly and predictably jump to the conclusion that Shrikant was "hen-pecked". He wasn't so at all. He just wasn't competitive or insecure as far as his wife's status and fame were concerned. They loved each other in their own fashion, even if the relationship was hard for outsiders to fathom. He rarely attended her concerts, claiming he understood very little about Indian classical music. This wasn't true at all. Shrikant was Sumantai's most discerning critic in private. And she respected his opinions. It was Manik's husband who had no ear for music nor any interest in it. Ramesh worked for a nationalised bank and played carrom with the colony boys for relaxation. Manik and he led a placid, eventless life, absorbed in the activities of their young children.

Mangalabai couldn't stand either of her sons-in-law, though for different reasons. Even though both of them had been selected by her after careful scrutiny, she found Shrikant arrogant and unworthy of someone as accomplished as Suman and she disliked Ramesh's utter mediocrity. She made it a point to let her views be known to her daughters, saying, "I don't have to be a hypocrite with my own children. Both of you deserve better men — especially you, Suman." The two women didn't mind their mother's pronouncements. She had always been strident in her criticisms. Mangalabai hardly liked anyone and made sure she said so. She claimed she lived only for music. And music lived for her through her daughter Suman. And yet, Mangalabai had resolutely refused to attend any of Sumantai's concerts all these years, claiming she didn't want to demoralise or distract her daughter. "After all, people are bound to compare," she'd say with a tired wave of her hand. And they did. If these comparisons bothered the haughty Sumantai, she gave no hint of it. In countless interviews, she'd say,

"Whatever I am is because of my mother. It is her gift that she has passed down to me. I am fortunate that she is my guru, my inspiration. But I also know I can never achieve her greatness."

Mangalabai was going to be 75 shortly. For her 75th birthday, a few admirers had decided to organise a modest function to honour her. They'd asked Sumantai to sing on the occasion. Sumantai had refused, claiming she was suffering from an acute throat infection. "I would have loved to...but my doctors have forbidden me...and you know after what happened to my mother's vocal chords, I'm terribly nervous."

The organisers had been disappointed and surprised by her attitude. But not her mother. She'd cackled with glee when the convener of the function had conveyed the news to her. "Of course, Suman won't sing in front of me. She won't dare to. I'm not surprised at all. Vocal chords, huh! She doesn't have the guts to face the true music-lover's verdict. That's all." Then, as an inspired afterthought, Mangalabai had added, "Why not ask Manik? The poor thing has been waiting for a chance for so many years. She can't really sing — but she does try hard. And she's so sincere...so sincere."

Manik had panicked at the thought. She'd told her husband and children as they sat down for their simple evening meal, "How can I do it? What will Sumantai think?"

Her daughter had scoffed, "What will tai think? What does it matter? She has decided to develop throat trouble to avoid singing. You have no such problem. Besides, our grandmother, aji wants you to do it."

Manik had looked uncertainly at her husband, hoping he'd back her up. Instead Ramesh had chosen to agree with his daughter. You must go ahead and sing. You shouldn't care about tai's reaction. Has she ever cared about yours?"

Manik had looked down into her thali. She hadn't touched the rice or vegetables. "If you want the truth, I'm nervous. I don't think I can do it. People will laugh at me. Compare me to aie and tai."

5

Ramesh said firmly, "Let them laugh. You are doing this to honour your mother — not to seek awards or regards."

Manik shook her head, "You don't know tai's rage. She won't talk to me again."

Her daughter asked, "But have you discussed aji's decision with her? Maybe she won't mind?"

Manik kept quiet and listlessly shovelled some rice and dal into her mouth. The family fell silent for a while. Manik went into the kitchen to fetch some chappatis and ghee. When she returned, she announced, "I'll do it. I'll sing for aie."

Ramesh looked at the children delightedly but kept quiet.

The function was organised in a large school hall in Girgaum. It was an unostentatious, dignified affair with about there hundred lovers of classical music present. Mangalabai was in fine fettle that evening. She'd groomed herself with care (her daughters had always known her to be a vain woman). Dressed in a simple, beige Maheshwari saree, she'd refused to take her walking stick along, saying, "I'm not a helpless old woman. I don't want to take it to the function." Instead, she'd leaned her weight on the arm of a young male disciple who had been only too honoured to help. Defying tradition and custom, Mangalabai, a widow for twenty years, had worn flowers in her hair and filled her frail, pale wrists with glass bangles. At the sight of her mother dressed like this, Manik had stared worriedly at her and in that one moment understood the sporadic rages Mangalabai was prone to fly into for no apparent reason. It was anger against her husband for having left her in this state — denied by society and convention to embellish her broad, flat forehead with a red bindi, denied a woman's right to string summer blossoms over her nape bun, wear brightly-coloured sarees, jewellery or anything else that might attract attention. Male attention.

Mangalabai had been a good-looking woman in her youth — tall for a Maharashtrian, fair, with grey-green eyes that Marathi-speaking people described as "manjri', cat-like. Her slightly hooked nose, thin lips and long neck leant an aristocratic air to her

6

appearance even though she came from a modest, middle-class background. When her husband had been alive, Mangalabai had gained renown as much for her superlative singing as for her flamboyant style of dressing. She had worn garters under her flimsy nine-yard saree, and polished pump shoes on her feet. Her chignon had invariably sported some elaborately jewelled hair ornament, while her fair arms had been covered practically upto the elbows with gold and glass bangles. She had always preferred a long mangalsutra, to the more traditional short one, which she had displayed over her clothes. Her forehead had been filled with kumkum, the size of a one-rupee silver coin. Mangalabai's other weakness was attar — even now she hoarded her collection of tiny glass vials from which she refused to let her curious daughters take even the smallest of sniffs.

For her felicitation programme, Mangalabai had virtually bathed herself in her favourite rose attar. Manik drew closer to her and breathed in deeply. "Aie you are smelling so good...just like...just like..." Mangalabai completed her sentence for her. "Just like when your baba was alive and he'd take me to the cinema...yes...just like that." She swept past Manik and onto the stage where she was received ceremoniously by the reception committee. Large satin banners announced the significance of the occasion. The hall was overflowing with her admirers. Manik waited in the wings. There were speeches to be made, garlands to be given and a shawl to be presented. The singing would come only after that. And Manik figured most people in the audience would leave by then. After all they'd probably come to listen to the absent daughter — Sumantai — not a poor substitute. Her.

Mangalabai delivered a thundering address. She'd decided not to prepare a formal speech since she didn't want to wear her thick-lensed cataract spectacles. But she had rehearsed her lines well at home. She spoke of her humble beginnings, of the time she had been kicked around by uncaring gurus; of the difficulties she had had getting concert engagements; of her terrible deliveries which had interrupted her fledgling career; of a husband who had been

7

frequently sick and in need of hospital care; of raising her two daughters — no son — single-handedly; of her eventual triumph and great success.

Then Mangalabai broke off and sipped some water. She took her time to resume. People in the audience thought she'd overstrained herself or perhaps was overcome with emotion. But when she spoke again, her voice was stronger than ever. She spoke of Sumantai and then of Manik. She spoke not as their mother but as a critic, analysing their respective styles, talking candidly about their weaknesses and strengths. Dramatically, she announced, "I now invite my beloved daughter Manik to join me on the stage. She has shown both courage and love by being here and agreeing to sing. By that act alone she has vindicated herself in my eyes. It will not matter whether her voice breaks or holds, whether she sings off key or on, or even whether she sings at all. I have discovered something today about her and about myself that is more precious than any public performance. I have discovered a daughter's love for her mother."

And then, Mangalabai folded her hands and begged for permission to end her speech. Everyone present was far too overwhelmed to deny it to her. Manik herself held on to her daughter and sobbed. Mangalabai, dry-eyed and proud, indicated the function was over. She summoned her young escort and prepared to leave. As she passed Manik in the darkened wings, she stopped briefly to pat her. "Never mind, child, I hope you aren't terribly disappointed by my decision. You'll realise one day that I did it for you...to spare you public humiliation. The stage is not for you. Go home now. Look after your family. They need you more than you need music."

And Mangalabai was gone.

Two

THE MOTORCYCLE

PESI SHOULD never have got married. That's what everybody said. Everybody who knew Pesi, the Parsee colony's pampered bachelor boy. Single till his fifty-first birthday and none the worse for it. But not only did Pesi get married, he chose a Hindu bride. Mohini. A hundred per cent Hindu. And still a girl. Compared to Pesi, that is. She was nineteen. It was an absurd thing for both of them to do, said the relatives of the bride and groom. Mohini could easily have waited another five years—even ten before making up her mind. These days so many girls—working girls—got married in their late twenties. Nothing wrong with that. Better, in a way. The girls were more mature and experienced. But Pesi. What on earth had made him do it? People had always envied him. He had a nice, big subsidised house belonging to his old parents, a doting mama who fed him his favourite foods everyday, no responsibilities, no problems. An easy life. Nobody was sure what exactly it was that Pesi did for a living. Mama said he went to the share market. Pesi himself just laughed. Papa was far too "ghela" to talk. In any case, nobody ever asked Papa anything. They never had. Not even when he had been younger and all there.

Pesi had just one passion in life — old cars and motorbikes. At Nana Chowk, where he lived, Pesi had befriended the Goan owner of a large garage. Alfie was Pesi's best friend. They met daily at the workshop over Irani tea and brun pao. Occasionally, Alfie allowed Pesi to test drive one of the vintage cars lying with him. And he looked after Pesi's old Harley for free.

It was in Alfie's garage that Pesi first met Mohini. She'd come riding up on her new scooter, complaining that she was having a bit of a problem kick-starting it. She thought Pesi was a mechanic. Not that Pesi minded — it happened to him all the time. It was the grease he invariably picked up on the floor of the workshop as he peered into the insides of ancient beauties. It was also his dishevelled appearance — the khakhi or white drill pants and the blue checked shirt he always wore.

"Khodai," Mama would scold, "People will think my only son has no clothes. How can I tell them there is a cupboardful—all English. St. Michael's shirts. Untouched. God only knows when this mad fellow will learn to dress properly. It is the company he keeps. All these macapau friends. No proper Parsees. I say to him, "Don't wear English shirts if you don't want to. But at least utilise the Bombay Dyeing Company shares I have. Every year they go waste. Then I have to give them away to Shirin aunty and those horrible daughters of hers."

Pesi pretended to be a mechanic when Mohini came. He often did that with customers. And some had begun asking for him by name. "Give us that Bawaji Pesi — he knows how to fix things." Mohini's scooter was cute. Like her, Pesi thought as he examined the ignition. She smelt good too. He sniffed lightly—it was a floral fragrance. Or Camay soap. Abruptly, he asked her, "Have you bathed with a Camay soap by any chance, miss?"

"Yardley Lavender," Mohini replied distractedly, adding, "Please hurry up, I'll be late for college."

"Wilson?" Pesi asked.

"Yes, how did you know?" Mohini exclaimed.

"I guessed," Pesi said, handing her the keys with a flourish.

"Are you sure it will work now? It's new. Brand new. It's so embarrassing when it dies on me in a traffic jam. Everybody stares...."

Pesi smiled. "That's because you are so pretty, miss. People must be staring at you—not at your scooter."

That was when Mohini looked at him sharply and said, "You aren't a mechanic, are you? Oh God! You must be the boss. Do you own this garage?"

Pesi laughed. "Relax, miss. It's O.K. I don't own the garage, but I'm the owner's friend — that's him, Alfie."

Mohini thanked Pesi profusely and asked how much she owed him for his efforts. He waved her on with a cheery, "My pleasure, miss. Come back again. Soon. In case your scooter needs something." He was astonished at himself. Women left Pesi cold. Always had. He found them so... so...silly. Almost foolish in their idiotic preoccupations. He'd liked a girl cousin once, but that had been a long time ago. When they were — what? Nineteen or twenty? Then Armaity had gone and married Behram—a pompous Chartered Accountant. She had moved into a smart flat on Malabar Hill, and hardly ever visited their baug after her wedding. And she never invited Pesi to her home.

Apart from Armaity, Pesi had liked the wives of friends. Well brought up Parsee ladies with fair napes showing under their short hair; dainty, manicured hands and narrow feet shod in low-heeled shoes. Yet he hadn't felt the slightest regret at not being married to one of them. They were all right to meet at the club or over a late Sunday lunch. But after a point, he couldn't bear to hear the sound of their voices as they chattered on about school admissions and the price of malai kulfi at Parsee Dairy Farm. Mama had tried — and hard — to fix him up with eligible girls. Now, the only "girls" going were widows or divorcees, generally with a child or two, in search of a home for themselves and their liabilities. They weren't interested in Pesi at all. Besides, one look at his formidable Mama and poor old Dada in his reclining chair, and the girls fled, knowing that sooner or later they'd have too look after the two old people — nurse them, feed them, bathe them — since ayahs from the Parsee General Hospital now expected to be paid over three hundred rupees a day. Plus food. And rest.

Mama would grumble to Pesi about them later as they sat at the old, carved dining table and finished up the remaining mawa

11

cakes. "These girls today are too much. They expect everything — good house, servants, jewellery, clothes, ayahs for their children...even pocket-money for themselves. They want to be treated like Memsahibs—and give nothing in return. What do they take us for — fools? We are not running some charitable institution here. I want a proper wife for my Pesi — one who will look after him when I am no more."

Pesi would console her by offering to open another bottle of Duke's Lemonade. "We are happy the way we are, Mama," he'd say, "I don't need a wife. A woman means trouble."

Mama would nod in agreement and reach for another cake.

Pesi's romance with Mohini moved at a pace that surprised everybody, including Pesi. Three days after their first meeting, he pulled up his Harley at the corner of Wilson College — he'd spotted the little red scooter. In any case he'd memorised the number. Mohini was nowhere in sight. He parked and went towards the scooter, telling himself he was only checking to see if it was working alright. Crouched near the pedals, he heard Mohini's voice, "Hey! That's my scooter. What the hell do you think you're doing?" He leapt to his feet and smiled sheepishly. Mohini's face softened, "It's you. Hi!"

Pesi's hand flew to his hair—he wore it long and with side-burns (a hangover from his college days when everybody kept sideburns). "Just checking. Is it working properly? I was passing by...and noticed it here."

Mohini said jauntily, "Hop on. Let's ride down to Chowpatty and find out."

She took off at such speed, Pesi had to hang on to the sides in order to stay on. His hair was flying in the sea breeze as Mohini careened down, weaving her way in and out of the mid-morning traffic. Pesi leaned towards her and took a deep breath — yes, it was Yardley again. An old woman's soap. Why did this girl like it so much? He decided to ask her.

"Oh...I don't like it at all. I mean, it's O.K. My mother got a gift-pack on her wedding anniversary. She's allergic to Lavender and so she passed it on to me."

With a start, Pesi realised he'd never smelt a Hindu woman before. He'd always imagined they exuded a different sort of body odour — a combination of ghee, masalas, hair oil, talcum powder and that particular puja smell most Hindu shops reeked off — incense and camphor. This girl...well...she could have been a Parsee with that smell. A Parsee from a good home, that is. Many Parsees smelt of moth-balls, Dettol, eggs, rose-water and vanilla essence. But mostly, they smelt musty.

Mohini was a particularly high-spirited girl, Pesi noted in a pleased sort of way. And quite modern too. Unlike other Hindu females he noticed around him, she wore skirts and blouses — the skirt length not too short or too long, her legs neatly waxed, without a stubble, her feet pushed into casual pumps. Maybe she was a half-Parsee. It was hard to tell from her accent—she spoke English rather well, without saying "no yaar", "yes yaar" all the time. Her nails were nicely polished and pretty. Mama always said, "you can tell a woman's background by her nails". Going by that, Mohini couldn't have been from a low-class family. Those girls always had oil in their hair and that smudgy black thing smeared in their eyes. Parsee girls only wore lipstick and rouge — light pink, usually, to match their complexions.

Without warning, Mohini spun the scooter around and headed back in the direction of her college. Pesi hadn't had such a good time in years. Spontaneously, he shouted above the din of the traffic, "Shall we eat an ice-cream somewhere?"

"Sure," she yelled back, spinning her head around and nearly crashing into the car ahead.

Pesi took her to the Cream Centre. He noticed everyone staring—the place was crammed with students, some of whom knew Mohini. "Why are they looking at us?" he asked.

Mohini laughed, "They must be wondering what I'm doing with a buddha," she replied.

13

It was the first time Pesi became aware of his age and the difference between theirs.

Mohini placed her warm hand over his arm and said reassuringly, "It's O.K. Let them stare."

Later, while finishing their cups of butterscotch, Pesi told Mohini, "I know I'm old enough to be your father...but I like you...not as a daughter, you understand. Don't worry, I'm not married...nor am I a frustrated widower or anything. I'm just a confirmed bachelor...a happy one. Would you like to make friends with me? Go out sometimes? Or...do you have a jealous boyfriend?"

Mohini shook her head vigorously, "No one, ...forget it."

Pesi got off the scooter, "See me again? Soon?"

Mohini nodded, waved and was off.

A month after that ride along the sea-front, Pesi declared his feelings as they stood under the fly-over at Marine Drive, eating freshly-roasted ears of corn. "Look Mohini, I know you'll find what I'm going to say ridiculous. I understand, but I'm going to say it anyway — I love you. And...and...I want...to marry you." Before she could respond, he turned his face towards the traffic, away from her and said into the wind. "You can say no. It's O.K. say no."

Mohini leaned forward and took his hand in her own. "And what if I say 'yes'?"

Pesi swung around and lifted her up into the air, as passers-by stopped to stare. Mohini's eyes were shining mischievously, as long strands of hair whipped her face in the strong breeze.

"Let's celebrate. And then I'll go home and tell Mama," Pesi announced joyfully.

Mohini tapped him on the shoulder and asked, "Who will tell my parents? They will die of a heart-attack."

Pesi dismissed her fears. "Don't tell them in that case. Let's just do it. They'll have to accept once I am your husband."

"What about my college?" Mohini asked.

"Continue, where's the problem?" Pesi replied pleasantly.

"Where will we live?" Mohini pouted.

14

"At home...with Mama," Pesi told her.

She pulled a face. "They'll hate me. I'll hate them."

Pesi considered that and said, "Definitely. But so what? You'll be with me."

Mohini looked doubtfully at him. "By the way...do you work or anything. Go to an office? Business? I don't know one single thing about you."

Pesi put his arm around her. "You won't starve — that much I can promise you. And you'll have fun — with me. We'll eat a lot, travel around...and open our own garage."

Mohini's eyes twinkled at that. "Our own garage? Promise?"

"Promise." Pesi repeated.

And off they went — Mohini to college and Pesi to Mama.

"It's not possible. That Hindu girl has done black magic on you. Khodai! Marriage — and that too to a non-Parsee. Have you gone completely mad? Or are you so desperate for...for...sex. Go to a prostitute, dikra, if you have to satisfy your urges. But mark Mama's words—these sort of ridiculous affairs do not work. I won't call it a marriage since nobody in our community will recognise it as one. And mind — you won't be able to show your face at a Parsee wedding or funeral if you do it."

Pesi had anticipated all her reactions. He sat down in his favourite rocking chair and looked at his mother calmly. In the fading light and with the strange shadows of the window-grill casting patterns across her face, Mama resembled one of Macbeth's witches. Her crooked nose was turned away from her son. He studied her strong profile with the broad flat forehead and defiant chin. Her breasts, heaved with anger. Pesi geared himself for another one of her breathless attacks. They were usually quite dramatic. Mama would roll her eyes and start panting like a Labrador who'd been over-exercised. Generally, she staged these shows when she felt particularly neglected by Pesi — if, for instance, he'd forgotten to get her her favourite Khari biscuits from the Irani bakery down the road after two requests. Or if he skipped the morning-evening ritual of kissing her 'good morning' and 'good night'. This attack was scheduled perfectly. Mama had timed it with his departure. She clutched her throat and started to gasp, swallowing great big gulps of air. He thought of the large fish in the Grant Road bazaar near his home. Before Mama could get into the second phase of her performance, when she reached out weakly for support and collapsed onto the nearest chair, Pesi fetched her a glass of water, placed it on a table near her and left the house. Mohini would be waiting near the Fire Brigade Station. Till she'd come into his life, Pesi hadn't missed not having a phone. Now he wished he had one so he could talk to his beloved between meetings.

Mohini was dressed in jeans. She looked even younger — sixteen, maybe? "What did Mama say?" she asked eagerly.

Pesi grinned. "What I expected her to. And your parents?"

"I haven't told them. And I'm not going to. They'll die."

Pesi's smile froze. "So then?"

"So then...we'll go to the registrar's office and do it. No problem." Mohini grinned.

"And you'll come and live with me after that? In my house?" Pesi asked uncertainly.

"Obviously. What else? Do you want me to check into a girl's hostel?"

Pesi chuckled, "Wait till you meet Mama...you might want to do just that."

Mohini laughed. "Wait till she meets me. Ha!"

Pesi looked into her eyes. "You won't be mean to her or anything, will you? She's quite old now. Health problems. All kinds of problems. I'm the only son...she depends on me...for everything."

Mohini put her arm around Pesi companionably. "Why should I be mean to her? Unless she is mean to me...I'm not Mother Teresa but I'm nice to people who are nice to me. If she's horrid, I'll be horrid. Don't worry, we women know about such things. We can handle it. Leave Mama to me — I'll straighten her out in a week if she acts funny."

Pesi was only too relieved to be left out of the bout. He was a peace-loving chap. Hated scenes. Hated arguments. "Just like your Papa," his Mama would taunt, "can't fight like a man — always running away from responsibility." Now that Mohini had told him categorically that she didn't expect him to play referee he felt freed of an enormous burden. "In that case, let's do it immediately. I'll get Alfie as a witness. And one of his mechanics. You get two friends."

Mohini whistled excitedly. "Just like they show it in films. Shall we elope to some place—Matheran?"

"No," Pesi said firmly. "I'm not a coward. Let's stay right here."

Mohini looked around for his motorbike. "The quickest way to do it is to go to the Arya Samaj. Do you have some money on you? Five hundred or so?"

Pesi dug into his jeans pocket. "I have money...always carry at least a thousand bucks in case the bike breaks down."

Mohini opened her sling bag. "Good. I also have some. Took it from my mother's cupboard — just in case. And look — extra clothes."

Pesi laughed. "I can't wait to see Mama's face. Must take photographs when we go home."

The officiating priest at the Arya Samaj hall in Girgaum looked bored and disinterested as he went through the twenty-minute ceremony mechanically. Pesi overheard him telling a crony, "Some mad Bawaji has brought this young Hindu girl as his bride. Hope he hasn't drugged her or anything." Pesi let it go. The moment was far too important and delicate...and if Alife or his boys had overheard, they would've rolled up their sleeves and punched the man there and then. Pesi looked across at Mohini, radiant and glowing. "This ceremony...it won't make me into a Hindu or anything, right?

She whispered back. "There's no such thing as 'making' anyone a Hindu, silly."

17

Pesi still had his doubts. This was supposed to be a secular sort of place where anybody could get married, irrespective of their religious beliefs. But it looked suspiciously Hindu, nevertheless. And of course, the area was full of Hindus. Even though Pesi had grown up in Bombay he had never had any Hindu friends — close friends, that is. Somehow, even in school, he'd stuck to other Parsees. He'd known a Gujarati boy once, even gone to his house a few times, but he'd felt odd and uncomfortable. The family had been nice to him and all that — offered him snacks, Ovaltine...it was the smell that had bothered him. And this place smelt exactly the same. Perhaps the odours were wafting across from the Ganesh temple next door. Or maybe the Police Station had a small shrine where the cops worshipped. But the narrow lane leading up to the Arya Samaj building reeked of....of....Mohini, in a way. It was no use fooling himself. He had married a Hindu girl. Not all the imported soaps in the world could change the way she smelt. He would have to come to terms with that—the sooner, the better.

They signed some papers. Everybody clapped. Mohini produced two garlands from a small package made out of dried leaves and tied with string. There it was — the inevitable Hindu touch. Not that Parsees didn't exchange garlands — but those were made of spider-lilies and roses. These were strung from flowers that exuded an over powering fragrance — a fragrance so sweet it was making Pesi nauseous. Mohini also produced a box of sweetmeats — pedas made from reduced milk and cream. Pesi loathed pedas (pronounced "pendhas" by the Parsees). Why couldn't she have bought chocolates instead?

Alfie and Peter (his mechanic) pounced on the box. "Boss, let's go for a big peg," the garage owner suggested. "My treat, boss— your marriage."

Pesi looked at Mohini. She agreed immediately, "Let's. But before we do that, I want to go to the temple. Do you mind, Pesi? You don't have to come inside with me."

Pesi looked at his brand new wife. "Why shouldn't I come with you? But....will they let me in?"

Mohini pulled him by the arm, "Don't be mad — of course they will. It isn't an Agiary where only Parsees are allowed. Hindu temples are for everyone."

Pesi shrugged. "But what about my shoes? Will I have to remove them?"

Mohini said impatiently, "You can't go in with dirty shoes—that's obvious. Look...forget it. Wait for me at the entrance, O.K.?"

Pesi and Alfie stood awkwardly on the narrow pavement outside the small, modest temple on the main road. Devotees were thronging there for the aarti. Pesi felt awkward — almost like an intruder. This was the first time he'd come this close to a temple. It was so noisy and crowded. Hundreds of people were drifting into the courtyard—screaming kids, housewives, men on their way home from work, widows and widowers from the neighbourhood, students, pregnant ladies. Heaps of discarded footwear were stacked by the entrance — torn, worn-out slippers, scuffed shoes, sandals with broken heels. Pesi noticed the sad state of the footwear on view and thought that Parsees were far more particular about the sort of shoes they wore. Plus, they'd never go out in chappals or open sandals, like the Hindus. Why, even in the privacy of their own homes, Parsees always kept their feet shod in velvet slippers that covered their toes. Pesi recoiled at the thought of all that muck sticking to Mohini's pretty feet. There was squelchy mud everywhere — and nobody seemed to mind.

Mohini entered to the sound of clanging bells. Pesi put his fingers into his ears to plug them. That was another thing — Hindus were so noisy. They didn't converse, they shouted. Even in worship, they created a din. How was a person supposed to reach the almighty in the midst of such a commotion? Prayer required silence. Communion could be achieved only though concentration. And, Pesi pondered, their temples were invariably filthy. If these people couldn't keep God's abode clean, how could anyone expect them to look after their own homes?

Pesi stared disgustedly around him. He could see Mohini's outline through the grill. Her eyes were shut, her hands folded. He could also see the squat, slightly comical figure of Ganesh buried under mounds of garlands. Mohini — his wife — was praying to that figure? Pesi turned away. It was important to respect other people's religions — especially one's wife's. But he could see it was going to be hard. Pretty hard. Not that he himself was religious. But Mama — oh God — Mama was a borderline fanatic. Especially of late. She'd taken to saying her prayers at all hours. The little "divi" she kept on the small altar in her room was lit through the night. She made sure to adorn the landing outside the front door with auspicious rangoli patterns. And she read her religious books diligently. Mama had also joined some sort of a sect that believed in communicating with the dead. Reams of cyclostyled literature on subjects like 'The After-life and You' arrived in the mail. Mama pushed off for seances every fortnight. Fearing Pesi's scorn, she refused to discuss what went on there. She conferred with the neighbourhood dasturs, and started subscribing to the 'Parsiana'. "We Zoroastrians are dying, dikra," she'd tell Pesi over frilly mutton cutlets. "It is upto the next generation to keep our community alive." Pesi sometimes wondered whether that was a pointed remark, intended to prod him into matrimony with a woman of child-bearing age from their community. Pesi smiled. Well, Mama dear was in for a major surprise.

Mohini emerged from the temple looking peaceful. She offered him some prasad — a few grains of sugar and a piece of coconut. Pesi declined hastily. He couldn't bear to have any — not with all those flies buzzing around. Mohini insisted on putting a small piece of the half-bitten coconut into his mouth. Pesi reluctantly allowed himself to accept it. When Mohini wasn't looking, he removed it surreptitiously and threw it onto the dusty ground.

"I saw you," Mohini said accusingly, "You can't do that — it's a sin."

Pesi took her arm and steered her firmly out of the compound. He paused long enough to remove a sheet of tissue paper from a tiny packet he always carried in his pocket ("Just in case something dirty happens"). He wiped his hands and mouth carefully. "You

20

must be more careful about what you eat," he told Mohini. He reached across to make the freshly-applied sindhoor a little more symmetrical.

"Don't," Mohini pulled away, "the priest has put it there — it's not meant to be wiped off."

Pesi shrugged, "It doesn't match what you're wearing. Besides, it's looking very messy."

Mohini grinned broadly. "Stop behaving like a bloody Bawaji," she said. "I thought you were different... that's why I married you."

Pesi stared down uncertainly at his toes. At that moment, as he saw Mohini stepping into her strappy shoes, looking entirely comfortable in that strange, almost surrealistic, setting, the sound of cymbals combining with the monotonous mumbo-jumbo being recited by bare-chested priests in the background, he knew that maybe he, Pesi Agboatwallah, had made a major blunder. A wife was very different from a motorcycle. He should have stuck to his Harley.

Three

THE FAIR ONE

HE LIKED her arms. Smooth, fair, hairless, graceful, and in perpetual motion. He could watch her and them for hours as she went about her daily chores, a frown of concentration creasing her noble brow. Noble in his eyes, that is. Everything about her appeared noble to him. Starting with her being a Parsee. How elegant she looked in her flower-printed "house frocks"— so different from his own saree-clad spouse. And so "un-wife like", too. Unless, he reasoned, all Parsee wives dressed this way. But how would he know? Five short months in Bombay weren't enough.

He interrupted his shaving and looked swiftly across at her bedroom door. The curtains were still drawn. She wasn't up yet. He'd noticed she was a late-riser. Never awake before 9 a.m. Often, he'd see her husband's car pulling out of the neighbouring compound. But, the bedroom curtains would still be in place. He wondered about her life with the balding, bespectacled man with whom she shared her home. Surely, she couldn't have had anything in common with him. Medicine of all professions. She didn't look like a doctor's wife at all. He thought of all the doctors he knew. Dull, preoccupied, unromantic fellows. She looked romantic. The sort who probably read Keats. And played Chopin on the piano. He'd visualised her house hundreds of times in his mind. And he was sure she had a piano in her living room. A piano and lace curtains. She probably had her afternoon tea there served to her in style as well by wonderfully trained servants who knew how to pour correctly.

He lost concentration briefly. In any case, the shaving mirror needed replacing. He'd had it since his first posting in New Delhi. It had travelled with him to Calcutta. And now here it was hanging from an ugly nail hastily hammered into the door frame that led into the small balcony facing his fair neighbour's flat. That's where the morning light came flooding in from — pale yellow and slightly filtered. So different from the Delhi light and the Calcutta light for that matter.

He could hear his wife Indu in the kitchen. The children had left for school. The house was quiet except for the sound of his wife arguing with the newly-appointed servant-girl. It was going to take Indu some time to adjust to Bombay. South Bombay at that. But not because it was an unfamiliar city — oh no, they were both pucca Bombaywallahs. Born and brought up here, as they say. It was just that they'd lived away for so long — nearly ten years. Besides, during their earlier stay, they'd lived in central Girgaum. With his brother's family. Girgaum was so different from the Oval where they'd been sanctioned this smart flat. All his colleagues had been so envious. "Good for you! Godbolé," they'd said, "think of us, living in Ghatkopar. Sheer hell." Well, he hadn't done anything special to deserve this. It had just so happened that it was the only available flat. And he'd got it.

His wife had been nervous, initially. "Such an expensive area. Everything will cost more — even the vegetables," she'd said.

"Never mind," he'd assured her, "think how much we'll save on commuting. No monthly train passes for the children. And I'll actually be able to walk to work." Funny how the government functioned, he thought. Getting a flat in one of these buildings was next to impossible these days. People were willing to pay lakhs of rupees for a similar one. And yet, here he was, a middle-level officer in the Ministry actually occupying a three-bedroom flat in a posh area like this.

He took a quick look around his own bedroom. Even to his eyes, it looked exceedingly shabby. Navy blue curtains hung lifelessly from a springy wire fastened to two hooks on either end of the window. The unpolished, ungainly furniture was on hire from the common government pool. He paid ten rupees a month for the double bed. Ten for the cupboard and five for the table on which he kept all his files.

From what he could see of her house through the fluttering curtains, she had a large, comfortable bed with several lace-edged pillows on it. There was an upholstered armchair near the door on which she often sat plucking her eyebrows. He could also see one half of a carved cupboard with two full-length mirrors on each door. Sometimes, when she allowed her noisy children into the room and they threw open the curtains some more, he could spot a dressing table with an oval mirror. It was laden with bottles. Once, just once, he'd seen her applying some sort of cream over those wonderful arms of hers. She'd taken her time, lovingly stroking each arm as she rubbed the cream in slowly. He had felt instantly aroused at the sight and continued to cherish the pretty image. He'd also felt vaguely ashamed. Just at the moment, Indu had walked into the room with his bath towel and he'd whirled around guiltily to face her.

Indu was a simple woman. They'd been married for fifteen years. An arranged marriage. "Semi-arranged", actually, as he took care to clarify when asked. Which meant that they'd been allowed two supervised meetings and some conversation with the option to say "no" either way. This was a far bigger privilege than any of his colleagues had enjoyed. In his mind, there had never been any question of saying "no". His bride had been fair, delicate and fine-boned. Like a Ravi Varma calendar painting. He had felt instantly protective towards the tiny girl dressed in blue, who had sat stiffly on the sofa, her small, neat feet together, hands in her lap, eyes appropriately lowered.

Godbolé didn't have much of an opinion of himself. His mirror told him the truth. He wasn't a good-looking man. But he was vain all right. Of medium height and with an average build, Godbolé resembled any middle-class Maharashtrian man. He was proud of his thick black hair which he groomed with Brilliantine and took immense care of in the mornings. For years he'd used this particular brand of lavender-perfumed Brilliantine which imparted an impressive gloss after he ran a comb through his neatly trimmed, side-parted hair. Everyday, he examined his elongated nostrils carefully for nose-hairs. With a pair of pointed nail scissors, he carefully clipped the strays and then looked into his large ears— those hairs were worse — bushy and long.

Sometimes, he stayed by the mirror for a few extra minutes, hoping to catch yet another glimpse of the 'Fair One', as he'd mentally dubbed her. On some lucky days he saw her preparing for her bath. Those were the moments he particularly valued. There was something so enticingly intimate about a woman's bathing ritual. He even enjoyed watching his wife as she gathered her faded towel from the clothes line, looked for her underthings, picked a fresh saree from the small heap on the bed, reached for a white petticoat (it was always white, irrespective of the saree's colour), a matching white blouse (again, always white) and hair-oil. Once or twice, he had asked her to let him into the bathroom to watch her bathe. Indu had been horrified, "What is there to see?" she'd enquired, her voice slightly shrill. "I bathe like you bathe. Like everybody bathes. I don't want you in the bathroom."

"Why not?" Godbolé had persisted.

"Because...Because...I'd feel embarrassed...it's not nice for a husband to look at his wife like this."

Godbolé hadn't given up. "But why is it not nice? Who says it's not nice. I think it's nice. Please...just once. I want to see how you wash your hair."

Indu had sounded most irritated as she had snapped, "Haven't you seen thousands of women washing their hair under taps by the roadside? I wash it in exactly the same way. No difference."

Godbolé had eventually stopped pestering her. He'd even stopped thinking about it. In any case his wife always bolted the bathroom door, "in case the children come in". But he knew what the lock was actually meant for. To keep him out.

Would the 'Fair One' be objecting too, he wondered. To her

husband—if he ever wanted to be in the bathroom with her?
Looking at that "Baldie", he doubted it. Why did such ugly
uninteresting men win all the beautiful women? God was most
unkind and unfair. Did that fellow even appreciate his wife's
charms? Did he notice the way she fussed with her hair, for instance,
with her lovely arms extended way above her head? Her neck
arched gracefully? Her long fingers twirling the short strands into
place? How well Godbolé knew each small gesture! He could
visualise her getting out of her robe in the bathroom. She looked
the sort of woman who luxuriated under a shower—like models in
TV advertisements. His own wife preferred a brisk bucket-bath.
He thought of the 'Fair One' soaping herself like those models —
lovingly lingering over each part of her anatomy. Did her full
breasts have pink nipples like the foreign women shown in *Playboy*?
    At this point of his reverie, Godbolé would force himself to
stop. It wasn't good to feel so aroused over a woman who was not
your wife. Besides, he found a woman's buttocks more erotic than
her breasts. He couldn't permit himself to visualise hers too vividly,
though he was certain they were smooth and white, like polished
alabaster orbs. Velvety to the touch. Large and firm. So were his
wife's, if it came to that, he consoled himself. He had never
understood how women with small, flat buttocks could be considered
attractive. For a woman to be a woman in the real sense of the
word, she had to have child-bearing hips — wide and soft and
fleshy.
    Godbolé walked smartly to his new office. He had been given
this great chance and he wanted to prove himself to his superiors
though he didn't really think much of them. Particularly that man
Shah. Such a show-off. And so nosey. Maybe he was only trying
to be helpful, but Godbolé couldn't bear his constant questions:
"Have you and the Mrs. settled in properly? Have you got a ration
card yet?" What did he think? This wasn't his first posting, and
Godbolé knew how to organise himself. Maybe Shah was hinting
that he wanted to be invited over to the house for a tea party or
something. Well, that wasn't going to be possible. They didn't

even have enough cups and saucers yet. The nice ones had been carelessly packed and had broken in transit. He'd pointed this out to Indu but she had flared up. As always.

Indu had a shorter than short temper. Any small excuse—even just a hint of criticism — and she'd let fly. Godbolé was genuinely scared of upsetting his overly sensitive, highly-strung wife. Once she got angry, she didn't speak to him for days. It was awkward — especially in front of the children. And then later in their bedroom, she slept turned away from him after placing a large bolster between them. Small things upset her. Things that weren't even his fault. Like when the milk had curdled and she had had to send someone to get more from the market. Or when the sweeper had reported late for work. Or the washerman had forgotten a pillow-cover. Godbolé had tried to reason with her. These things were not all that important, he'd said. But she hadn't listened.

"No. For you, nothing is important", she'd snarled. It would have been different if he had been the sort to complain. Godbolé didn't particularly care if the pillow-cover was there or not. And he was perfectly willing to go without milk in his tea for one day. But Indu was fanatical about such things. Sometimes he wondered whether she used these little lapses as an excuse to get back at him. For what though? And why? Godbolé had always been a little baffled by his wife's rages. It had occurred to him that perhaps he wasn't the man she'd have really liked for a husband. That maybe she'd been forced into saying "yes", accepting him after the formal approval from his side. Funny, but even in this day and age, "the girl's side" had to wait for the "boy's side" to okay the match. Maybe Indu had had someone else in mind? Another more dashing man? A neighbour, perhaps? Or a distant cousin? Or maybe none of them, but a dream figure...far removed from what he himself was? But then, did Indu really know him after all these years? And, for that matter, did he know his sharp-featured wife? Deep down? They lived out their daily routines, taking care to keep strife at bay. But that was about all.

Godbolé appreciated the fine things of life. And liked a few indulgences now and then. He responded to the sad beauty of a dying sun as it sank into the sea. He read poetry — classical British verse. Occasionally, he strolled into an art gallery, especially if there were "nature studies" on the walls. Indu became impatient with such talk. She turned her face away and began to write her daily accounts furiously in a plastic-covered diary that had been given gratis to him during Diwali by shopkeepers seeking continued client support. Godbolé, for some reason, hated the sight of it. And the thought that his pretty wife's writing was restricted to entries in the diary's ugly, lined pages. Mind you, Indu was not dumb. She was quick and fluent on occasions, which made him feel ashamed and proud at the same time. Ashamed because he often underestimated her. Proud that she hadn't let him down in front of colleagues.

Colleagues. Most of them were perfectly hateful. And hostile too. Godbolé felt like a misfit amongst them. His office seemed to be staffed with mediocre minds. "Head clerks", as he dismissively described them. What did they know or care about the vast world outside? Most of them were stuck in their robotic, suburban existence. Taking a fast train to work. Another, back home. Gossip and free tea in between. And bribes under the table. He knew they didn't like him even though he came from the same region. He was Maharashtrian. Like them. And yet, they treated him like they treated outsiders — officers from Delhi, for instance. Or from Madras. "Punjabis" and "Madrasis" as they were derisively categorised. Godbolé figured his colleagues were jealous of him. Jealous of his big flat in a posh area. Jealous of his nice-looking wife who spoke English. And jealous of his competence at work.

Godbolé lingered near the open balcony for a few extra minutes. He couldn't bear to leave his home without a final glimpse of her. Sometimes God granted him his wish. He saw her drying her hair or hanging up her towel. He considered it an auspicious sign. An omen. Today, he wasn't lucky. He waited a whole five minutes, his briefcase in hand. Indu looked at him impatiently. "Aren't you going?" she asked without bothering to hide her irritation. "Yes, yes, I'm going," Godbolé assured her. "My entire day gets upset," she added, if you don't leave on time. I need the room to be free — can't you see the sweeper is waiting? If you don't go on time, everything gets delayed."

Godbolé all but ran guiltily out of the house. He couldn't bear Indu's wrath. Or her expression when she was in such a frame of mind. He thought he saw a flash of pink behind the curtains as he cast one final glance. But he could as well have imagined it.

Once he'd asked Indu whether she'd noticed the woman in the next building. "Which one? The fat woman with no chin or the other one with big teeth?" Indu had asked absently as she shelled green peas for dinner. "No...I mean the fair one. You know...the Parsee lady right opposite?" Indu had looked up. "Well...that's the one I meant — she has big teeth. Huge teeth. Her entire upper row sits over her lower lip...spread out like a fan."

Godbolé winced at the description. Strangely, he hadn't noticed the size of her teeth. Indu made her appear monstrous. But then, Indu did have an especially cruel streak in her. She rarely spared anyone.

After a few minutes, Godbolé had once again raised the topic: "She must be getting bored in the house with no work to do." Exasperated, Indu had asked, "Who?"

"That woman...the same one. The one you just said had big teeth."

"Huge," Indu confirmed.

"How many servants does she keep?" Godbolé continued even though he knew the answer.

Indu snapped, "Three or four. I haven't kept a count. Most people in this area have three-four servants. Only we don't. I'm not blaming you or anything. But Mrs. Aggarwal next door was asking me the other day how I managed with just one."

Godbolé sighed, "That's the problem of living in such a flat. We were better off in our old colony. At least there the neighbours

were in the same position as us. Everybody in the same boat.
Nobody had money to burn. Maybe I should request the office to
give us another flat. This area is far too expensive for us."

Indu stopped shelling peas. "See...I knew you'd take it this
way. I can't open my mouth without your misunderstanding me.
I was not complaining. But since you raised the topic of servants,
I told you what the neighbours said. That's all. As for that Parsee
woman — all she does is sleep. Nice life, I'd say. Get up in the
morning. Eat and sleep. That is when she isn't dressing up and
going out. The amount of scent she uses, my God. I can smell it
here—imagine—that too, over all the cooking aromas. That's how
strong it is."

Godbolé was immediately interested. "How often does she go
out? And with whom? Where?"

Indu resumed shelling peas, stopping occcasionally to grumble
about their staleness or to remove worms from some of the yellowing
pods. "How do you expect me to know? I'm not a detective. She
generally goes alone in the car with her driver."

Godbolé was tempted to ask, "And how does she dress on
these occasions? Have you ever seen her in a saree?" But he didn't.
He tried to visualise the 'Fair One' in a saree. It would have to
be one of those floaty, flimsy, flowered ones. What did they call
the texture? Georgette? Chiffon? And she'd wear a sleeveless
blouse, of course. He thought of her armpits if she raised her arms
for something. Smooth to the touch. Little hollows of ivory, Godbolé
mused. She had no hips. Sarees required a hip-line. Something
curvaceous from which to hang. Otherwise, they resembled
curtains— limp and shapeless. Indu had wonderful hips. The 'Fair
One's' were compact, narrow — but not flat. Maybe she looked
best in frocks. Once, he thought he'd caught sight of her on a
Sunday afternoon, going somewhere clad in jeans. The image had
amused him. Godbolé didn't like women in trousers. It defeminised
them in his eyes. Took something away from their innate grace.
But she'd looked quite nice. And tall too. Much taller than
she appeared in dresses. Her eyes had been hidden behind large

sun-glasses, her hair carefully coiffed. Maybe she had been going to some fashionable ladies' tea party or to the races.

Once, Indu had also been invited by the governor's wife for an 'At Home'. Godbolé had been most nervous. How would she conduct herself in front of such educated, sophisticated ladies? How would she look dressed in her simple clothes, her hair in an old-fashioned nape bun, her face free of make-up? All these things had bothered him, but they hadn't bothered his wife. She'd briskly taken out a freshly ironed cotton saree, draped it quickly, worn her best pair of slippers, folded a few notes into a handkerchief, tucked them inside her blouse and left confidently enough. Godbolé had sympathised. Poor woman didn't know what she was letting herself into. Anyway, he hadn't wanted to prejudice her. But his nervousness hadn't escaped her sharp eyes. "Why are you so tense?" she'd asked, "I'm not going there to be surveyed by a prospective bridegroom or anything." Godbolé had denied being nervous. But he knew he hadn't fooled his clever wife.

Often, he feared she was too clever for him. And that she found his company boring. It was just that they didn't seem to have much in common. Indu was a prosaic woman with few passions. It showed in their desultory love-making. If he was in an amorous mood, she wasn't. And she never gave any indication that she felt like going to bed with him. Admittedly, he wasn't very accomplished in this department. He knew it. He had read books. Seen photographs. Heard other men discussing techniques. But that wasn't his fault. Indu had been the first woman in his life. His first sexual experience. And it wasn't as if she had known a man before either. She'd told him plainly that she did not enjoy sex. She didn't like the physical intimacy of the act. Plus she found male genitals repulsive. He'd been hurt by her words. And thoroughly discouraged. Indirectly, she had told him she found him wanting in this department. Or maybe not. Perhaps she had implied that sex was for the lower species. An animal preoccupation. And that any man who indulged in it for reasons other than those of procreation was in some way a pervert, a deviant, a beast.

Over the years, Godbolé had established a pattern. Sunday afternoons. It never varied — except on those Sunday afternoons when Indu was bleeding. In which case, she indicated her condition by placing a pillow between them. Otherwise, after lunch (mutton curry and rice) and before his siesta, Godbolé untied his pajamas, lifted up his wife's saree, took down her underwear and did it. Her eyes were always tightly shut when he looked down at her face, and there were furrows of deep annoyance creasing her forehead. She lay rigidly under him, her limbs stiff, her hands clutching the sides of the bed, her legs splayed out at any awkward angle. The minute he rolled off, she pushed her saree down hastily, jumped off the bed and rushed to wash off any evidence he might have deposited on her thighs. This brusque brushing away of their joining together physically always affected him. It was like a slap. A snub. But he dared not talk about it. Indu's contemptuous silence was preferable to her open scorn.

He was certain the 'Fair One' was dissatisfied with her husband. They looked mismatched. What could that clumsy oaf be doing in bed to keep his beautiful wife happy? Not much . Of that Godbolé was certain. She looked like she had hidden fires between her thighs. She was probably the sort of woman who emitted little noises when she was aroused, who kept her eyes open, relaxed her legs and welcomed a man in. Not any man. But a man with a certain finesse. Godbolé did not delude himself that he was that man. But he could clearly picture the appropriate lover for her. Someone resembling Gary Cooper, for instance. Or Stewart Granger. She had the pale good looks of a silent screen heroine herself. A combination of Greta Garbo and Jean Harlow. Godbolé laughed at his own exaggeration. He was an old-fashioned man. Even his fantasies were outdated.

Godbolé was going to be late for work again. This had begun happening far too frequently nowadays. He had to stop lingering at the window like a love-lorn swain. Even his boss had noticed last week. "Godbolé," he'd said sharply, "sleeping too much, eh? Can't get up in the morning or what?" Once in his office, his mind tended to drift a great deal. This was something new. He'd sit staring at the same file for half-an-hour with nothing really registering. In the old days, colleagues would comment on the speed with which he disposed of his paper-work. What's more, he always did it so competently. He knew all the rules, laws and bye-laws. He went into each case thoroughly. "Your grasp is very good, Godbolé," his ex-boss had complimented him. Godbolé had accepted his words complacently. He *knew* his grasp was not just good but excellent.

He ordered another cup of tea. This was also something new he'd started. One cup after another. Over-brewed and too sweet. No wonder he was suffering from acidity. Indu used to turn her face away each time he belched. But he couldn't help himself. The extra cups also meant extra kilos. Guiltily, Godbolé patted his belly. No good, no good, he reprimanded himself. He'd stopped his evening walks too, these days. Why? Because he didn't want to miss seeing her. She was generally in her room at that time. Later on, she often went out with that...that...man...that husband of hers. He knew when they got home by the sound of the car. Even in deep sleep. Godbolé got up with a small start when he heard the sharp click of the car doors opening, and the rasping cough of her husband as he fiddled with the car keys. He'd never heard them exchange a single word. Not a single one. He'd strain his ears hoping to catch a sentence or two, but so far, there had only been silence. It had pleased Godbolé.

On Sundays, Godbolé would position himself on an armchair near the balcony and pretend to read the papers. That was the time the two of them were together in the room. With the door locked. How did he know? Because he could hear the servants knocking. If the day was particularly hot, their room would be sealed and the air-conditioner switched on. In a way, it provided Godbolé some relief from his vigil. He knew he wasn't likely to see her till late evening. When, possibly, after tea and pastries, her husband would emerge in his balcony after throwing open the doors. On these occasions, the man was generally clad in his Parsee undershirt, his

34

hair dishevelled. Godbolé tried not to think about it but he imagined what he'd been upto with the 'Fair One'. She never joined her husband on the balcony. Godbolé wasn't at all surprised. With an ironic smile he reminded himself that Indu had to be coaxed to sit by his side in their other, bigger balcony. In fact, she always found an excuse to avoid doing so. Funny, how she preferred her hated household chores to half-an-hour with him. "What is there to say?" she'd query, "What do you want to talk about?"

In her own way, Indu was very much an individualist. In his more affectionate moments, he thought of her as his "stubborn little wife". When angered by her, he railed against her obstinacy. "It's all there on the tip of that sharp nose of yours," he'd shout. And regret the harshness of his tone later. With some satisfaction he'd witnessed the 'Fair One' fighting with "Baldie" once or twice. Or rather, he had seen him gesticulating wildly, his voice raised, while she reclined on the bed in a queen-like fashion and impassively filed her nails. He'd wondered what provocation she'd given her husband — denied him intimacy on some flimsy excuse? That was what women did — they withheld pleasure when a man needed it the most. Indu invariably turned away on the days he came back looking for relaxation — or maybe that wasn't the right word. What Godbolé sought was comfort. Warmth.

Indu always misunderstood his intentions. Some months ago, he'd asked her, "Do you find me that repulsive?" And she'd replied witheringly, "I find all physical contact repulsive. Now that we've had our children...what more is left?" So far as Indu was concerned, that was her final word on the subject — not open to debate. Godbolé had withdrawn into himself scrupulously avoiding even a passing touch and going to the extent of shrinking away while walking past Indu in the narrow passage that led from their room to the bathroom. If she noticed, she didn't comment. This was Indu's usual way of dealing with emotional issues — she'd leave them alone, pretend they didn't exist, and then wait for them to disappear.

As it happened, Godbolé forgot all about his resolve one night, about a month or more later, when, after a small victory in the office, he came home feeling like Atlas and longing to boast about his triumphs. For a change, Indu was receptive and attentive. She even seemed enthusiastic as he recounted the debate he'd got into with his boss, repeating sentences for added emphasis and closely mimicking Mr. Satish Batra's speech down to the frequent, "I'm say". Indu went about her bed-time rituals smiling pleasantly, combing her long hair in smooth, graceful strokes and finally getting out of her day's saree into the soft, well-worn cotton one she preferred for the night. Dinner had been delayed that night so that Godbolé could watch a TV programme on "The Changing Face of Indian Commerce". Generally, this would have driven Indu up a wall with impatience — but that night she'd indulged her husband, even getting him an extra cup of tea as he sat on "his" armchair in front of the set.

The sight of her silhouette framed against the door frame as she undraped her crushed saree excited Godbolé. Forgetting that he'd sworn to himself that he wouldn't make a move till Indu asked him to, he reached out tenderly for his wife. To his amazement, she responded. Indu left her discarded saree on the floor and moved into her husband's arms. Godbolé wondered whether to make some appropriate comment...combine it with the standard endearments he reserved for these encounters. But he thought better of it and opted for silence. He patted his wife's "noble" forehead. Tentatively, she put her arm across his chest. He traced the outline of her body with his fingers. Indu didn't stiffen or pull away. Encouraged, Godbolé held her face between his hands and kissed her — first on her left cheek then her right. In the past, this would've been the signal for her to turn her face away jerkily, shut her eyes and hold her breath. Indu never permitted her husband to kiss her on the lips. But that night she did. Her mouth was soft and yielding under his. The pressure of her soft palm on his back was firm, deliberate. Something had changed. Godbolé didn't particularly want to know what or why. Indu indicated with her half-shut eyes that she wanted the lights in the room to be switched off. Reluctantly, Godbolé rolled out of bed and walked

36

towards the plastic switch board. His pajamas were making him uncomfortable. His vest was constricting his chest. As he reached for the light switch, he glanced out at the 'Fair One's' room — a reflex action. He saw her clearly. Distinctly. She was nude. He looked again quickly. Yes...there was no mistake. She was stark naked and brushing her hair in quick angry strokes. Godbolé turned away. There was nothing left to see. Not really. He turned the lights out and went back to his bed. It was warm and welcoming. The light across the compound was still on when Godbolé finally went to bed. Suddenly, it had become just another light. Some poor insomniac's little beacon. It had nothing to do with him. Nothing at all.

Four

THE DECISION

"YOU'LL BE arriving on Cherry Blossom Day," Mohan had told her over the phone. As always, the sound of the his voice — soft, reassuring, loving — cheered up Manisha. But not enough for her to feel entirely confident about the trip. Even though she had been to America before — five times. And she'd enjoyed all her trips, including the two months she'd spent living in New York. But this wasn't going to be like any other trip. She couldn't even call it a holiday. Manisha was about to leave a large segment of her life behind to join her husband who had accepted a job in Washington. "Why Washington?" Manisha had groaned the day he'd come home waving his appointment letter.

Mohan had looked at her, surprised, "That's a strange reaction. I thought you'd be excited. Just imagine, we'll be getting out of this dump finally."

Manisha had stared around their comfortable flat thinking to herself. "Dump? This place? It's home for heaven's sake. Our home. How can he call it a dump?"

Seeing her crest-fallen face, Mohan had walked up and hugged her. "Look, it's a great opportunity. A new life. More money. And it's the United States of America we are talking about, darling. Not the backwoods somewhere."

Manisha didn't — couldn't — tell her husband how badly-timed the move was for her. The last thing she wanted now was to relocate. She was enjoying her job at the bank. There was more money in the marriage now. Her relationship with her mother had improved. The servants had finally settled into a workable groove. She'd made friends with the neighbours. And she was ready to have a baby. How could Mohan have taken such a unilateral decision? Of course, they had been talking about a change of jobs for more than a year now. And Manisha had known all along just how keen her husband was to get out of India and back to the United States where he'd spent six happy years as a student. But the reality of the impending move hadn't struck her till this moment. And she didn't have the heart to tell him she didn't want to go. In fact she hated the whole idea.

She liked living in India. She felt secure and comfortable here. She didn't care if they didn't make more money. She didn't care if they lived in a flat and not a home. She didn't care whether Mohan made it in the fast lane or not. Dammit, all she wanted was their life as it was. Plus, a baby. Strange that the maternal urge had finally caught up with her. Manisha, at one point, had been pretty sure she preferred her status the way it was — unencumbered. But then, that's the way she'd felt about marriage too. And Mohan had changed all that. Maybe her making up with her mother was responsible for this new "baby thing" that had gripped her. They'd started to speak to each other after nearly ten years of silence. And bitterness. Today, Manisha mourned the wordless decade they'd allowed to come between them. She longed to make up for all the lost time, though somewhere at the back of her mind she'd come to terms with the possibility that it was too late now. A hardening had taken place in the interim. A mutual hardening of feelings and attitudes. It had become virtually impossible for the two of them to talk to one another without a careless sentence sparking off an ugly argument. Manisha sincerely wanted to change all that. Become more... more...what was the word — caring? It frightened her that she harboured such strong feelings still. Feelings that bordered on hatred, resentment and loathing. It wasn't right to feel this way about one's mother, she'd reprimand herself. A child generally reversed roles in later life. Manisha wanted to feel protective. And

40

loving. Only she couldn't. And that induced guilt...self-recrimination. Manisha invariably ended up feeling lousy about herself each time she met her mother. Mohan's Washington job would mean another break — a long one — just when the two of them had begun to reach out and connect.

The night Mohan broke the news to her, Manisha lay by his side stiffly. If he sensed her distancing, he gave no indication of it. Over dinner, his eyes had been unnaturally bright, his body language altered. He'd talked excessively and flapped his arms around discussing the terms and conditions offered by his new employers. "It's a pretty good deal, darling," he'd exulted, "better than I'd bargained for." And then added hastily, "Fortunately there'll be enough money...you won't have to work." Manisha had resented that. For one, he'd forgotten to say that in any case, without a work permit, who'd employ her? And secondly, with her basic qualifications, what sort of a job would she have been able to get? A baby-sitter's? A store assistant's?

Manisha knew she was being too hard. After all, she had encouraged Mohan to apply. She'd even been excited during his preliminary interviews. What had she secretly hoped for? That he wouldn't make it? That finally, he'd stop trying to get to America and come down to earth? It was probably just that. Manisha had been so sure Mohan would fall flat on his face, she'd been willing to back him up, even push him. "Anything to get this American bug out of his system," she'd told her mother. "Let him find out for himself how tough it really is. Mohan isn't a student anymore. He keeps talking about his campus days. Well...that was then. Ten years ago. The story has changed...."

It didn't seem like that to Mohan. He'd reverted to college slang. He'd pulled out his old moth-balled sweaters and coats. He'd started reestablishing contacts with "buddies" he'd roomed with. Manisha had observed it all indulgently, patiently. She'd been so sure that he'd be rejected and finally forced to accept the fact that his future was in India. Once, she'd even said to him, with an uncharacteristically cruel edge to her voice, "Come off it

Mohan — you lack the killer instinct. Even if you do get the job, you won't be able to survive there. Don't you read anything? Those people are tough and competitive. They'll gobble you up."

But Mohan had barely listened. He'd been far too busy planning. Abruptly, he'd cut her off and announced cheerfully, "I've found a travel agent who's offering cheap fares. Really cheap fares. Your ticket will be practically free."

Manisha should have spoken up then. She should have said, "You go. I'm not coming." But she'd kept quiet, still certain that she'd be proved right eventually. Mohan and she would stay put. Right where they were. And she'd have her baby.

Manisha's mother stared at her daughter thoughtfully. Soon, she would be leaving. There were very many things she wanted to tell her, pass on to her. She might never get the chance again. She herself was old — not old enough to die, but who could tell? Manisha was still impetuous, still immature. She'd hoped marriage to an even-tempered man like Mohan would have calmed her daughter down. If anything, Manisha had become still more restless, often unable to sit still or concentrate on simple conversations. With sorrow, the old lady thought of the ten wasted years, filled with suspicion and acrimony. It had been Manisha's doing — the cause a minor misunderstanding. At least, that's how it had begun.

Manisha had accused her mother of "taking sides" — favouring her younger sister in a trivial argument. And for ten long years, she'd nursed the grudge, refusing to compromise...apologise...make up. In that period, her sister had emigrated to Canada, her father had died, but Manisha's fury had not abated.

Relatives had hoped the rapprochement would come at the time of Manisha's marriage to Mohan. Mohan himself had come over to meet his bride's mother before the ceremony and seek her blessings. But not Manisha. "I will go to see her when I'm ready...and I'm not ready now," she'd said stubbornly. She'd also made it known that she didn't want her mother to attend the wedding. Mohan had found that particularly harsh, especially after meeting his mother-in-law-to-be.

"Come on, darling. She isn't such a witch. I liked her. She was good enough to see me," he'd argued.

But Manisha had shaken her head and said, "Call her if you want to but remember, it will make me desperately unhappy. You don't know how she traumatised me." Mohan had sensibly left it at that in the hope that his wife would soon realise the futility of her rage.

Manisha's irrational outbursts had puzzled Mohan. He had found it hard to figure out why his "sensible" wife sometimes flew off the handle without the slightest warning. But he had learnt to deal with her moods with admirable equanimity. The trick, he reminded himself, was to stay calm, not argue and fetch her a glass of water. That generally worked. When Manisha was in the throes of one of these black periods, nobody could reach her, not even Mohan. In the past her mother had rather tactlessly dismissed these radical mood-swings by saying her daughter was possessed — at least temporarily. She had half-meant it too. Confronted by her attitude, Manisha would isolate herself for days on end, locked in a private world filled with brooding self-doubts. "Sulking again?" her mother would taunt, watching her daughter's pinched, tortured face closely.

And now it was time for Manisha to go. Mohan was waiting anxiously in a cold, semi-detached house in suburban Washington. He'd picked their new home with great care. He knew his wife wasn't accustomed to living in isolation. She'd grown up in Bombay — she was used to the bustle of a big city; she needed the noise, the chaos, the madness that Bombay provided so generously. Downtown Washington could have scared her — it would've scared anybody. The posher areas in Georgetown were way beyond his salary. The place he finally found was in a predominantly white, "safe", yuppie locality, conveniently close to a shopping mall.

Though Manisha was anything but a manic shopper, Mohan knew that her first weeks in a strange city would be depressing, friendless and empty. He'd be at work from eight to eight — and she? Mohan knew how much his wife detested housework. One of her first thoughts when the Washington job came up had been, "Will we be able to afford a maid — at least a part-time one? Don't expect me to clean the toilets."

According to Manisha, most Indian men thought of their wives as nothing more than glorified domestics. She'd made it very clear when they married that she didn't fall into that category. "I happen to have a mind. And I plan to use it. If you're looking for someone to cook, clean, keep house and bed you too, look somewhere else," she'd warned Mohan. Her attitude had amused him and he had reassured her that just as she didn't consider herself an "average" wife, he too wasn't an "average" husband. "I want my woman to be a companion, a mate not a maid," he'd said fervently. And he'd stuck to it.

Manisha's disdain for domesticity had been duly respected with Mohan effectively running the house and handling the servants. It was he who decided the daily menus and looked after stores. He handed out salaries and kept track of expenses. What Manisha earned, Manisha kept. Given her schedule, she didn't have much time to spend at home anyway. Their neat but impersonal apartment was a place to come to for the night; a bed to rest their weary selves on. "I'm not house-proud," Manisha would declare to friends, a defiant edge to voice.

"It shows," her mother would comment, casting her eyes over a house which while not looking exactly neglected, didn't inspire anybody either. It resembled an efficient guest-house or a fussy bachelor's well-maintained apartment — which, in a sense, was exactly what it was. Manisha had no idea what her kitchen contained. And it didn't interest her either. Mohan, on the other hand, was not only a good weekend cook, but he took his food seriously. Manisha was indifferent to meals. As she'd grumble exasperatedly, "Food is food. Dinner is dinner. So long as it's hot and filling, it doesn't matter what it is."

Mohan, ever-sensitive to his wife's idiosyncrasies, had made sure their Washington home had a well-stocked kitchen with every modern convenience. He'd investigated the neighbourhood mall and found out exactly what was available. He'd told her over the phone, "You won't have to worry about cooking when you get here. It's all under control. I've filled the fridge with enough meals to see us through two months. Besides, once you get into the micro-oven habit, even you won't mind popping ready-to-eat dishes into it. Believe me, it's easy."

Manisha's mouth twisted into a small sneer. Mohan was trying too hard to sell America to her. What the hell, he needn't have been so impassioned. She'd been there, for heaven's sake. She knew how things functioned.

Her mother, overhearing one of his calls once, had pointed out to Manisha just how considerate her husband was. "Try and appreciate the effort he's making to see that you're comfortable. You sound so ungrateful," the old lady had commented.

Manisha had flown at her furiously. "It's easy for you to take his side. Obviously, he has to be considerate. I never wanted to go, remember? It wasn't my idea. He could've found a job here. He could at least have tried... I hate the thought of moving. I know I'm going to detest America. Don't be surprised if I decide to come back."

Her mother had shaken her head and kept silent. No, she wouldn't be surprised if Manisha came back. She would be surprised if she left.

Mohan located a small nursery near their house. He'd noticed the way other residents had filled their homes with plants. Often, when he parked his second-hand, shabby car next to the gleaming BMWs any Volvos in the driveway, he'd see young couples in attractive kitchens, getting dinner ready. It was such a pleasant sight — framed against the large windows, energetic, fit-looking blondes, their hair carelessly held back in ponytails, stirring foods in saucepans with wooden spoons, while their husbands pottered around mixing huge bowls of salad. Most of the young marrieds who were his neighbours had gigantic dogs but no children. He'd hear jazz playing. He'd smell food cooking. And he'd imagine these perfect people making perfect love later in the night.

Mohan was missing Manisha desperately. Missing her caustic remarks, her sharp retorts, her frequent nagging, even her aggressive quarrels. Most of all, he was missing her familiar body in bed. Mohan liked Manisha's skin and often told her so. "I love the texture, I love the colouring," he'd say, lovingly stroking her thighs. If his attention flattered her, she rarely articulated her feelings. But he could tell from the way she shifted her body and slid closer to him, or the manner in which she rested her head against his arm while he watched the news on TV, that Manisha was responding in the only way she could. And Mohan loved her all the more for it.

He'd picked their new bed with care. He knew Manisha liked a large one with lots of pillows. He also knew she didn't like to share blankets. Or snuggle with him through the night. Manisha was like a cat — content to be on her own. Bodily contact was restricted to the minimum. Once their love-making was over, she preferred to shift to her side of the bed and stay there, turned away from him. Mohan had got used to that, even though he longed for a night in which she'd stay in his arms, her soft, whipped-cream like skin touching his, her warm breath moving the hairs on his chest with each exhalation, her fingers resting lightly on his arm, her hair tumbling over his face, her thigh interlocked with his, her belly fitting neatly into the curve of his waist, her breasts moving against his side, the nipples grazing him gently.

Mohan pushed the images away as he looked at the newly installed bed uncertainly. Maybe Manisha would disapprove of the blond Scandinavian wood. Or maybe she'd hate the height of the mattress. It was possible she'd dislike the bamboo print of the sheets. Or she'd take a strong objection to the pastel-coloured duvets. He regarded the dhurries on the floor critically. He'd bought them in Bombay. Somehow, they didn't fit here. But Mohan had exhausted his limited budget. They'd have to do for the next year or so. He'd also positioned a carnivorous-looking plant near the dresser. Manisha didn't like plants. At least she didn't like them in the bedroom. She'd often said they emitted carbon dioxide at night and were bad for health. But Mohan hadn't known what else to fill the empty space with. Besides, the plant did look so dramatic, reflected in the full length mirror fixed to the bathroom door. Never mind. If Manisha really hated it all that much, he'd shift it out into the hallway. Ah! she'd like that area of the house at least. It had parquet flooring and an old hat-stand he'd picked up in the flea market. He'd also hung up colourful art prints. And invested in an expensive lampshade. This was after all the entrance to their little home — it had to look welcoming and cheerful.

The bedroom walls were still bare. He wanted to involve Manisha in the decisions. Maybe she'd prefer putting up photographs. Manisha had a good eye for black-and-white work, mainly portraits. Or maybe she'd prefer wall-hangings. He was going to leave that to her. Mohan was particularly proud of the built-in-cupboards in which the lights came on automatically when the doors were thrown open. He'd taken care to arrange his clothes neatly on the shelves. He also liked the utilities closet with the washing machine in it and enough storage space for suitcases. This was something he missed in their Bombay flat, where there was not an inch of space to spare.

Mohan strolled into the spare room and looked at it critically. It had enormous potential — but right now it was empty — minus even a camp-cot or a rug. Stark and empty. Though he had used the attached bathroom a few times and hung up cheerful shower curtains in it. The room overlooked a small park — a wooded one. He could see the evergreens and grassy knolls, a welcome sight for someone accustomed to grey concrete and peeling walls. Mohan had been tempted to dump all the unwanted things here and lock up the room. He knew that was exactly what Manisha would've done — pushed cartons, blankets and packing cases into a corner and left it at that saying impatiently, "It's not as if we need the room tomorrow or anything. What difference does it make?"

But to Mohan, it did make a difference. He'd decided to fill the room with large branches of cherry blossoms for his wife's arrival. In fact, he'd planned different flowers for different rooms. And little notes everywhere to demonstrate how glad he was to have her with him again. He'd also planned their first dinner with care. Manisha would be too tired for them to eat out. And chances were, she'd be depressed. So he'd decided to cook her favourite dishes himself. Not that Manisha was a big or enthusiastic eater, but she did enjoy interesting salads and she was a sucker for *biryani*. Mohan had done a trial run using Madhur Jaffrey's invaluable cook-book. The results had been more than merely edible — he'd licked the casserole clean. Mohan had also investigated the wines available at the nearby mall, and picked two Californian ones. He'd bought bright red candles and a new table-cloth. He'd wondered about a 'Welcome' sign strung up in the living room and then decided against it. Manisha could be quite unpredictable in her responses. It might have irritated her.

Mohan was particularly pleased with the way he'd organised the living room, combining some Indian furniture with comfortable sofas bought from a discount store in the downtown area. The room looked friendly and not oppressively ethnic. Mohan had kept in mind the fact that they'd eventually be entertaining American friends here. The best way of breaking down barriers and assimilating oneself into a new culture was to blend in and not bellow your identity. Mohan was proud to be an Indian, but now that they were in America, he wanted to belong. He wanted to be like other professionals. He didn't want to be eternally labelled, an immigrant from India. He didn't want to run yet another "curry joint" for curious American colleagues, eager to sample "authentic" Indian cuisine.

Mohan was certain Manisha would approve of his overall game

plan. She was quite a practical sort of woman. She'd understand quickly enough that to make it here and get quick acceptance, it was important to act like the Americans, behave like them, even think like them. Though that would take some time. Even at the office, Mohan was still a little out of sync with the informality of the language used. He'd known it as a student, of course. But at that stage he'd attributed this casualness to the universal attitude adopted by students. But even way back then, he'd been one of the first overseas chaps to merge his identity with the others on campus and pick up all the latest slang. He'd also consciously made American friends and not stuck to either other Indians or Pakistanis. Mohan had made himself popular in a short time and he'd done so by adopting tactics that were subtle and non-threatening. He intended to do the same now.

Of course, he was worried about Manisha and how she'd adjust. She could be difficult at times. And stubborn. He'd sensed her resistance, but then he also knew that she was the kind of person who resisted any change. Period. For her, continuity spelt security. And even Mohan realised how major this change was going to be for his wife. Anyway, it was just as well she'd be coming now when the weather was so delightful — almost as warm as in India. He'd told her to pack her woolies, but not buy a coat — that they'd do in America once the store sales started. Right now, he too was doing fine with his Indian shirts and light wool jackets. He was longing to show her around, "do the sights".

Washington was such a pretty city — a lot like Delhi. Broad, tree-lined avenues, impressive Government buildings, lovely homes with gardens...and basically the same sort of people — obsessed with power and politics. Mohan had known before he got here that it was a predominantly black city — but he hadn't realised to what extent till he started to live in Washington. Not that he was scared of them or anything — but he wasn't sure what Manisha's attitude would be. That's why, even while choosing this place he'd asked around discreetly and made sure there were more whites than blacks in their complex. It had meant spending more money but then Manisha's safety was of prime importance to him. He'd heard the most horrifying stories about break-ins, robberies and in other areas, rape. He had made sure that their new house was well-protected and in an area that was predominantly middle class professional. There was enough security too and visitors were carefully screened. The first few nights he'd been awakened by strange noises on the roof. Later, he'd discovered they were made by falling twigs and scurrying squirrels. He'd made a note to tell Manisha that — she was a light sleeper. Very light. Even a slight change in his breathing pattern was enough to wake her up — and keep her awake, which invariably led to her being irritable the next morning and complaining of a lack of sleep. He'd checked and rechecked the thermostat in the bedroom too. Sometimes it acted up and the room got over-heated. He'd called in an electrician to take a look — it had turned out to be just that — a look, but a very expensive one.

Mohan had fallen in love with the bathroom though — it was like something straight out of a fabulous catalogue. Not too large — but larger than anything he'd known in Bombay. With a sunken tub, gleaming mirrors, attractive cabinets and granite flooring. And the lights! There were at least a dozen bulbs that went on at the press of a single switch, bathing the room in a warm, golden glow. Mohan had played with them like a child and stared delightedly at his multiple images in the many mirrors. Manisha was going to love this, he knew it. She had such a weakness for hotel bathrooms with their powerful showers and marble flooring— this one was fitted with the latest shower-head which one could adjust to the desired pressure. Mohan enjoyed the strong gush of hot water as it poured over his brown shoulders. It felt as good as a regular massage. Compared to the pathetic trickle that emerged from their Bombay shower, this was bliss. He imagined bathing with Manisha — one of his favourite fantasies, though one that she consistently discouraged. This bathroom was made for it. They could listen to music, sip wine, stand under the powerful shower together, soap themselves sensuously and then soak in the tub after sprinkling a generous amount of bath oils into the warm water. Mohan had splurged on fragrant gels, crystals, shampoos and soaps. The bathroom looked so pretty with matching towels and a colourful bath-mat. It was only a matter of days now, but he could hardly wait to show it all off to Manisha.

"I'm not going... I've changed my mind. I can't do it..." Manisha's mother stared expressionlessly at her daughter. The announcement didn't surprise her at all. She'd seen it coming from the moment Mohan had signed his contract and accepted the new job. Manisha stuck her chin out and looked at her mother, "Well?" she said, a trifle too loudly, "Why aren't you saying something? Why aren't you reacting?"

The old lady picked up the slim remote control panel and flicked on the television. Manisha walked over to the set and deliberately switched it off. "I want to talk to you — don't you understand? This is important."

Her mother continued to stare blankly ahead. After a long silence she turned to Manisha and said quietly, "Divorce. That's what it comes to. You don't want to live with your husband any longer. That's it."

Manisha shot to her feet and said in a shrill voice, "Why must you always be so harsh with me? Would you have talked like this to your other daughter? Who's talking about a divorce? All I'm saying is that I cannot go and live in Washington. That's all."

Her mother walked slowly away from her into the tiny kitchen. She came back with a red plastic basket filled with green peas and wordlessly started to shell them. Manisha, her eyes blazing, her breathing heavy, paced the room restlessly. "I should never have told you. I should have known how hostile you'd be. You've always been this way with me. Always. Even when I was a child. Did I use the word divorce? No. I only said I can't go there. Is that such a sin?"

Her mother mechanically shelled one pod after another. Finally, she spoke, her voice even, her eyes steady. "When a wife decides not to go and live with her husband — for whatever reasons — she is breaking her marriage. At least that is what I believe in. You cannot have a marriage when two people are living separately, leading their own lives. Am I right or wrong in assuming this?"

Manisha sat down heavily across her mother. "I don't want to get into this right and wrong business. It wasn't fair of Mohan to have taken this job. He should have thought of my feelings. My life. My priorities."

Her mother asked, "And he didn't? You mean he did all this without your knowledge? You didn't know he was going to Washington? He didn't consult you? Is that what you're telling me?"

Manisha shook her head vigorously. "No, It's not that. Mohan did consult me at every stage."

The mother stopped shelling the pod that was in her hands and said, "Then?"

Manisha replied, "Then what? I didn't have the heart to discourage him. He was so keen on it. Besides, his career was going nowhere here. He'd started getting demoralised. How could I tell him then that I didn't want to go?"

The old lady resumed shelling, "It would have been more honest. Also, more convenient. If you'd been frank, Mohan would have known what to do — which decision to take. Stay back and save the marriage. Or go there without you. What you've done now is dishonest."

Manisha switched the TV back on. A Game Show was on, with plenty of rowdiness and applause. "The girl in red is winning," she said dully. Her mother didn't look up. Manisha continued, "I know what you're thinking. That I'm selfish. Self-centred. You've always thought that about me...haven't you? Just because I wasn't a hypoerite like my sister. You couldn't see through her act, that's all. But I could and did. Sickening, the way she manipulated you. Played the Holy Martyr. Don't expect me to be like that. I'm different...have always been."

Her mother had nearly finished her task. "You don't have to tell me. I know. Besides, how does your sister come into this? We are not talking about her..."

Manisha burst out, "You've always been cruel to me... judging me all the time...comparing the two of us. Had she faced a similar problem, you wouldn't have sat there with those bloody peas. You would have put your arms around her and told her it was o.k. You would've stroked her hair, made her put her head in your lap. You don't care about me at all, do you?"

Her mother was walking back to the kitchen slowly, balancing the shelled peas in one hand and the basket containing the pods in the other. The passageway to the kitchen was dark. The old lady rarely switched on lights unless it was imperative. But she knew her way around her small flat very well. Even though one of her eyes was cataractous now, and her step unsteady, she could get around unaided... padding softly like a sure-footed cat. As she was doing now. Suddenly, without warning, Manisha flew at her, knocking the peas from her hands. As they scattered all over the tiled floor, the old lady stumbled and fell forward. It was unfortunate that a stool had been left carelessly in the passage by the washerwoman who'd earlier used it to hang up the wet clothes to dry. She tried to reach out for support, but missed her balance, falling over its sharp edge. Manisha watched in horror as her mother's boney body collapsed in front of her, the limbs splayed helplessly. Manisha found herself looking down at her mother's exposed legs and thighs, as her saree climbed up to her waist and her body writhed in pain on the floor. How emaciated she looked, Manisha noted. How weak she had become. What had happened to the once proud, strong, sturdy-limbed, straight-backed woman who could unaided lift a drunk's dead-weight up three flights of stairs, clean his vomit, change his clothes and go straight in to the kitchen to prepare the next meal for her two frightened little girls?

The old lady was obviously in pain. But she stared back at her daughter steadily, her gaze unblinking and even. Pitiless still Manisha thought to herself, "Even now, she won't ask me for help...even now. Damn that pride of hers. Where did it ever get her?" Her mother was beginning to moan softly now. She was doubling up, and yet, her hands were groping forward like claws in an effort to retrieve the disobedient peas. Manisha stood rooted to the spot, unable to move. She felt no remorse as she watched her mother drag her body towards her room. She thought of her sister and what she would have done under these circumstances.

Mohini would've rushed forward to hold the fallen woman, cradled her in her arms, sobbed into her neck, lifted her up bodily, placed her gently on the bed and then, after ensuring she wasn't grievously hurt, summoned the doctor. But then again, such a situation would never have arisen between Mohini and her mother — they loved each other, understood each other and accepted one another unconditionally. All the concessions denied to her applied to Mohini. All the harshness reserved for her was reversed in Mohini's case. Why? What had she ever done to deserve such discriminatory treatment?

Manisha bent down and started to gather the peas. "Don't. Stop," her mother rasped. "Those are my peas. Don't touch them." Manisha ignored her command and continued with the task. Her mother had managed to drag herself a few feet. Now she was close enough to an old reclining chair to use its arm as a lever to prop herself up. Manisha watched coldly. The room was dark. It was dusk outside — a time of day her mother detested. The "in between" time as she put it, neither here nor there. Neither day nor night. Manisha stood silently in the door-frame. She could've reached out and switched on the light — that's what Mohini would've done instantly. Mohini was the sort who switched on all lights wherever she went. But the shadows created in that dimly-lit room were starting to fascinate Manisha. For a moment, she wondered whether her mother was going to die. Her breath was coming out in gasps. One hand was clutching her side. But the eyes — the eyes continued to blaze. She was staring hard at Manisha. It was obvious she wanted to say something. The look on her face was malevolent. Another malicious remark, mused Manisha, before prompting mockingly, "Say it... go ahead. Get it out of your system once and for all. Tell me why you hate me so much. What is the special poison you've held in your heart all these years."

Her mother struggled to climb into the low chair. She lay back and shut her eyes — those powerful eyes that had once frozen Manisha in her tracks with one carelessly thrown glance in her direction. The old lady threw her head back against the wicker work of the chair. Her chest was heaving and a wheezing sound escaped from her open mouth. Her frame looked shrunken and distorted, her legs arranged at an awkward angle. Abruptly, she opened her eyes, propped up her head and began to speak in a firm, loud voice that sounded unnatural to Manisha's ears. "Listen to me, you foolish woman. Flesh of my flesh you are, but that is all...nothing more. You were conceived on a moonless night — perhaps that is why I have harboured only dark thoughts about you. A moonless night...and a very hot one. You were also fathered by the devil himself — a devil who came to me whenever there was hunger in his groins and lust in his heart. I didn't want you. I never have. Whether I live or die now, I have cursed you since the day you tore my loins apart and entered this world. My curse shall remain till you're alive...and if I can help it...it shall also follow you into your next life."

Manisha's body was quivering and she felt a strange chill travelling down her spine. Her voice had altered as well when she spoke in the thin, uncertain voice of a child now. It had a slight lisp to it. She found herself stuttering as she asked, "But...was it my fault? Why did you blame me?"

The mother was silent for a long time before she said, "Had your father's seed not entered me that night and left me burdened with a new life inside me, I would have left him and run away. That is what I had planned to do. By taking birth inside my womb, you ruined my life. Permanently. I became enslaved. Chained to a man whose very breath I loathed."

Manisha was whimpering, "You could've got rid of me...you could have, if that was how you felt."

"No," her mother thundered, "I tried. And failed. That wasn't my destiny — you were. As my belly began to bloat...as I felt you moving inside me, with each kick of yours, I felt some part of my life draining away. And with it, hope. Do you know what it is to live without hope? I was young. And beautiful. I had my dreams. I wanted another life with another man. I could've had it — but for you."

Manisha thought of her mother as she used to be — an attractive, strong woman with fine features and a supple body. Yes, she could have got any man. And escaped.

But what about Mohini then...why was she born? Was she too another horrible mistake? Another ghastly miscalculation? And if so, how come her mother didn't hate her even more? Manisha desperately needed to know the answer. Almost as if reading her thoughts, her mother's voice reached her, "You are wondering about Mohini, aren't you? Wondering why I had her?" Manisha shook her head dumbly, unable to articulate the one question that had gnawed at her insides all her life. The old woman looked away dreamily and smiled. "Aah....Mohini, Mohini, Mohini. She was different. Mohini was my revenge on that wretched drunk. My precious secret..."

Manisha took a few steps towards her mother, but the old lady stopped her in her tracks with a sharp, "No...stay there. And don't ask me one single question because I will not tell you. Do you understand? I will not. It is my secret...mine alone. It will stay with me. And die with me."

Mohan took one final look around his new home. There was a satisfied smile on his face. Even his finicky, difficult wife would find it hard to turn up her nose at it. Two days from now, the house would look different, smell different — her familiar cologne would linger in each room. The closet in the bedroom would exude the heady fragrance of her perfumes permeating the soft, silk fold of her sarees. There'd be lipsticks and cleaners on the dresser and

Manisha's array of heeled slippers arranged in rows on the shoe-rack. The ironing board would look different too with her nighties, bras and panties piled up on it. Of course, Mohan knew Manisha would rearrange a few things — not because she was all that interested in the way the house looked but more to assert her presence in it. She'd also find several faults with, say the kitchen cabinets or the plumbing. But, Mohan reasoned, that was the fun and challenge of being married to a woman with a mind of her own. He'd have felt bored with a doormat — a woman who meekly agreed with everything he said and did.

He opened the fridge to see just how well-stocked it was and to check whether he'd forgotten anything. He scribbled a note to himself not to forget to pick up fresh lettuce on the day of her arrival. And he'd tell her on the phone when she next called to remember to pack her *puja* agarbattis (he had still to locate a good Indian store here). Mohan had earmarked a spot for his wife's gods — a small niche in the wall close to the kitchen — that would do nicely. Two days, just two days left. He switched on the TV to keep his excitement under control. He watched the flickering images without really seeing anything. He was about to switch channels but stopped himself — it was a habit Manisha loathed. Thank God for good television, Mohan thought. At least Manisha wouldn't get too bored — there were so many options to choose from.

Mohan fell into a light sleep. He was woken up by the bedside phone ringing insistently. It was her. It had to be. Who else would call at this hour? Excitedly, expectantly, he picked up the receiver and sat up in bed, "Darling....?" he said.

A dull voice at the other end repeated words he was sure he had misheard. "I'm not coming, Mohan....can you hear me? I'm not coming to Washington....I can't...forgive me...I'm really sorry. Goodbye, Mohan... don't call me back."

Mohan was certain he was hallucinating. He looked across at a small silver frame with his wife's photograph in it. There was some mistake or this was Manisha's idea of a silly prank. One of her bad jokes, intended to tease him and get him all worked up. He hung on, uncomprehending, to the dead line for close to five minutes, waiting for her voice to resume the heard conversation and tell him she was just kidding. But all he got was a long engaged whine. Mohan replaced the receiver slowly and went to the bathroom. He needed to wake up. A glass of water would help.

Manisha looked around her bedroom for the few remaining traces of Mohan. There were still quite a number of them around. Systematically, she began filling up carton with the things he'd left behind. It was going to be hours, maybe days or even months, before she got rid of them. And him. She glanced at herself in the mirror and touched her stomach. Something told her there was life inside. Manisha was far too busy clearing up things right now. She'd pay attention to the new development tomorrow. And then make a decision. Just like her mother had so many years earlier....

Five

THE TRIP

RITIKA WAS a woman with wild and uncontrollable longings. It had always been this way with her, ever since she was a child growing up on the outskirts of Delhi. Her parents had long given up trying to understand their self-willed youngest daughter, so different from the other children. So different in fact that her timid mother often wondered under which particular celestial conjunction she'd conceived her. Ritika looked different, acted different, behaved different. She was unlike anybody her family had ever known — with an untamed, limitless imagination that made people around her dizzy. It got Ritika into a great deal of trouble too as a schoolgirl. And even more of it as an adult, especially since her husband, locked in a world defined by money and yet more money, didn't have the foggiest notion about his sweet, docile wife's secret life peopled by dangerous men and breathless moments. Hiten only saw a restrained and respectable woman who kept a clean, efficient house and was a wonderful mother to their three children.

But recently, Ritika's fantasies had started to scare and worry her. She'd begun to panic at her own thoughts, agonise over the eventual consequences of actions not yet taken. Because she knew she was going to do it — fulfil at least one of her recurrent dreams, that is. Before it was too late — too late to live the life she constantly yearned for. A life lived on the edge...nervously...but oh so deliciously. Ritika was sick of the self-deception. She'd started to feel more and more like an imposter. And like all imposters, she knew it was only a matter of time before she'd be found out and exposed. Not that she cared about the outcome of such a prospect in her more reckless moments. On the contrary, she hankered after it. "God, I hope it happens soon," she'd think to herself as she supervised dinner. "I can't keep up the pretence much longer." Pretence? What pretence? Nothing had changed as far as her behaviour was concerned. She didn't neglect to perform any of her duties. She loved and cared for her family. She said all the right things at the right moment to the right person. She was admired for her skills at "managing" everything so efficiently without neglecting anyone or anything. Friends often asked *her* advice on how to perform the perfect balancing act. She'd overheard one or other remarking, "It's amazing how she does it. Just look at her— so in control, so on top of the situation. And look at me, for instance—one minor emergency and I promptly fall apart."

Ritika enjoyed stringing women like them along — offering advice on time-management to harried careerists, giving tips on smart investments to housewives with small, private incomes, helping a mother understand a difficult child better, counselling a distraught wife on how best to cope with a neglectful husband without nagging. Yes, Ritika could do all that most convincingly even as her mind continued to race with fevered images of unlikely situations, unspoken conversations and untamed couplings with strangers at twilight.

It amused and aggravated her that her husband suspected nothing, knew nothing, understood nothing. He saw in her only what he wanted to see — a loving wife who behaved herself at parties, unlike some of the other bitches, a conscientious mother who didn't skip a single PTA, and an obliging bed partner who rarely said "no". Hiten was a simple, self-satisfied man whose idea of a marital crisis didn't go beyond his wife's refusal to attend a business dinner with him because she just wasn't "in the mood".

"There's no question," he'd once thundered when Ritika had trotted that out as an excuse. "Moods don't come into this. It is your duty as my wife to accompany me whenever and wherever I go...after all, it's for *our* sake that I'm doing all this. Do you think I enjoy going to all these boring affairs?" Ritika had bowed her head and assumed a penitent expression — she'd become very good at doing that without further argument, she'd gone to her cupboard and busily started looking for an appropriate saree. How easy it was to fool her husband—to appease him, distract him, and forget about him.

Sometimes Ritika wondered whether there was something seriously the matter with her. Did other women "suffer" from a similar syndrome? Whom could she ask such a crazy question to? Ritika imagined phoning her friend, Anisha — the only real friend she had, — to ask, "Do you sometimes feel so strongly attracted to a stranger that at that particular moment you know — you just know — you'd leave your family, your husband, children, everything and run away with him?" It had happened to her. She remembered at least one incident clearly....

Hiten had decided — uncharacteristically — to take her along on a business trip abroad. They were to spend four days in Dubai—a place that had always intrigued Ritika—before leaving for London. The thought of travelling with as boring and unadventurous a companion as Hiten was something Ritika had reconciled herself to. At least he was pleasant enough, if not exactly inspiring. Besides, a new place always fired up her imagination and made her pulse race. The possibilities—oh God—the possibilities, she'd think excitedly even when at the back of her mind she knew only too well that each trip would be exactly like the previous one—uneventful and crammed with shopping for the kids. And yet, as Ritika packed, she had visions of unexpected adventures, unplanned happenings. Hiten, of course, only experienced the usual excitement most people display at the prospect of going abroad. "I'm warning you," he cautioned his wife good humouredly, "No shopping this time. I'm not a rich man, remember."

Ritika had grinned tolerantly at that husbandly remark. Shopping! He actually thought she was all charged up about shopping! Ha! What did she care about a new lipstick or the latest perfume? What a fool Hiten was to think she'd be smiling her secret smile over something as mundane as shopping.

On their third day in Dubai, exhausted, dehydrated and desperately bored going from one glittering shopping mall to the other, Ritika had longed to catch her breath and drink a tall glass of iced tea. She'd tugged at Hiten's shirt sleeve. He'd looked irritable and tired too, as if all the walking around looking for cheap electronic goods was her fault.

"Now what?" he'd asked shortly.

She'd pointed to a small self-service cafe and said, "I'm thirsty. Can we catch our breath a little?"

He'd consulted his watch—a gesture she found particularly irritating—it wasn't as if he had an appointment to keep and they were running hopelessly behind schedule because of her. Reluctantly, he'd agreed. They'd staggered towards the chairs and collapsed tiredly, scattering their bundles all over.

Ritika had her large sunglasses on. She was dressed in clothes she despised — clothes she wouldn't have dreamt of wearing in Bombay—tights and a casual shirt. She sat at a small round table and looked blankly ahead of her while Hiten went off to get her tea. She noticed a small, chic shoe shop adjoining the cafe. It had an unusually attractive window display. Whoever had arranged the hay and rocks over painted sand must have been awfully artistic, she concluded idly, comparing the different textures and colours. The shoes were different too — not the usual strappy sandals and chunky platforms so in vogue then. These were beautifully crafted works of art in jewel tones — rich purples, deep pinks, velvety greens, iridiscent blues. Classical shoes, moulded to caress the foot snugly. Some had tiny windows cut on top, others were laced up in front. The heels were graceful and sculptured, the leather, matt-finished and unblemished. Ritika couldn't take her eyes off the footwear, poised so delicately over rough-hewn rocks. She couldn't remember shoes ever looking so seductive. She imagined how wearing one of them would feel — the leather brushing against her skin, her toes fitting snugly inside, her ankle resting lightly on the well-balanced heel.

And shoes were not even a fetish with her. To add to it, Ritika had problem feet and a buniyon distorting her left big toe. It was one of the reasons why she disliked travelling. Her feet experienced enormous fatigue even before she left the airport. But these shoes looked so heavenly...so pretty...almost too pretty to be worn. At least, far too pretty for her singularly unattractive feet. So what? she thought defiantly. I know I'll never own such a fine pair—they probably cost a small fortune — but at least I can dream. She continued to stare, lingering over each handcrafted detail. Just then, a man with a long, easy stride walked out of the shop. She noticed him immediately. He noticed her too. He was one of the best looking men she'd ever seen. And frighteningly elegant in a studiedly casual sort of a way. He walked a short distance to an adjoining shop and came back briskly. His eyes caught hers again.

In real life Ritika rarely reacted to men — strange men — this strongly. But this man *was* extraordinary. To begin with, he sported a neatly-tied pony-tail. Normally, Ritika would have mocked a grown man with a similar hair style. And this chap was no spring-chicken. He had a much-lived face — angled and sharp. This ought to have made the pony-tail seem still more incongruous, almost foolish — he certainly wasn't dressed like a hippie. On the contrary, his clothes were conservative and expensive-looking. Loose grey trousers and an open-necked blue shirt. He wore tan-coloured brogues on his large feet. But then, he was large too — over six feet tall. And broad. Ritika quickly tried to think who he reminded her of — some Hollywood movie star? An archetypal gigolo from a European film? No. Then it came to her — he resembled a Giorgio Armani advertisement — the one that featured a mature man with a weathered face. A man who looked like he'd slept with hundreds of women and would sleep with hundreds more. And yet, not an obvious Lothario. Not a vain, empty-headed Lover Boy but a man of refined tastes and acute sensibilities. A thinking man. A sensitive man. Someone who probably played the flute for relaxation. Ate strawberries after sex and painted his lover's

63

toe-nails fire-engine red while she slept.

Hiten came back crossly saying. "No iced tea. They don't have it. Why don't you drink a Pepsi like everybody else?"

The spell was broken, but not entirely. Absently. Ritika said, "O.K. I'll have a Pepsi. Sorry about the tea."

And Hiten was off again. Ritika's eyes went back to the shop entrance. She knew he'd walk out soon. Very soon. And he did. Her heart skipped a beat and she began to wonder whether he'd come up to her and ask, "Mind if I join you?" He probably thought she was alone since Hiten had been in a queue most of the time. She obviously looked interested. Ritika blushed at the thought. Maybe she was giving out all the wrong (right?) signals. The man must have concluded she was a tourist — one of those bored, rich wives, on a shopping junket. He probably saw (and slept with) several of those. How terrible. She stared as he strode off again. His back looking as inviting, as sexy as his front. Perhaps even more so. Mentally, she stripped him of his clothes. She visualised what his bottom must look like — taut and well-muscled, though it was really quite hard to tell through the loose lines of his impeccably cut trousers. She liked his loping walk. The way he'd causally rolled up his sleeves. The neat bow around his pony-tail. The broad, square forehead. The cheekbones like priceless calcium deposits. The eyes — deep-set and as blue as the Mediterranean. This man was a cliché. Alarmingly good-looking. A three-dimensional designer ad.

Then why was she reacting so foolishly? She, who was not the sort to go for lookers and never had been. She, who rarely devoured men with her eyes (most weren't worth the effort). She who didn't see herself as a particularly sexual animal (all that unaesthetic heaving and huffing). And here she was going weak at the knees over a man who looked like the jacket of a Mills & Boon romance (without that pony-tail, of course). Now, he was walking back towards her...staring hard...sizing her up? She could've looked away. Feigned disinterest. Pretended she hadn't noticed him in the first place. But she didn't. Instead with great deliberation, she removed her sunglasses and placed them on the table. She held his eyes steadily with her own, almost challenging him...beckoning him to take the initiative. He didn't. He walked back into the shoe store. Ritika felt bitterly let-down. Perhaps he was the owner. Maybe he was trying to entice her to enter his shop—see him on his own home ground. She actually considered it. Hiten? Well, that was easily taken care of. All she had to do was park him at the table with all the shopping and say lightly, "Will be back in just a moment — spotted something cute — but don't worry, I'm not buying, just looking." And she'd saunter off unhurriedly...perhaps never to return.

Ritika dejectedly watched Hiten walking back with a small plastic tray loaded with paper glasses of Pepsi and ice. He'd thrown in a packet of potato crisps for himself. Hiten looked so vulnerable...so unsuspecting...so, so silly, as he negotiated his way past manic shoppers to where she was seated. Her impulse was to pick up her bag briskly and announce to Hiten, "This is it. I'm leaving you. I can't stand another minute of monotony. And the predictability. I'm bored out of my wits. I'm off." But she knew she wouldn't do it. Not now. Not ever. She smiled sweetly at her husband and said in her submissive wifely voice, "Sorry for the trouble. But I *was* dying of thirst."

They sipped their drinks in silence. Rivulets of sweat were trickling down Hiten's face. He needed a shave. He looked almost shabby in his semi-holiday gear. The T-Shirt was too tight. His paunch was showing. The bald patch on his head too. The whites of his eyes looked yellowish. There were blackheads over his nose. She thought of his bottom — it was ugly. Discoloured, rough to the touch. Large and completely lacking in any sort of muscle tone. It jiggled each morning as he walked nude from the bathroom to his cupboard. Ritika had always had a thing about men's bottoms. She'd noticed the one featured in the "Obsession" fragrance ad.

It had been perfect — firm, round high, compact. She was certain the shoe shop man's would be similar. As she drank down her Pepsi thirstily, she imagined what he might be doing inside the shop at that moment. Maybe he was a salesman. Maybe *he* had a fetish for women's feet. Maybe he worked in a shoe shop so that he could caress hundreds of anonymous feet attached to strange women. Ritika didn't want him to see her own ugly ones. No, there was no way she was going to walk into his shop.

He came out again. This time, he was accompanied by a woman. He looked in her direction and smiled a small, ironic smile as he caught sight of Hiten. She got the message, and shrugged. He shrugged, too. The woman with him took his arm possessively.

Was she his wife? Ritika immediately imagined them in bed together and hoped they'd be entirely incompatible. The woman with him looked brassy and hard. And the way she clung to his arm revealed her insecurity. She also looked ill-tempered and impatient, deep frown lines criss-crossing her forehead. The lipstick was all wrong—a bright orange that clashed with her colouring. Her hair seemed bleached and coarse. Ritika looked at her clothes — too tight, too short, too obvious. But she probably had great breasts. The legs were passable though the ankles were too thick. Actually, it was her manner that wasn't attractive—bossy, pushy as she looked this way and that, her hands holding on to his arm like grasping claws. Before they crossed the street and disappeared from view altogether, he turned around for one final time and looked at Ritika. With such intensity, it was as if they had made love. Ritika's hand—the one that was holding the straw — suddenly dropped to the table with a loud thud. Her eyes lost their shine. The corners of her lips drooped, and the colour drained from her face. She felt exhausted. And old.

Hiten was staring at her strangely. "You look ill. Are you all right?" he asked.

She looked past him at the rapidly shrinking flash of blue in the distance. She shook her head. Hot tears started to well up in her eyes. Ritika felt a dull pain growing in her heart. It was hopeless. It really was. If only she could have had one glorious hour with the man. Just one. Not even an hour of sex. Just conversation. And kisses. And cigarettes. And laughter. And touches. And jokes. One hour. She'd have untied his hair and buried her face in his neck. She'd have opened her mouth to receive his tongue. She'd have stroked his back. And made love to his face. One hour. That was all she wanted from life. One hour of being a hundred per cent alive. A hundred per cent herself. One hour free of pretence. No acts. No duties. No obligations. No strings attached. No memories. No future. No regrets. Especially, no regrets.

She composed herself and turned towards Hiten. He was still looking at her, this time with genuine concern. "Maybe we should try and see a doctor. You look pale," he said. Ritika straightened her narrow shoulders, pushed back the hair from her eyes, stuck her chin out, inclined her head and smiled a slow, mysterious smile before saying, "I'm fine. Absolutely fine. Never felt better. Really." She wasn't exactly lying, either.

Six

THE TRANSFER

WHEN POOJA'S father was transferred to Bombay from Calcutta, she was eleven years old. Bombay meant just one thing to her — Hindi films. Even though her friends seemed more interested in them than she was. "Gosh! How lucky!" they'd exclaimed when she'd broken the news to them. "Now you'll get to meet all the heroes and heroines. Madhuri Dixit and Jackie and Amir and Karishma."

Pooja had pulled a face and said disdainfully, "Who wants to meet them? I want to go to Bombay because it is big and beautiful — and better than Calcutta."

Pooja's father worked for a paint company in Calcutta. The transfer to Bombay was going to be a major career-break for him. Till then, they'd lived in his father's (Pooja's grandfather's) home near the lakes and led a predictable enough life. Pooja's mother, Piyali, a plump and sexy woman in her late thirties, dreamed of becoming a lecturer in a college some day. Only, she couldn't find the time, what with an eight-year-old son to take care of plus an invalid mother-in-law languishing in a room upstairs. Pooja liked living with her grandparents. She particularly liked her parchment skinned thakurma. The old lady told her stories, braided her hair and allowed her to spend the hot afternoons in her cool room when Pooja's mother needed to rest undisturbed. Pooja was definitely going to miss her grandmother. But not her school or friends. She'd also half-hoped to leave her brother behind and said so to her mother.

Little Khokun was an over-energetic brat with a prematurely developed ego. Pooja's mother further contributed to his exaggerated sense of self-worth by endorsing the little boy's views on himself. Khokun was as fat and arrogant as Pooja was stringy and sensitive. She detested her brother. And often, her mother as well. Her father, she barely knew since he was away such a lot. And her grandfather she feared, especially in the late evening when he'd roar at the servants after consuming two large pegs of rum. "For my bronchitis," he'd explain to relatives if they ever visited.

The father and son hardly spoke to one another, which pained Pooja's thakurma. Pooja's mother stayed away as much as possible from the old lady, repelled as much by the antiseptic smell in her room as by her mother-in-law's saint-like acceptance of her own suffering. "I wish she'd be miserable...I wish she'd complain...I'm tired of her smiling face. What does she have to be happy about?" she'd ask her husband irritably. He'd ignore the remarks saying, "So long as she stays out of your hair, so long as you get to run the house independently, why crib?"

Piyali was truly the real mistress of the house. She gave the servants instructions on what to prepare for their meals, she ordered the supplies and she decided on which fish was to be bought each morning. And yet, Piyali resented the fact that she was living in a house not her own while her friends occupied smart flats and threw weekend parties. She'd complain to her husband, "Look at Anita...look at Ronjona...see what freedom they have. How will you ever rise in your company if you don't entertain clients like your colleagues do?" Patiently, Prodip would point out that they did do their share of business entertaining — not in his father's house perhaps, but at the two clubs they were proud members of. "Yes...but can we have dance parties like those others? Or Sunday lunches? No. Can I pursue my career? No. Do I have a life of my own outside this house? No. I feel tied down and frustrated."

Pooja would occasionally overhear these arguments between her parents and wonder about her mother, her father, marriage in general. Life, as she perceived it, was as perfect as it could be.

70

Sure, she had an obnoxious brother, but they had a TV in the living room (bought by her father) and now they even had access to cable programmes. Her father didn't have his own car yet, but so what — thakurda let him use his old Ambassador. Her mother wore good clothes — at home too. And Tangail sarees with pretty borders when she went to the market or out with baba. And salwar-kameez suits from small boutiques when she had to go out in the evening. She even visited the beauty parlour once or twice a month to have her eyebrows threaded and face bleached. Pooja's friends thought her mother pretty, in fact, she was rather good-looking. A little blousy after the birth of her son, but presentable enough.

It was a pity Pooja hadn't inherited her mother's large, expressive, "fish-eyes", nor her thick wavy hair. But while her mother was dusky ("dark" according to the old lady), Pooja's skin was lighter ("like our side of the family," thakurma said). Pooja's mother had a large mole near her nose that Pooja had loved touching as a child. It had annoyed Piyali since she hated that mole, especially the tiny hairs that grew out of it. Pooja's brother Khokun was allowed to touch it, however, since Piyali said it was an old habit from the days she used to nurse him. Khokun had refused to give up the breast till he was four years old and his teeth hurt his mother's sore nipples.

Pooja didn't mind all this. She was so used to Khokun receiving preferential treatment that any other attitude tended to surprise her. Her secondary status was something she took entirely for granted. "After all, Khokun is a boy," her thakurma would nod, if Pooja ever complained of discrimination. "Get used to it from now — accept the fact that men are superior because if you don't, you'll feel miserable later." Pooja often puzzled over that remark. Superior? In what way? Khokun was far from superior. He was a dud. A spoilt, fat dud. And when she thought that of her brother, she wasn't being mean. She was merely stating what was obvious to the world.

Khokun didn't want to move to Bombay. "What will I do

there?" he howled while his mother gathered him to her ample bosom and rocked his plump body consolingly. "Ssh, Khokun. You will love Bombay. Imported chocolates. Video games. Foreign clothes."

Khokun was unconvinced. "I get all that in Calcutta. I don't want to go. Tell baba I'm staying back. I won't leave."

Pooja watched in silence. She knew this was only a mini-rehearsal before the real scene — the one Khokun would stage for a full-house after her father came home. She sighed and went in search of Suchi, her best friend, who lived next door. She half-hoped her baba would consider Khokun's request seriously and leave him behind. Maybe her mother too would prefer to stay back. Then Pooja would be free. Free of the two of them. Free to find herself in a new city away from the embarrassment of being "just a girl" in a family fixated on the male gender.

They arrived at Santa Cruz airport on a muggy October day. Pooja's first reaction was, "My God! How hot it is."

Her mother sneered, "Why? Did you think we were going to Europe? Bombay is only Bombay, not Paris."

Khokun, hanging on to a jumbo-sized bar of Toblerone chocolate, continued to whimper (he'd snivelled through the flight). He kept up a steady refrain of "I hate it. I hate it. I want to go home. Take me back to Calcutta."

Only Pooja and her father seemed curious and expectant. "Baba," Pooja nudged him, "will we see any film stars along the way after we land or pass any of their homes?"

Her father shook his head before saying, "But don't worry...I'll arrange a visit to a studio through my old friend. Also from Calcutta. He's now a big man in films. Art director. He'll take you."

Pooja nodded her head. She had enormous faith in her father unlike her mother who, overhearing their conversation, sniffed derisively, "Huh! Every Bengali in Bombay think he's a big man."

Khokun bit into a sticky chunk of his chocolate and stared glumly ahead, refusing to take the slightest interest in his new surroundings.

They were to stay in the company guest house till a suitable flat could be found for them. Pooja's father had been to Bombay several times and she marvelled at the confidence with which he gave directions to the taxi-driver. "Avoid Dadar... stick to the main road, past the Prabhadevi telephone exchange," he said. He turned around to tell his family, "Bombay is not like Calcutta, you know. People here work very hard. No time to waste. See how beautiful the roads are."

Just then, they passed a small mountain of mud where one section of the street had been untidily dug up to lay new telephone cables. His wife pointed to it and said, "Look, just like Calcutta. No difference."

Pooja squeezed her father's hand and smiled at him, adding softly, "The buildings are nice. Really big. And quite clean."

Khokun screwed up his eyes tight and refused to look at anything. Pooja wondered about their temporary home. What would it be like? She imagined a 5-star hotel suite with thick egg-shell blue carpeting, fancy sofas, three of four air-conditioners and satin drapes. In reality it turned out to be like any ordinary transit flat — functional without being fancy. Pooja did a quick check, taking care to hide her disappointment. She came out into the tiny sitting room to report, "There's a geyser in the bathroom — imagine, a geyser. Now we won't have to heat our bath water over a stove."

Her mother was half-lying on a cane chair, breathing heavily. "Go to the kitchen — if there is one — and see if there's at least a fridge in there. I'm dying of thirst." Pooja's father was busy dragging heavy suitcases out of the lift without any help from the man who ran the guest house.

Piyali muttered, "In Calcutta, people are not so unhelpful. They don't stand there and stare while the bosses do all the work. Well, what can one expect here? This is Bombay, after all."

Khokun was absorbed in excavating a misplaced lollipop from the small overnight case he'd carried on the plane. Pooja went into the bedroom and sat on the low, narrow bed. She tried to switch on the bedside lamp. It didn't work. The covers smelt strongly of mothballs. She started to sneeze. Her mother called out from outside. "Look at that girl — not even a few hours in a new place and she has caught a cold. I hope we won't need a doctor this time. It's my bad luck — wherever we go, this girl falls sick and spoils everything."

Pooja was used to being referred to as "this girl" by her mother, who rarely called her by her given name. And unlike most other Bengali children, Pooja didn't have a "dak" or pet name either — the standard endearment used by the family over the other more formal name. Not that she minded. She liked being "Pooja" — it had a sweet, appealing sound to it. Pooja, Pooja, Pooja. Prayer. Prayer. Prayer. Even though Pooja knew she wasn't an answer to her mother's, her father liked to call her that. So did her friends at school. Khokun was forced to address her as "didi", which he did reluctantly. Most times though, brother and sister left each other well alone. When Suchi asked Pooja why she didn't get along with Khokun, she answered simply, "Because we have nothing in common".

They didn't. Pooja was a dreamer, a poor eater and an introvert, Khokun, a brash, selfish bully used to having his own way. Sometimes Pooja wished she had a sister, another girl in the house to talk to, to play with. Once, she'd made the mistake of saying so aloud, when the family sat together for dinner. Her mother had hit her forehead dramatically with the palm of her hand and exclaimed, "Hey Ma! Don't even joke about it. Another girl? Are you my enemy that you're cursing me this way? One is bad enough. Already I worry myself to death over your marriage. It's not going to be all that easy finding a husband for you. Look at yourself — so thin, pale and sickly. Which man would want to be stuck with a lifelong patient, tell me? And you're talking of a sister. No, no, no. May Kali ma spare me."

Her father had exchanged a conspiratorial look with Pooja and blinked his eyes rapidly to indicate she was not to take her mother's outburst seriously. Despite that, Pooja's eyes had filled with tears and she'd left the table without finishing dinner. Her mother's voice had rung in her ears. "Just look at that girl. Defiant. That's what she is. Leaving a whole piece of fish uneaten. Expensive fish at that. Does she know I paid a small fortune for it this morning? No value for money. And too much pride. It's not good for a girl to have this much pride. Will it be tolerated in her husband's home? Will she dare to throw such tantrums there? Never. She does it here because she knows her father will put up with it. Well, it's fine by me. It's his money that's paid for the fish after all. Not mine."

Pooja walked into the small balcony and looked around interestedly. She decided there and then that she was going to like Bombay, and her new school.

Inside the house, the phone was ringing and her father was far too preoccupied to pay much attention to his family. Khokun was complaining of a stomachache again as he rolled around on the bed, kicking his legs in the air and howling. Her mother was examining the bathroom critically, sniffing and grumbling. "No soap. No mug. No towels. Where have we arrived? God knows what sort of food we'll have to eat now. Whether we'll get fresh water fish in this city."

Pooja came back into the room and said brightly, "Ma, there are lots of good shops here — I've seen them in the ads. Let's go shopping tomorrow. I need new jeans."

Her mother whirled around, "Is that all you can think of? Fashion? Jeans? Here's your mother worried about basic necessities and your brother suffering so much. And you are talking about jeans."

Her father, noticing the stricken expression in Pooja's eyes, came over and said softly, "Meet me after office tomorrow and I'll take you out."

"I heard that," the mother screamed. "Always planning things behind my back, always talking about me. Am I your enemy? Go ahead and buy her jeans. Buy her the Taj Mahal too. But remember, if things get out of hand, I won't be there to control this wilful daughter of yours."

Pooja wondered why her mother always disowned her by saying "your daughter", to the father. Hadn't she carried her in her womb? Once, in a crying fit, she'd shouted, "Are you really my mother? I don't believe I've come out of your womb. Why do you hate me so much? I'm sure you're my stepmother. You're lying. You don't want me to know the truth."

Her grandmother had interfered at one time and reprimanded her daughter-in-law, "What are you doing to this poor child? You should have killed her in your womb itself if you didn't want a daughter. Why do women give birth to unwanted children? It's not Pooja's fault. Aren't you a woman yourself? Or did your mother treat you like this too?"

Pooja often recalled that scene and strangely enough, it invariably ended up with her feeling intensely sorry for her mother. There was so much pent-up anger in her, it puzzled Pooja. What made her so unhappy? So discontented? From what Pooja could tell, all of them enjoyed a good life. Her father was a pleasant man, and the grandparents weren't monsters. Plus, there was Khokun — her mother's most-prized trophy. Maybe Bombay would take care of it all.

But Bombay didn't. A month after their arrival, they moved into a cramped flat at Colaba. It was supposedly a new construction but the plumbing was terrible and the lifts hardly worked. Pooja's mother had lapsed into a permanent state of depression and babbled on all day about how sick Bombay made her. She walked around the house with her saree pallav pressed against her nose. "The stench from Sassoon Docks with all that rotting fish lying there is going to kill me," she told everybody. She wept on the phone to her sister in Calcutta, "We live near a fishing village. They dry fish on the dirty roads here. People walk all over them with shoes on. Dogs piss on the prawns. Beggars pick them up by the fistful. Nobody cares. And the stink — worse than Calcutta's Tangda district. There it's only animal hides drying, one gets used to that. Here it's rotting fish. When the tide is low, it's worse. People do their big jobs along the beach. Yes, they shit in public. The stink gets even worse. My husband has brought me here to die."

Pooja was enjoying her new school as much as Khokun was hating it. They were together in one building for the first time, since Pooja's father had picked a co-ed school, not out of conviction but convenience. "It makes it easier to drop them in the morning. And Pooja can bring back her brother by bus in the afternoon."

Other kids, as kids everywhere generally do, poked fun of both Pooja and Khokun for the first few days. "Your accent is so funny. Are you sure you're speaking English? You sound like you've got a laddoo in your mouth." They were merciless with Khokun, calling him "Fatty Bombola" and pushing him around during gym classes. Pooja decided to handle it by laughing at her tormentors. Khokun whined all the time, requiring physical persuasion to go to school each morning. Their father was far too busy making an impression on his boss to pay too much attention to what was going on at home, which made their mother still more miserable. Her first visit was to the fish market nearby. She came home reeling. "People in this city eat the sort of fish our cats in Calcutta would reject. Have they no refinement, no taste? And look at what I've bought for hundred rupees. Two gulps and it will be finished."

Her husband smiled, "Then let's eat vegetables from tomorrow. I don't mind."

Pooja nodded enthusiastically, "I like vegetables".

Her mother glared at both of them. "I've been raised in a family that ate good fish twice a day. Twice. Even our servants were given fish heads to cook. Do you think I could ever consider eating vegetables? And just look of the vegetables. Come with me to the market — I'll show you. Miserable. Wilted leaves, hardened turnips, shrivelled up radishes, sorry-looking potatoes and misshapen onions. No variety at all. The size of the potols has to be seen to be believed. Like shrunken ping-pong balls. What am I going to cook? What will poor Khokun eat? He's going to starve here, poor boy. Mark my words. And he'll fall sick." Pooja's father looked at his son eating the large pile of rice on his plate.

"Pickle, I want pickle," he was sniffling.

"Nothing tastes good here, not even the mustard oil," his mother added. "As for neighbours — huh — do you think anybody is bothered? I'm alone in this wretched flat all day — has anybody come to see me? Offer help? No. In Calcutta we wouldn't have had to cook for a week — everybody would've brought food and made us feel welcome. And look at Bombay servants — they come to work dressed like film stars and expect to be treated like royalty. Are they doing me a favour by working in my house? That's how they behave. What arrogance! And what fancy notions! Thousand rupees — she asked me for a thousand rupees. I thought she was joking. Instead of my interviewing her, she was interviewing me— the cheek of it! 'Do you have a separate TV in the servants' room?' Is there cable TV in this building? I need two hours to go downstairs every evening, plus a weekly off.'" Piyali mimicked the maid. "The woman thought she was a maharani. I felt embarrassed looking at her face — lipstick, powder, kajal. Can you believe it? Am I going to employ a maidservant or a queen?" Pooja, at that very moment, was seized by an uncontrollable fit of giggles. "Stop that," her mother screamed, "before I beat you black and blue."

The real crisis in the Ghosh family arose when Mrs. Ghosh was invited to join the building kitty club. In Calcutta, she'd been accustomed to meeting an informal group of ladies off and on without the constraints of belonging to a formal club.

In any case, a club in Calcutta meant just one place — the club your husband was a member of. Or clubs if he happened to be upwardly mobile and ambitious. She remembered his interview call for the elite Calcutta Club and what nervous wrecks the two

of them had become. By then, he was already a member of the
Saturday Club and on the waiting list of "Tolly" (as the verdant
Tollygunje Club was referred to). The "call" had involved
preparatory work. He'd worked on the all-important selection
committee members for months, courting them assiduously over
gin-tonics and beer, trying desperately to make a good impression
on them. Piyali had done her bit as well by inviting the wives of
prominent members to lunch in the hope that their husbands would
sign on as "seconders" on the wives' recommendation. The father-
in-law had been completely baffled and had asked bluntly at the
dinner table, "Why do you want to be a member of so many clubs?
Isn't one enough?"

The son had answered shortly, "You won't understand. It is
important from the business point of view. These are the places
where all the contacts are made. If I ever want to change jobs in
the future...this will be the best way to impress new bosses."

The old man had shaken his head and said, "In our time, if we
wanted to impress our superiors, we did it through our work."

Piyali had flashed a warning signal to her husband. This was
how most arguments started and ruined dinner. And, today she had
taken care over the meal, spending hours to make sure the coconut
milk for the prawn curry was of the right consistency — neither
too watery nor too thick, and free of pulpy remnants.

Of course, she wanted to get into the Calcutta Club herself.
Some of her friends were members and it made her feel small when
they discussed weekend events or beer sessions on holidays. But
she wasn't at all confident about the interviews. Prodip was a
reasonably smart man, but when she compared him to Shefali's
husband, for instance, he seemed too mild and diffident. Perhaps,
too decent. In today's world, a man needed to be pushy...
aggressive...ambitious. To make a good impression, the two of
them rehearsed for days, even inventing right-sounding social patter
and memorising the names of different wines and liqueurs. Though
Prodip was an occasional smoker who bummed the odd cigarette
from colleagues, for this occasion he'd invested in an imported

pack of Marlboros and had stood in front of a mirror blowing smoke rings in the air with tears streaming out of his eyes. He'd asked his wife to show him what she planned to wear that evening. She'd brought out a new synthetic silk salwar kameez, and a traditional Tangail saree (the one she'd bought for the last "Puja" festival). He'd looked uncertainly at both and said, "I don't know — do you think green really suits you? And that salwar kameez makes you look very fat. Why not buy a new saree — maybe a light blue one? You look fairer in blue." She'd rummaged through her cupboard but hadn't been able to come up with a thing that met with his approval.

It had been her turn to review his clothes. "Oh, I'll wear my dark blue suit, of course. It fits me best. And that imported shirt — the one I got from London. Stripes. It looks British. And goes with the maroon tie."

She'd taken her time to consider before saying, "But the collar of the shirt — isn't it tight? You said you couldn't wear a tie with it because your neck got caught in the buttonhole."

Prodip had shrugged, "I don't mind being uncomfortable for a few hours. I don't have a better shirt."

Piyali had offered to get him a new one the next morning on her way back from the market. "I'll pick up a Zodiac — I've seen the new ads in *The Telegraph*. Very good. Some with white collars. Some without."

Prodip had dismissed the suggestion with an impatient shake of his head. "The London shirt is fine. I feel all right in it. Remember — don't speak unless someone asks you a question. Don't laugh loudly at a joke. Don't yawn. Don't fidget with your saree. Look interested without being inquisitive. Don't express any opinions. And don't, for God's sake, eat anything and everything that's offered to you...even out of nervousness."

Piyali had looked at her husband witheringly. "And you — you just make sure you don't drink too much. You know what an ass you make of yourself after even the third beer."

And so they'd presented themselves to the committee — she

in blue and he in grey. It had turned out to be a painless encounter that they'd passed with flying colours. Though it hadn't prepared Piyali for what she had had to undergo in order to make a favourable impression at her maiden kitty party in Bombay. Her husband had tried to console her. "It's nothing to get worked up about. It's a casual sort of afternoon where a group of ladies meet and chat and eat. That's all. You be charming and friendly and they'll accept you."

Piyali had hesitated a little before breaking it to him that this wasn't going to be a free lunch. "Each woman has to contribute five hundred bucks," she said.

Prodip had yelled, "What? Why? You mean you have to pay for your lunch even when some woman has invited you to her home?"

Piyali had explained that it didn't work quite like that. "When my turn for the kitty comes, I'll get back all the money. It's one way of saving."

Prodip had retorted, "I don't understand. What are you saving?"

"I get a lump sum when my name is drawn out, when my turn comes — so if there are ten women contributing five hundred each, I'll get five thousand rupees over ten months."

Prodip had laughed, "Well, if you were to deposit that amount in the bank each month, you'd still save five thousand in ten months plus earn interest on the amount."

Piyali had shaken her head in the way she often did when she wanted him to know that women thought differently from men, and said, "You won't understand. It's our way of doing things. In any case, it you don't want me to join the kitty just say so. Or, I could always ask my sister for a loan. Five hundred rupees are nothing to her..."

He had left the room saying, "Yes, yes, yes, ask her. We know how rich and generous she is, don't we — go ahead and take it from her. Leave me out of your kitty nonsense."

Piyali had decided to wear the newer of her two dhakai sarees — the one that had been given to her by her sister. She looked at herself in the hazy mirror. Would these Bombay women find her hopelessly unsophisticated? Would they think her saree old-fashioned? What about her thick, dark hair? Should she try the Chinese girl behind the Taj Mahal Hotel? Or would she be far too expensive? She had stared at her unpolished nails — she assumed most of the women she would meet would have manicured ones. And they'd have neatly threaded eyebrows, bleached moustaches and waxed arms. It was too late for all that now. But at least she had nice gold jewellery from Calcutta. Bombay gold had a different colour, a different sheen. It looked far too brassy, too yellow. She was doubtful of its purity. It couldn't be 23-carat, no matter what those sly jewellers claimed. She brought out her day-time set and scrutinised it with pride. Her sister had chosen it. She had such fine taste. Piyali envied her for it. And for several other things too, of course.

Aarti had married a businessman — and not a Bengali at that. But how happy she was in her nice Dover Road flat. No children to worry about. Membership at four clubs. Holidays in "bilayat". Countless beautiful sarees and enough gold jewellery to last five lifetimes. Each time they met, Aarti showed her something new — a kitchen gadget, fax machine (one at home, one at the office), laser discs, CD player. My God! That husband of hers really spoilt her. Each time he went to Hong Kong, he came back with a suitcase full of presents — lovely nighties, frilly panties, nice bras and so many bottles of perfume.

Aarti was a generous woman — she didn't mind passing on a few things to her sister. But Prodip minded it a lot. "Why do you accept charity from your sister? We know she is married to a rich man, but that does not mean she has to show off. God knows how that brother-in-law of yours makes his money — though I have a fairly good idea."

Piyali had thought her husband was mean to say such things. Maybe he was just jealous. Anyway she felt grateful for all the clothes Aarti gave her and she felt no shame in using them.

When she walked into Mrs. Ramsinghani's seventh floor flat, she couldn't spot one familiar face. There were about ten women sitting around langourously, drinks in their hands. As she entered, all of them stared at her, sizing her up, pulling out mental calculators to assess her worth. She stood uncertainly at the entrance, not knowing quite what to do. Was she supposed to hand over her contribution of five hundred rupees to someone straightaway? Could she just walk in and sit down? Or was she expected to introduce herself while she waited for the hostess to show up? Her agonising suspense ended when an enormous ball of shiny, smelly satin silk swooped down and enveloped her in a suffocating hug. Piyali, gagged, overwhelmed by the stale aroma of the strong perfume Anita Ramsinghani had doused herself with. Two sticky kisses on her cheeks later Piyali was taken by her arm and introduced to the others as "the new Bengali lady in our building — she is very artistic".

Piyali blushed as the women appraised her, with little squeals of "oh, really?" thrown in. A man servant appeared with a tray filled with piping hot cocktail samosas. The women pounced on them hungrily, clawing at the small deep-fried snacks like cats attacking a basketful of mice.

"So...Mrs. Ghosh, isn't it? What do you do? Just a housewife?"

Piyali wasn't sure what the acceptable response to that was. Should she explain her background? That she wanted to be a lecturer? And that as soon as she'd settled her kids, she'd look for a job in Bombay? That is, if she didn't suffer a nervous breakdown before that and decide to go back to her mother's home in Calcutta? She didn't say any of this. Instead, she smiled non-commitally and confessed, "Yes...I'm just a housewife".

Dozens of questions followed, most of them intensely personal. The women got her name consistently wrong, even though it was simple enough. They made little jokes about all Bengalis looking alike and talking alike. "If they aren't Chatterjees then they're Mukherjees. How do you people keep track?"

Piyali watched and listened but did not participate. She felt disoriented and dizzy. Perhaps it was all that perfume in the room. Or all those vivid colours. The women had strange straw-like hair, and very red mouths. They spoke too fast and laughed too much even when nothing funny was being said. One small group was shuffling two packs of cards efficiently, another lot was gossiping about a regular member who was absent that afternoon. ("Poor thing, how could she come when she knows that we all know about her husband's affair with his secretary?")

To her left, a woman had pulled out a blue velvet tray and spread out pieces of jewellery on it. She was discussing weights and prices per gram, making charges and wax content. Two ladies were busy pushing thick gold loops into their fleshy ear-lobes as they studied their images in a hand-mirror. She overheard the fatter of the two saying, "My husband will kill me if I buy one more pair of earrings. Do you know he nearly had a heartattack the last time he peeped into my cupboard? But it's o.k. I won't ask him to pay for this. I'll take it out of the housemoney."

The other woman, in a purple-and-gold saree, shrieked in mock horror, "House money? So much? Won't he find out? My husband is such a bloody miser — he counts every ten buck note and makes me explain if a couple are missing."

The hostess fluttered in and out of the kitchen carrying plates of food. "Just snacks, girls — the main courses are coming out later." She seemed nervous and anxious as she screamed at her maid servants and rearranged the flowers for the nth time, "Useless women," she kept cursing, "can't rely on them at all".

Piyali didn't care for the snacks. They were far too oily, besides being impossibly fiery. Mrs. Ramsinghani came and sat down heavily next to her. "You must be getting a little bored, no? It's always like this for the first few times. But don't worry — after six months or so, you'll start enjoying yourself. Hey where's your drink? No drink? What's the matter? Scared of your hubby? No probs, yaar. Have vodka or gin. No smell, nothing."

Piyali shook her head and shifted uncomfortably. Mrs. Ramsinghani had onion and garlic on her breath, the most awful body odour and was sweating all over Piyali's crisp dhakai saree. Piyali's head was reeling with the noise and the overpowering kitchen smells. She thought she would faint. She leaned back against the plastic-covered head-rest of the sofa. Mrs. Ramsinghani placed greasy fingers on her forehead and asked solicitously, "Not well, dear? Oh...oh...maybe you are you-know-what. Does your hubby know? My, my, good news, good news! Shall we tell the girls? Let's hope it's another boy — you have one, already, don't you? Yes, I've seen him. A little overweight, poor fellow. Must be eating all your sweet-sweet Bengali food. Tell me — when are you calling us over for dinner? We want to taste your fish-dish — but please, no mustard oil, all right? We people don't like that horrible smell."

Piyali shut her eyes. She felt she was going to black out. It reminded her of the time she'd been given general anaesthesia when an abcess on her thigh needed surgery. She thought of Aarti and how she would have conducted herself on such an occasion. She knew she hadn't made a good impression on these Bombay women. She had noticed them staring at her, their plucked, penciled eyebrows arched in disgust and surprise. She had always known it. Why hadn't her husband listened to her when she'd said she didn't want to go to Bombay? She thought of her mother's home in South Calcutta — cool, calm and neat. She wanted to go back. Go there. And stay there. Who needed her here, anyway? Not Pooja — she'd settled in splendidly. Not her husband — his office had claimed him body and soul. Not even Khokun — he was fine so long as his chocolate supply didn't dry up. The kitty party had given her the answer. Before she passed out, she saw the imposing Howrah Bridge floating in front of her eyes. She was crossing it slowly. Steadily. Along with thousands of others. But they weren't strangers. Not at all. They all belonged to Calcutta.

85

Seven

THE BAR MAN

SANTOSH WAS back in Bombay after close to fifteen years. He barley recognised the city he'd once been a hero of. Swashbuckling, sought-after, upwardly-mobile, with a swanky company flat on Peddar Road, Santosh had been the captain of the rugby team at the Bombay Gymkhana and each time he had walked off the field and into the main club house covered with gooey mud, the rugby shirt sticking to his well-muscled, hard body, the shorts climbing tantalisingly up his taut, hairy thighs, at least five women had sighed audibly and reached for their cool nimbu-paanis afraid of swooning at his filthy feet.

And now, as he swaggered into the familiar well-lit, plant lined corridor, the city he hardly recognised, didn't pay any attention to him either. All he got were a couple of disinterested glances from young, glamorous mothers clad in spangled T-shirts and bottom-hugging jeans. He glanced at his reflection in the smoked glass sheets encasing the bar and dining room. Instinctively, he tucked in his gut — not that he'd let himself go — but there were two extra inches sitting obstinately around his midriff now. He checked his hair-line and patted the few wispy strands he groomed so carefully each time he went to the men's room. Gone...nearly all of it. And to think there had been a time he couldn't run his own fingers through the thick, glossy mop on his head. More than his altered silhouette, it was the shining pate that had let him down. Aged him. Though he'd tried it all — herbal oils, special creams, hair tonics purchased abroad. He'd even considered grafting — till he'd recoiled at the sight of a colleague's head — it resembled a freshly-sown corn field after the hair-job. No. That was out.

Santosh strode into the men's room. He was sure he'd find a familiar person in there. This was crazy! Was fifteen years all that long a time? As he stood facing the urinal, his mind went back to the days when he'd be in the shower-room close by, singing bawdy rugby songs with the boys after a match. Celebrating. Rejoicing. Confident in the knowledge that freshly-showered, combed and perfumed, he'd walk out to drooling fans of both sexes dying to buy him a drink in the cool, wood-panelled bar with its old hunting scenes lining the walls. How he loved his Club! It was his second home — the place he headed for right after knocking off from his functional office by the sea. The place he rushed to first thing in the morning for some brisk sets of tennis, followed by a shower and a quick breakfast, before he hit his office cabin at 9 a.m. Always on time if not early. Always the driven executive, already busy at his work-table as the others trickled in. The Club took care of his lunch too. A hurried affair with clients or colleagues, it was generally a toasted sandwich or a plate of chow mein. And then, of course, he'd be back after work for his obligatory forty lengths in the pool before exhausting himself on the squash courts. Sporty Santosh. Yup, that was him. He looked it too. Looked great. Everybody told him so — even the drunks at the bar, who generally spent their time tearing everybody to pieces, especially the jocks who strutted around aggressively and came on strong with the girls. He was "one of the guys". They liked him, even if they often envied him his seamless success with the women. And other men, of course. Those fastidiously dressed fags with solitaires in their ear-lobes (left? right? Santosh could never be sure). They hung around him hungrily, pouting even when they knew he wasn't "thataway". He really wasn't. Not even during those nine nasty years in an exclusive boarding school in the hills up north. Nine years of resisting , resisting. As he repeated to the senior boys, he was not a "launda".

Santosh considered himself lucky that he hadn't been raped. The only reason he'd been spared, was thanks to his left hook. Santosh was a tough kid, and an accomplished boxer....tougher than most of the older boys. He'd fought off at least fifteen of them during those agonising first two years till finally the message had penetrated. Though that hadn't stopped younger boys from developing massive crushes on Santosh. He was, after all, the star of his batch — the captain of the football team, a gymnast, a basketball player and...and...a pretty good actor too. But he knew how to handle worshipful youngsters. Besides, he was inwardly flattered by their adulation. He could have taken advantage of his position, as most other chaps did. But Santosh had his principles. He loved repeating that he'd never crawled into a senior's bed and offered his butt, and he wasn't about to take anyone else's now that he was a senior himself. Not that he hadn't been tempted. Even now when he recalled his first meeting with Chetan ("The Princeling"), he felt himself drawing in his breath sharply.

Chetan had been the most perfectly proportioned, the most divinely chiselled, the most outstandingly sculpted human being Santosh had ever seen. After leaving school, he'd been around, travelled, seen life. But he still hadn't encountered anybody even remotely like Chetan. It was in the aristocratic air of arrogance he exuded, the slightly twisted lines of his mouth, the meanness of his narrow, fox-like yellow-green eyes, those high cheekbones...the long brown hair, the slightly crooked aquiline nose, the disproportionately large (as compared to the wonderfully balanced planes of the rest of his face) ears, the long, strong neck, the proud tilt of his head, the faint sneer...the challenging, steady gaze, the flat, noble forehead.

Chetan had a champion swimmer's V-shaped body — strong torso, narrow hips, powerful arms. And a tanned, wide back in which each muscle rippled and glistened under the sun when he emerged from the school pool like some ancient god — a creature of such dangerous beauty, people were afraid to go too close to him. But Santosh had. Drawn by a force he couldn't resist and

didn't want to. And when he had got close enough, he had found
Chetan waiting. At that moment of recognition, Santosh had recoiled
and almost turned back. But Chetan's strange eyes had held
him...frozen him, as he rose silently like a lithe jungle cat and
crossed the small distance between them in five easy strides. He
was a dancer, an enchantress, a mythical animal stalking his prey.
He had moved around Santosh slowly, deliberately, never leaving
his eyes, encircling him in an invisible web, moving with the grace
of a sleepy leopard, till Santosh had felt his knees giving way, his
head reeling as he reached out blindly, desperately for something
to hold on to — to steady himself against. And his hands had
found Chetan. Santosh had been powerless. He knew he didn't
want to fight as Chetan's mouth sought his with unexpected
tenderness. Even love.

It was a secret both of them had guarded closely. Nobody but
nobody had gotten to know of it — not even the nosiest prefect.
Santosh marvelled at how they had managed to keep their
relationship private, given the complete absence of privacy in their
school. But they had succeeded because it was an unspoken pact
between them — an oath never really taken. It had mattered too
much. They had valued what they shared too much. And while
Chetan had been dubbed "the slut" after Santosh and he eventually
broke off, for Santosh it had been the only homosexual encounter
of his life.

He had often wondered what had become of Chetan. For a
while he'd even tried to keep track of him.

He knew Chetan had been sent to England for his "O" and later
"A" levels. He also knew he'd later gone to America and acquired
a degree in art history from Stanford. But nobody could enlighten
Santosh on what had happened after that. It was rumoured that
Chetan had married an English girl (an adoring junior) he'd met
in California and they'd produced three sons in quick succession.
If he had visited India during that period the visit had been kept

so private that only his immediate family had known his plans. But Santosh hadn't forgotten Chetan.

He couldn't. He'd wanted to, of course. Especially after school when they had gone their separate ways, but the memory of Chetan came back to him at the unlikeliest of times. Chetan came alive in Santosh's dreams in which, strangely enough, Chetan was still an athletic school-boy and Santosh his contemporary adult self. There was no guilt in these recollections. Just longing and nostalgia for the intensity of an ardour once experienced and then lost for good.

Santosh strode into the bar the Gymkhana with an air of preoccupied purpose. He had a couple of hours to kill before his next appointment. He decided to spend them in the Club instead of at his hotel. After all he still coughed up his annual membership fee even though he didn't utilise a single facility. The old bartender was gone ("a job in Dubai" his replacement mentioned). And Santosh couldn't recognise any of the stewards either ("new management, boss," the bartender mumbled, "and too much union trouble"). Santosh looked around interestedly. He missed the earlier warmth and cosiness of the place. The renovated bar was impersonal, gleaming and sterile — like any bar in a busy airport lounge. The old one had had character — with stained glass panels, wooden beams, silver trophies and charming gouaches on the pale green walls. Besides, it had been the sort of bar designed for serious drinkers, which automatically eliminated women — unless they were like Sula — the khasi woman married to a tea man who could out-drink, out-smoke and out-swear most of the males seated on the rickety bamboo bar stools elbows resting on the polished counter. She was gone too ("Died, boss. Cancer. Terrible how she suffered"). The "regulars" were missing as well.

Santosh checked himself. What did he expect after so many years? There was no point in badgering the bartender. He couldn't have known any of those fellows — apart from the Maharajah of course. Everybody knew him because of his monumental size. He'd become a part of Club lore. A permanent fixture who routinely wept into his vodka-tonics and narrated the sad story of his life to whosoever cared to listen. It was the same old "My wife doesn't love me," with occasionally a small variation, "She loves my son." The Maharajah's third marriage to a flashy airline stewardess had seemed absurd to everyone but the besotted bridegroom. With grown children from his previous marriages, he'd gone ahead and brought a nubile bride home with expected consequences. She'd taken up with her stepson right after the official honeymoon was over, leaving the Maharajah to seek whatever small consolation he could wrench out of his bar buddies over rounds of beer bought by him.

Santosh stared at all the new faces around, looking desperately for at least one from his past. Everybody looked so young. So animated. So alive. Especially the women. Their air of supreme confidence scared him somewhat, reminding him of the time he'd tried to strike up a conversation with a strange woman in the bar of the Hilton in New York only to be rebuffed in icy, very-easy-to-understand terms. But she'd looked so friendly and warm, he'd thought to himself in utter puzzlement later. And it wasn't as if he'd made a crude pass or anything. He wasn't that unsophisticated. Maybe she'd mistaken him for an "Average Indian Male" — the frustrated, uncouth first-timer to the West who imagined every woman on the street was easy game. Santosh had never forgotten the look of utter contempt in the woman's eyes. The females he saw at the Club today weren't all that different if you overlooked their colour. They were dressed the same, made up the same, and from the few lines of conversation he'd overheard, they even spoke the same language. Mainly marketing jargon liberally sprinkled with current buzz words.

He had a few these in his office — many rungs junior to him, of course. They fascinated and frightened him. He often wondered what they were like outside the office environment. Specifically, what they were like in bed. He'd joked about it once with a male

92

colleague only to be told smugly, "They're great, man. Just great. They prefer being on top. Which means less strain for us." Santosh had felt foolish. As if he'd given himself away — all but confessed that he hadn't scored with any of them. He, Santosh, the man regarded by other men as something of a Casanova, the one with the sure touch. But he hadn't scored with anyone in a long, long time.

Santosh looked around at the men. He vaguely recognised two or three executive-types. Thinning hair, he noted with some satisfaction. And paunches. Grey whiskers and bad teeth. He stole a quick glance at himself in the large mirrored screen behind the bar and perked up his shirt collar unconsciously — a gesture from his college days that had once driven the girls wild.

His life had had its lows all right, but he wasn't exactly displeased with the overall score-card. Career-wise at least, he couldn't complain — not really. Apart from that solitary setback when his Brit boss had victimised and humiliated him, Santosh had risen steadily and become something of a "burra saab" himself. Colleagues commented on his cushy lifestyle — the fancy expense account, the travel, the perks. Santosh rather enjoyed the look of envy he glimpsed in their eyes when he turned up at office parties in his latest Italian sports shirt and faded jeans. The wives would look him up and down appreciatively, tilt their heads and tease, "Still single, handsome?" and Santosh would give them the familiar thumbs-up sign, grin and say. "Yes. And still happy." But was he really?

He started as a woman walked in with a small group of carefully groomed ladies. It was the perfume he recognised first. So familiar...so distressingly familiar. It had to be her. He wanted to stare....but he controlled himself. What if she didn't recognise him? What an ass he'd feel. He watched from the corners of his eyes, as the women moved towards the dining area, their starched, pastel-coloured muslin kurtas crackling as they walked. He could see her back now — broader than he remembered it. And the hair, significantly, shorter. Fool woman! Why had she cut it? And the colour. Oh no, no, no — had she too joined the henna brigade? It looked unnaturally red, though mercifully not carroty orange. Sushmita had gained weight all right but she still looked beautiful. Santosh watched the women as they fussed about the table, the seating, the uncleared plates and finally flounced off to a far corner to flop on a long settee against the wall. Damm! He couldn't see her now. But if he shifted from his position...maybe two seats down the left...yes...he could watch from here without her catching him staring.

Santosh was surprised at himself. At the first sight of her, his heart had started thudding uncontrollably... unreasonably. He'd said to himself, "You stupid jerk, behave yourself. After all these years, she still has that effect on you. What are you — some kind of an idiot? Stop behaving like an asshole. Stop right now." And yet his eyes had continued to trail her as she fussed around with the rest of the group. That wasn't like her at all, he mused. She was such a serene person. So placid and calm. Or had she changed beyond recognition too? Too? He hadn't. He was pretty much the man he'd been at their last encounter. Though maybe not physically. He ordered another drink and debated whether or not to stroll past her table casually, feign surprise, freeze, shrug, raise his eyebrows, stick out his left leg à la Fred Astaire, say, "Hey, hey, hey...if it isn't...?" and take it from there. Surely she'd dealt with a similar situation before. There must have been dozens of men...admirers...in her life since...or earlier. She was poised enough to handle nearly any exigency. And this would be simple enough to laugh away in case her friends wondered. She could smile that winning smile of hers, lower her voice conspiratorially and say, "He's...he's...an old flame that's all." The women in the group would then look critically at his retreating back, exchange glances, giggle and exclaim knowingly, "Oh...one of those...serial number?"

No, Santosh couldn't risk it. He hated the thought of making a fool of himself. And yet, had Sushmita been alone...waiting for someone...her husband, perhaps Santosh would have approached her confidently and risked the possibility of a snub. He wondered whether she was still married to the same chap. Knowing her as well as he did, she probably was. Sushmita wasn't the sort of woman to rock the boat too violently. Their affair had been a "major event" as she'd called it, and not one of her passing flings. It had lasted four years — as long as she'd been married at that point. And her husband had known about it all along — or so she had told Santosh the night they had finally broken up. That had been his final humiliation. The bastard had known. And kept perfectly quiet. A man does that only when a rival poses no threat to him. Santosh had looked into Sushmita's luminous, dark eyes (now tinged with a vague tristesse) and wept. She had remained dry-eyed and distant, as if she was already somewhere else with someone else. "It is another man, isn't it?" Santosh had whimpered, adding, "the chap with whom you go for long walks at the Race Course? I knew it. I knew it. I should have stopped that nonsense as soon as it started."

Sushmita had raised her eyebrows and mocked, "Stopped it? Goodness, that's ambitious."

Santosh had begged and pleaded ...even threatened. She'd looked into the far distance and pronounced, "October is truly the worst month of the year in Bombay — worse than May even, don't you agree?" With that, she'd picked up her elegant bag and floated out on a cloud of "Calèche". Her trademark fragrance. The same one that had wafted in and jolted him a little earlier. The same one that had penetrated his memory through the thick cloud of cigarette smoke, alcohol fumes, sweat and strong after-shaves that hung over the bar.

Santosh wondered whether she was still married. She looked terribly married, with an air about her that proclaimed that she was well-settled. Almost matronly. Her face was fuller and a few shades fairer than he remembered it. He couldn't see her arms through the long sleeves. He wondered if they were still as slender. Her midiff was definitely wider. Santosh calculated her approximate age (she was the sort of woman who was paranoid about revealing it). He figured that she would be touching forty-four. She looked younger than that. No noticeable lines under those wonderful eyes, no puffiness either. Maybe she'd remained a teetotaller — out of vanity more than any high moral principles. He remembered her nagging him, "Booze is bad for the figure, bad for the skin, bad for the eyes, bad for hair..."

He'd interrupted her with, "...but great for sex. And good for the soul."

Sushmita hadn't been a sex-oriented woman. And yet most men found her irresistible. Perhaps it was her aloofness that attracted them. Santosh had deluded himself into believing she'd achieved her first orgasm with him. Today, as he looked at her, so cool and in control, he wondered whether it was a lie she'd trotted out to several other besotted fools. Men were such gullible dolts when it came to sex. It wasn't enough that a woman was willing to share her bed with them — they wanted to impress her as well. She'd probably lied, Santosh concluded. After all, when a married woman claims she hasn't felt the earth move with her husband, she's only trying to make the lover feel superior. It was such a tragic ploy and one that every man ended up falling for. As if getting a woman to orgasm was a feat comparable to scaling the Everest. Besides, you only had her word for it. And Santosh knew what inveterate liars women were. They lied for the heck of it. They lied because for them it was the most natural thing to do. They lied because lying was fun. They lied to save their skins. They lied for survival.

She was sipping fresh orange juice. Was it spiked? And she was laughing excessively. That was new. Sushmita had always been self-conscious about her teeth and rarely liked to show them. But here she was, head thrown back, laughing full-throatedly. What was she finding so funny? She hadn't had much of a sense of humour. His jokes had invariably fallen flat on her. Those women with her didn't look all that lively...or was she trying to attract someone's attention?

Santosh looked at the other tables. The dining section was completely filled with predominantly young people — well, much younger than he was — eating quick, small lunches and talking animatedly between mouthfuls. Sushmita was looking at the Day's Menu and wrinkling up her nose. She summoned the Manager, who scurried over promptly. That meant she was the wife of a big shot. Maybe that dope of a husband had risen in his firm. But had he been a major player, Santosh would've heard of him. Or at least read about him in the business press. Maybe she had divorced him and married someone else or maybe she just lunched at the Club regularly and left fat tips (against Club rules, but then Sushmita didn't let such things bother her). Strange how they hadn't made eye contact so far. Some of the other women at her table had glanced in Santosh's direction once or twice. But not Sushmita. She'd barely looked around her. Not that it surprised Santosh. She'd often make fun of people with "restless, darting eyes", women in particular. It was a habit she found distasteful. He remembered her rapping him sharply across the knuckles with a fork and saying, "Stop that. Your roving eyes make me giddy. What or who are you looking at when I'm there sitting across from you?" He'd thought she was being egoistic. She'd explained patiently that that wasn't the case. "Eyes that keep roaming... straying...reveal a mind that lacks focus." And Santosh had obediently locked eyes with her and made a mental note of concentrating exclusively on Sushmita from then on.

He wondered whether the Men's Room had also been shifted. Most areas of the Club had become unrecognisable with all the fancy renovations and changes. He asked a passing waiter, who pointed to a door that was directly behind Sushmita's table. No. He'd wait. He couldn't risk walking past her. His legs already felt unsteady. Suddenly, Santosh's attention shifted to his over-full bladder. He could think of nothing else. The urge to pee was overwhelming. He imagined himself wetting his pants there and then — making a messy puddle around the bar-stool. Everybody laughing at him. *That* would attract her attention all right. Bring a smile to her serene face. And then he'd be asked to leave — or worse, someone would lead him off firmly, open the heavy glass door and shove him out. This was ridiculous. Santosh tried to concentrate on the slightly rancid peanuts and limp potato chips sitting in front of him. He felt like a little boy at a circus — the one crossing his legs and frowning instead of getting up and looking for a toilet. His bladder was going to explode....he had to do something about it. He got unsteadily to his feet and started to stagger towards the Men's Room.

He didn't make it beyond the third table. Suddenly, he felt a searing pain shooting up his arm. It went straight to his heart. Santosh gasped and reached for the nearest chair. He felt as if an iron wince was tightening around his broad chest. Someone was squeezing it tighter and tighter. Rivulets of sweat were running down his body and his breathing had become shallow. He wanted to shout for help. Sushmita's help. But only a strange, harsh, strangled bark-like sound emerged from his throat. Santosh fell heavily on to the parquet flooring. The dull thud shook a few tables though the noise itself was drowned out by the high decibel-levels of drinkers on their eighth round of beers. Someone two tables away jerked up when the floor shook and exclaimed, "Oops! What was THAT? Not another earthquake, surely?"

A woman giggled, glanced disinterestedly at Santosh and said, "It's nothing. And no one. Just an out-of-towner who's had one too many. Don't worry. He's not anyone we know."

Eight

THE FERN LADY

SHE WAS half-hidden behind a lush fern when Dheeraj first saw
her. The next time he looked, she was gone. Only the fern was still
there, teasing him with its fleshy, emerald-hued sensuality. "What's
wrong with me?" he asked himself, "how can I find a bloody plant
sexy?" Dheeraj went to the improvised bar in the corner of the
large living room for a refill. "Stop this, old chap. You're sloshed
enough," he reminded himself, "one more drink and you're out of
here." He stared morosely into his heavy whiskey tumbler and
swirled the rapidly melting ice cubes around the bottom. "There
lies my life," he muttered over-dramatically, "my watered down,
lousy life — like the bum scotch the host is serving. Nice and
fake."

A voice interrupted his boozy reverie. It belonged to Shweta,
the sultry wife of his wart-faced colleague. "Feeling sorry for
yourself, as usual, D.D.?"

He looked at Shewta in his standard unfocused sort of way.
"You know something? I used to think you were really, really
pretty once. What happened?"

Shewta laughed, "Still your old charming self, I see...Well,
D.D., I'll leave you to drown happily. By the way—the woman you
were staring at. She's married. Bottoms up, you swine." And she
was gone.

Dheeraj wandered into the tiny study and dropped heavily into
a leather armchair. It was a lousy party. All parties were lousy. But

99

he went anyway. Life itself was so lousy, how could it become any worse when there was quality booze going? But these days, people cheated even on that — watered down Scotch was still acceptable, but not this poison water. He decided to switch drinks. Indian rum — dark, strong, heady. Like that "Fern Woman". Dark? Well, she wasn't fair. He didn't like pasty-faced, anaemic-looking women. She had that lovely complexion his mother disparagingly described as "wheatish". Married, Shweta had said. So fucking what? Everybody was married. He was married too — well, sort of. Dheeraj remembered the last party at Wart Face's house a few months ago. His ex-wife had been present with her new escort and even newer hair. Short. And bleached. She resembled an out-of-work hooker. The poor girl was really quite an innocent, though. His present wife was away in Delhi. "Work, darling, work," she'd said tweaking his nose before leaving for the airport. "Mucho work". Like fuck, he'd thought to himself. "More like Mucho prick."

That evening, an out-of-towner had made the mistake of striking up a conversation with him. After the first few painful minutes, the man had asked, "Are you married?" Dheeraj had answered truthfully. "I'm between wives. There's one out there...another's away in Delhi fucking a client." The man had stared at him in utter disbelief and rapidly moved away. People in Bombay were used to him by now. At least people in this sort of crowd. Or the regulars at the Club. They indulged him most of the time ("Like they bloody well should", he'd say in indignation to anyone who challenged the view).

Dheeraj was considered something of a minor genius. Quirky, eccentric, impossible but talented. Exceedingly talented. Without him, it was believed, his ad agency would suffer if not actually collapse. His creatives were remarkable. "Amazing," said the groupies. Nobody could quite figure out how Dheeraj managed to deliver, given his Scotch-soaked brain and obnoxious manner. In his milder moments he'd assure whosoever was listening, "Hey, come of it. I'm not detestable. I'm brilliant. And drunk, of course."

Wart Face and he shared a strange relationship. They were partners who could barely stand each other, even in public. Yet, the equation worked in its own peculiar fashion at work. Wart Face handled finance and public relations, leaving Dheeraj to come up with all the dazzling campaigns. The turn-over at the agency was high. Youngsters who'd heard about the D.D. legend killed themselves for the chance to train with him. But if ulcers didn't get them first, impatience did. Dheeraj worked at his own pace, preferring to jot down campaign strategies on rough pads of paper late into the night, often insisting on his core team hanging around doing nothing...waiting to be summoned and briefed. Paper cups filled with Scotch and water were expected to be sent in to his spacious un-office-like room at regular intervals with occasional vegetable sandwiches from the cafe across the street. It was a life that suited Dheeraj just fine—long, lonely hours spent in a semi-deserted office, with classic jaaz playing on neat Bose speakers fitted into his book-lined wall cabinet.

Some women found Dheeraj's hang dog looks attractive. "He looks so sad. I think that's terribly sexy," a junior copy writer would sigh each time he passed her in the corridor. 'Club Wives' would try and match him drink for drink at the bar on Sunday afternoons pretending to be deeply interested in his welfare. Even the gays seemed to think he was irresistible. Dheeraj was frequently propositioned by one of the boys while washing his hands in the loo. Even though he was anything but sociable, Dheeraj accepted invitations to parties with alarming alacrity. "Why do you go?" Wart Face often asked him, "You look so bored and miserable. Besides, you are insufferable...."

Dheeraj asked himself the same question. Why did he make it to all these dreary affairs? For the booze? He had enough of that at his own home...or office. The broads? No dearth of those, either. Company...any company? Unlikely. Dheeraj was choosy about who he spoke to — and in any case, most people preferred to stay miles away from "that pompous drunk". Hanging around with people he couldn't stand had become something of a compulsion

with Dheeraj but it was still preferable to being by himself. Or
with his second wife for that matter — the one with the big tits
and small brain. And Dheeraj knew he was awful company these
days, often getting into avoidable brawls with arseholes not worth
the punch or shove he threw in their direction. Was it the attention?
The nasty reputation he actually enjoyed? Dheeraj was used to
both. But whether or not he revelled in either, was still unclear.

He spotted the "Fern Lady" at the dining table. She was loading
her already heaped plate with another helping of pillaf. "You eat
too much for someone so petite," he commented, spilling scotch
over her embroidered saree pallav.

"And you drink too much for your own good," she countered,
moving on to the chicken dish.

"Who the fuck are you to know what is good for me?" Dheeraj
mocked, following her round the table.

She continued to fuss, digging into a salad bowl, picking out
all the walnuts. "I am a wife. And I know."

Dheeraj watched aghast as she reached for fresh naans. "Wife!"
he scoffed, "Who needs one?"

She looked straight at him. "You do," she said in a friendly,
chatty way.

"I already have a fucking wife. Two, in fact. And believe me,
that's not what I need."

She bit into a kabab. "You need the right sort of wife. Someone
like me. Only, I'm married. Or else I would've made you my
project."

Dheeraj drank noisily, "What are you, some sort of a fucked-
up social worker? Stuff your project."

She moved away lithely, gracefully. He heard her say, "I'll
send you the laundry bill for ruining my new Chanderi. Or better
still, I'll just buy myself a new one and make you pay for it."

Dheeraj experienced a deep, strange pain as he watched her
blend into the crowd and become a golden blur. He wanted to walk
upto her, chase her, hold her and say, "Don't you dare talk to
anyone else tonight. They're all such fools, don't you see? Such

102

pathetic little fools. Talk to me. Stay with me. Don't leave."
Instead, he asked for a fresh drink and went out into the terrace
garden to clear his head. This was absurd. Lunatic. What was the
matter with him? He didn't know who the hell she was, and yet
he felt drawn to her with a strange sense of familiarity. He'd felt
more comfortable with a total stranger in those few minutes than
he had with practically anyone else in ages.

She was attractive, of course. But there were at least half a
dozen attractive women present at that party itself. Well-dressed,
expensively perfumed, with tinkling laughs and perfectly made-up
faces. Dheeraj noticed most of them were in silk salwar suits or
trousers. She was in the minority — clad in a saree. But it wasn't
the saree. It was her. Dheeraj found himself wanting her with a
desperation that was bordering on dementia. He told himself to
wait it out till everybody else had left. He couldn't bear the thought
of seeing her again. How could she waste her time on all those
fucking idiots she'd gone over to? The man she'd filled a plate for.
Her husband? Had to be. What could she possibly have in common
with him? If she'd only stayed at the dining table by his side...
given him just fifteen more minutes of her time...he knew he'd
have won her. Now the moment was lost. He'd never see her again.
He didn't even know who she was. Maybe it was better this way.
Damn! He knew it wasn't. Bloody hell. He was sure she knew too.

Dheeraj rushed back into the room. She had gone. He
contemplated killing himself. What was the fucking purpose of his
life, anyway? What did he have to live for? He was monumentally
bored. And fatigued. Nothing interested him—not even his much-
discussed "brilliance". He even disliked his newly done up home
with an intensity that was manic. Every inch of it reflected his
current wife's flamboyant taste. He particularly detested his ugly,
impersonal bedroom — the one she'd spent the most money on.
His money. It resembled a suite in an American hotel. Not deluxe
but three-star. Fake period fittings, heavy champagne-coloured
carpet, a wall of mirrors, French windows that weren't meant to
open, a fussy ceiling, satin bolsters on their king-size bed, quilted

pillows strewn everywhere and a writing table that looked as untouched as it actually was. And those detestable picture frames — acrylic ones, cork ones, silver ones, mother-of-pearl ones, filled with pictures of his ex-model wife, Monisha. And facing their monstrous bed — a gilt-framed formal portrait of her done by a leading painter — the one whose contempt for women was so hard to camouflage. It showed up in their eyes — cold, cunning, calculating and merciless. Like Monisha's.

He wondered what the "Fern Lady's" house was like. Did it reflect her personality or her husband's? Her husband. He couldn't bear to call him that. The man was probably an absolute jerk, Dheeraj told himself. He didn't realise the treasure he had in his home. He looked too thick, too self-absorbed. And he smoked cigars. Big, fat, smelly ones. Dheeraj was suspicious of any man who puffed away at those phallic-looking, atmosphere-fouling things. He'd noticed the men who loved them were generally short, stubby creatures with major ego problems. Small dicks, he concluded. Big hang-ups. Men who wanted to be noticed and taken seriously by other men. Men on futile power-trips. Tycoon-types minus the clout or class. Her husband looked a multinationalwallah. Maybe a Harvard man with fancy degrees. Or worse — someone from the London School of Economics, with a put-on clipped accent. It was hard to tell from his clothes. They were nondescript. "Party Shirts" from somewhere. And old-fashioned baggy trousers hanging below his belly. How could she — that utterly divine woman — bear to go to bed with such a beast?

Separate bedrooms. That was it. Dheeraj felt instantly better at the thought. He imagined her driving back in silence, resenting the cigar-smoke trapped in her freshly washed hair. He was certain that asshole must've kept up a monologue on the way. Something along the lines of "And then that Mehta fellow said to me, 'My public issue was over-subscribed,' and I said, 'Really? Last week your bankers came to see me. Their story was slightly different.' You should've seen his face." Dheeraj smiled...and her face too, you jerk. Look at it sometimes. Read it if you can. How the fuck

104

did she succeed in looking so sublime? So in control? So fucking happy? What was she happy about? Certainly not about her fucking husband? Maybe she had a lover, Dheeraj speculated. He was beginning to feel melancholy again.

If she did have a lover, there was no hope for him. Or wait a minute, a woman who took one lover could as easily take two or three. After a point, she generally stopped counting. Like his wife. Or rather, wives. But the "Fern Lady" was not like them. She looked wholesome and true. Like those antiseptic housewives in TV ads who fried perfect puris for their eager-eyed kids. Dheeraj pushed the image away. He didn't want to think of her as having children for some reason. Children induced guilt. At least they did in him. He'd always felt a bit of a heel seducing someone's mother — even when the mother herself was more than willing.

Maybe the "Fern Lady" was barren. That was it. Or better still, her husband was probably impotent. And she was yearning for her womb to be filled. Dheeraj decided he was the one who'd do it. Not that he was much of a kiddy-person. Far from it. Both his wives had agreed before the wedding that children would not be the issue. It had suited everybody just fine. Dheeraj had no time to deal with domesticity, while his wives had been far too busy with their own lives to even consider taking a break for baby-making. But this woman aroused the latent father in him. Yes, he definitely wanted to have a child with her. But what if she already had a couple hanging on to her saree pallav? Would she leave them with the asshole and agree to spend the rest of her life with him?

Dheeraj pulled out his little pocket-pad and wrote unsteadily in it. "'Fern Lady' — phone number and name. Tomorrow."

He didn't have to call her. She called him. Without any preliminaries, she said, "I have been worried about you since last night. Are you all right?"

Dheeraj felt his heart lurching clumsily against his rib-case, "Marry me," he said hoarsely, "I can't live without you. I'll kill

105

myself. I swear I will."

She laughed lightly, "Don't be utterly ridiculous. I told you, I'm already married. Happly at that."

"Bullshit. Bull-fucking-shit," Dheeraj exploded,. "If you are so fucking happy, why the fuck are you phoning me, huh? Who am I to you? Your fucking father or your fucking son? What difference does it make to you how fucking I am? I'm dead. Dead, without you. Does that answer your fucking, stupid question?"

There was a pause, and then he heard her say, "Didn't anybody tell you it's juvenile to keep swearing? I'm neither shocked nor impressed. Now, tell me are you o.k.? Yes or no. Stop behaving like a badly brought up child. A brat. You're much too nice a person."

Dheeraj clenched the receiver tightly in his hand. "When and where can I see you? How about right now? Right this minute? I can't breathe. I can't talk. The pain in my heart is killing me. I'll die of cardiac arrest in another two seconds if you say 'no'. They'll hang you for murder. You'll go to jail...your conscience will eat into you. Have mercy. See me."

"Fine," she said, "I'm across the road from you. In fact, if you risked your neck by climbing out of the window and walking along the ledge, we could see each other quite clearly. And perhaps exchange waves. How does that sound?"

"Cut out the fucking crap. By the way, what's your fucking name? I call you the 'Fern Lady'.

"Fern Lady? Why? Did I resemble one? Or was there a fern growing out of my head?"

"Never mind. What the fuck are you doing across the street? Don't tell me now. Let's meet immediately. You take the elevator down. I'll do the same. Then we shall both start to cross the street simultaneously — and then...and then...I shall grab you in my arms and stay that way till the cops come and separate us. Or you say 'yes' — whichever is sooner. So....I'm counting. By five, I'm out of here...One — two — three."

The woman laughed. "Stop it. I can't just drop everything and

106

walk out. It's impossible."

Dheeraj held back his anger. "So why did you call? You want to fuck me? Is that it?"

"I phoned because I was concerned about you. You looked so sad...so suicidal...if I may use the word. And for some reason, I held myself responsible. Silly of me, I agree, but that's it. The whole story. Forgive me if I conveyed the wrong impression. And now...good-bye." She disconnected.

Dheeraj stared in disbelief at the receiver. This was crazy. And he still didn't know her name. He'd probably never see her again in his life. Even if he did, she'd snub him, ignore him...or worse...laugh at him. He sat at his table stabbing pins into a pin cushion. He walked to the window and looked out. He could see nothing. No building at any rate. Just a glimpse of the sea in the far distance. He looked down. Fourteen floors below he saw cars, taxis, people — the usual scene on any week-day. Yes, the ledge was there — just like she'd said. Maybe her office was round the next corner. Dheeraj swung his leg out. The ledge was narrow but firm. He swung the other leg out. It was possible to walk on it provided there was something to hang on to. He looked at the wall adjoining his window. He couldn't see anything — no niche or protruding masonry. He gripped the window sill tightly with his hands. He could do it if he didn't look down and if he kept his steps absolutely steady — like those painters who scampered around from one level to the other rigging up bamboo scaffolding. If they could do it, he could do it too. Dheeraj took a couple of steps, keeping one hand on the window railing. For the next one, he'd have to leave that hand and balance himself just on his feet. Damn! He was wearing the wrong shoes — today of all days. He wished he'd worn his usual top siders. What he needed were rubber soles.

He heard a noise in the room behind him. Must be the bloody secretary with the fucking proofs, he cursed. Maybe she'd think he was in the loo and go away after leaving the papers on his messy desk. He waited. His eyes were shut. His heart pounding. He could feel the strain on his knuckles as he hung on with one hand and stretched out his other along the rough wall. Why wasn't the girl leaving? He waited for the small click of the door that would tell him she'd gone. He hoped she wouldn't linger to clean up some of the clutter. He thought he could feel the strength from his hand seeping away. He was beginning to feel dizzy. His feet were numb. He wasn't going to be able to hang on for much longer now. He screwed up his eyes tighter and began to see stars. There was no sensation left in his arms now. He wanted to fly...he was sure he could. All a matter of trying. Giving it a fucking shot. Yes, he'd fly. Soar. Glide. Float. Go where the wind would take him. He felt his fingers slipping...and he heard a voice. Her voice. "Hold him...hold his arm. He is going to be all right. He's safe now. I'll handle him..."

Dheeraj opened his eyes. He saw her. And then he saw the lush, green, fleshy new fern sitting smugly on his table. Bitch. Fucking bitch, he grinned as they started to pull him inside. Dheeraj reached out to grab the outstretched hand. Their fingers met briefly and then Dheeraj felt his own curling up...stiffening...and pulling away.

Nine

LINES

SIMRAN HATED sunlight. Or bright lights at dinner. "I belong to a very good vintage, but I'm not telling you which one," she'd say smilingly to guests as she raised a glass of champagne. It wasn't all that difficult though, to figure out exactly how old she was. All anybody had to do was ask one of her three strapping sons his age and then work back from there. Whatever it was, Simran was still a staggeringly beautiful woman. "Still," she'd snort. "I hate that word 'still'. What do you mean when you say 'still' — that I should be decrepit and ugly? I'm not a well-preserved pickle...nor am I all that old, you know."

Innocents who'd actually meant to compliment her would hastily retreat, mumble something stupid and move on to something or someone else, leaving Simran to hiss, "Still, still, still," under her breath. "Still" was a strange word to apply to her, as admirers agreed. But she'd been an acknowledged beauty for so long — practically all her life — that it was difficult to recall a time when her name wasn't the first one on everybody's lips when the topic of beauty came up. "Oh... a beautiful woman? Well, there's Simran Singh — you know the lady with the exquisite face? Used to fly for Air India in the good old days when they hired the best-lookers in the country. She *is* getting on — but she still looks good." Still.

Sometimes Simran got well and truly sick of her good looks. 'It's a curse to be born this way?" she'd sigh, gazing into the mirror, her long, heavily fringed eyes half closed, as if in so doing, they'd miss the new line around the full, well-shaped mouth, the latest wrinkle on her long, fair throat. Putting away her silver hand-mirror with a tired gesture, Simran would reach for one of her cream jars — strawberry for the face, apricot for her slim, elegant hands, plum for her elbows.

Beauty had become something of a burden for the attractive wealthy widow. As she'd explain to her favourite son Prakrit, during their frequent tête-á-têtes. "My status attracts men — the wrong men." He'd gaze adoringly at his divine-looking mother and wonder whether he'd ever be able to find a bride even half as lovely as her. He also wondered occasionally about the mysterious men she sometimes mentioned. All three boys frequently speculated amongst themselves about their mother's love-life. More specifically, her sex life. Did she...? And if she did, who with? And where? As Rahul, the eldest, would conclude, "She's still quite young...she can't have given up on it. Not so soon." Still.

Krishen, the middle brother, would say, "She looks good for her age..." and then add slyly, "sexy too... I mean she isn't fat or anything like other mothers."

That's when Prakrit would interrupt hotly and stop the conversation from going any further. "What mom does is her business. It's cheap to talk about our mother like this. As if she's just another loose woman."

The older two would exchange looks and mutter. "Man — you don't have to be cheap. Just normal. She's still in her forties, remember? She isn't all that ancient yet."

No, Simran was not "all that ancient", but sometimes, she felt it. Felt at least fifteen years older than her forty-nine. Especially during the long, lonely evenings when she tucked herself into bed at 10 p.m., with her latest night-cream slathered all over her face and a silver glass filled with freshly squeezed fruit juice (to combat nocturnal dehydration) by her side. That's when she'd catch sight of herself in the full-length mirror of her old teak cupboard and weep — something she hated to do, even when she didn't have the cream covering her face. With it on, it was even more distasteful for the tears coursed down her cheeks, creating little rivulets through the thick layers of cream, and Simran had to tissue them dry, without wasting too much of the expensive, imported cream.

Her sons teased her about her cream-mania. Twice a year, Simran travelled abroad. She had friends in England and Europe, who she claimed she liked to meet at regular intervals. But the truth was, she went to London and Amsterdam to buy creams — the latest, anti-ageing, anti-wrinkle, collagen-rich, lanolin-enriched gooey concoctions, whipped up by international cosmetic houses, only too aware of their clientele's collective obsession with youth. Her sons would watch her unpack. Simran removed each new jar with utmost care, treating it like precious, fragile cargo. There was a certain method to the way she carted back these potions. Not for her the careless dumping of new purchases in an open suitcase. Simran had a specially made felt-lined box with individual plastic pouches inside. "To prevent any spillage," she'd explain. Each newly bought jar was first stripped of all extra packaging. Only the literature accompanying it was preserved and carefully taped on to the cover. Next, the pouches were neatly labelled and the jars put in. Then the box was sealed with adhesive tape. "I'd hate to get my chiffons soiled," Simran would remark, "You never know...creams can be so messy. And they leave stains that never go." There were creams for under-the-eyes, over-the-eyes, neck and throat, lips and cheeks, knuckles and knees, breasts and buttocks. They came in different consistencies — rich and creamy, light and transparent, fragrant and odour-free. Simran loved her cache and splurged on it guiltlessly. "Once my looks are gone," she'd say sadly, "everything will be gone. What else do I have? And if I don't look after myself, who will?" There were times she missed having a daughter. A young girl in the house would have understood her preoccupations — not made fun of her.

Here sons weren't cruel — oh no — but she knew they didn't really understand her anxieties. As Prakrit had put it so bluntly when he was younger, "But Mother, why do you want to look good all the time? You are a widow — what difference is it going to make?"

Simran had recoiled at the harshness of his words. His brothers too had shut him up promptly and hustled him away saying, "Shut up, yaar. Don't talk such rot."

But Simran hadn't forgotten. What difference is it going to make, young Prakrit had asked. All the difference in the world, she'd wanted to say. The difference between being alive... and dead. What could boys know about such things? A daughter might have understood...condoned. How could a beautiful woman ever become indifferent to her own beauty? Each day her mirror told her the uncomfortable truth. Each day her reflection said, "Watch out. You aren't getting younger. Soon you'll be grey and wrinkled. Preserve what God has given you. Protect yourself. That's the least you can do."

Simran was utterly dedicated to her beauty routine. It drove her servants crazy and it amused her sons, but she stuck to it obstinately even when her spirits were at their lowest — or perhaps, more so then. Simran savoured the rigidity of routine. And discipline. She saw her strict adherence to her morning, afternoon and nightly rituals as something she owed to herself. Besides, how else was she supposed to fill the hours from the time she awoke at 9.00 a.m. till she retired thirteen hours later? Nothing ever varied about her schedules. She'd start her day with a warm glass of water to which the juice of a lemon and a spoonful of honey had been added ("good for the bowels and hence good for the complexion"). Next, she'd have weak tea with one toast of whole wheat bread ("fibre for the intestines"). Then she'd wander into the kitchen in search of "natural, kitchen cosmetics", as she called them — fresh milk cream with a pinch of turmeric during the dry, cool months, and slices of cucumber throughout summer. Occasionally, she'd vary those with honey or mashed fruits such as bananas, papaya, strawberries and peaches. "My facial fruit salad," she'd grin at the breakfast table, while the boys pulled faces and held their noses. Often, she had a masseuse come in and give her a body and head massage with freshly pressed almond oil ("To tone up the system — and just feel good. Do you mind?") This had nothing to do with her bi-weekly hair treatment with special herbal oil ordered from Calcutta, a routine expertly performed by her husband's old maid. She'd been doing it for Simran from the day she'd entered this house as a blushing, radiantly beautiful bride. Simran loved the ministrations of Savitribai — the feel of her gnarled, hard fingers as she massaged hot, sticky, green oil into Simran's long, lustrous tresses, always adding, "Keep your hair tied or it will attract the evil eye." Simran would shut her eyes as Savitribai's fingers moved over her scalp and later down her neck, over her slim shoulders in soothing, circular rhythmic movements.

Simran's daily bath was also a special indulgence. She hated quick showers. They didn't make her feel clean. Or at least clean enough. "Nothing like the luxury of a long, perfumed bath," she'd sigh, after emerging from hers, clad in a fluffy white towelled-robe, her skin aglow, her eyes shining. Simran loved her large, airy, plant-filled bathroom. She loved her array of imported soaps and lotions. The sweet smell of lavender bath gel, the aromatic bath oils exuding the fragrance of fresh apples, the milky after-bath fluids that clung in a transparent silky film to her arms and legs, the tiny crystal bottles of assorted colognes and fragrances. Simran was particular about not using clashing aromas. Which meant that selecting the deodorant for the day took a while as she decided on what her day's perfume would be, lemony, floral or something musky? Accordingly, she'd co-ordinate the rest of the range. It gave her enormous satisfaction when she finally emerged from her pretty, cheerful bathroom to enter her pre-cooled bedroom that her body was fresh, clean and smelling good from top to toe. As soon as she was reclining on her favourite chair, Simran would get to work on her long, elegant, scrupulously looked after feet. She had special foot sprays and talcs which she lavished on them after drying carefully between the toes. Simran never had to endure dead skin or in-grown toe nails, thanks to her bi-monthly pedicure appointment with Mr. D'Souza. He was such a dear, that man. He'd looked after her feet for fifteen years now. And done so with concentration...even love. She'd often studied his expression as he sat with one foot in his towelled lap, the other soaking in warm sudsy, water. It was the way in which he held her foot — almost reverentially — that touched Simran. When he buffed her toe nails, he did it gently with the surest of touches. And when he massaged the balls of her feet with rich cream, it was designed to induce in her a sense of drowsy well-being. Yes, Mr. D'Souza definitely earned the generous tip she always discreetly pushed into the pocket of his white drill coat.

For Simran, beauty was commitment. A life-long commitment. She owed that much to her creator, the divine being who'd blessed her with such physical abundance. Her sons respected her beauty regimen, even though she took care not to walk around the house with a ghoulish face-pack on. They never disturbed her on those occasions when she was locked in her bedroom for hours with her beautician — that nice Parsee lady with baby-soft hands who gave the world's most relaxing facials with light feathery strokes of her long, graceful fingers. Simran liked her seaweed special. It made her skin look translucent. While all that mucky-looking stuff was on her face and neck she resembled a character out of a scifi-film. She and Mrs. Pavri would laugh over how funny she looked with a green face. But they both knew just how wonderful she'd look two hours from the time she washed it off with warm water and applied a moisturiser over her tingling skin.

The same went for her monthly henna treatment. Simran hated the smell and consistency of henna. It reminded her of cowdung but she knew her hair required it, she was opposed to using hair dyes after having read an article on how dangerous some of them were. Cancer, the article said. She'd decided to stick to a mix of henna with tea leaves or coffee powder forever. "Safer, dear — and so glossy too," Mrs. Pavri had agreed. Ideally, Simran would've preferred to have her henna pack in the privacy of her bedroom, since the sight of it was so unaesthetic and repulsive. But then she didn't have the contraption that generated the all-important steam which made the henna work faster and better. So, she was forced to make an appointment with Mrs. Pavri at her small salon — the one she ran from her modest home in a Parsee colony.

Simran had to prepare herself for these visits well in advance. The approach to Mrs. Pavri's neat flat was what offended her. It was crowded, dimly-lit and dirty. She had to pick her way carefully past mounds of uncleared garbage with stray cats and dogs blocking her path aggressively. Of course, her old driver, Pyarelal, realising how all this bothered her, invariably escorted her right up to Mrs. Pavri's small foyer. And being the gentleman he was, he carried a baton with him to shoo the cats and dogs away as Simran tripped lightly behind him, holding up her chiffon saree delicately with one hand, and hanging on to her handbag with the other. She knew her visits embarrassed Mrs. Pavri who always apologised profusely for the inconvenience it caused her. But one had to do these things sometimes. Just as one had to go to the driver's quarters during Divali to distribute sweets and gifts to the children. Which reminded Simran, she had to organise some clothes for the next jumble sale. She'd give the money to Pyarelal and let him handle the shopping. It wasn't possible for her to go to whichever area these people bought their things from. As a matter of fact, she didn't have the faintest idea where such shops were located.

Pyarelal was such a find. He'd come to her over a decade ago, and had always been faithful and discreet. Loyal too. That's why she didn't mind indulging him, though over the years she'd lost track of the number of children he'd sired. That veiled wife of his looked permanently pregnant. Well...the poor things had no other preoccupations, Simram figured, why grudge them their couplings?

These days she just wasn't entirely pleased with her body. Though she had her yoga instructor come home twice a week and she never broke her gym appointment with the aerobics instructor, Simran was distressed to find signs of impending flab — loose tissue that refused to remain taut despite the massages and oils. "What does it matter?" she'd think to herself a trifly crossly, as she pinched her waist and frowned. And what did it matter, really speaking? Simran prided herself on the fact that unlike city socialites, who in their desperation to cling to bygone years, had

taken to wearing ridiculously short, tight ensembles, she had stuck
to what suited her best sarees. Not even "salwar-suits", as her
friends called those shapeless, tent-like camouflage clothes. Sarees
it had always been and sarees it would remain. She wasn't the
beach-going type either, so the question of strangers scrutinising
her crepy thighs didn't arise. But she knew she had them. She
knew her breasts were beginning to droop just a bit. She knew her
once tight stomach muscles were getting unreasonably lax.

Sometimes, Simran would pull out her old albums from the
walnut wood chest of drawers. She liked looking at photographs—
her photographs. People often commented on how she had
improved with age. "Like wine," she'd laugh and change the
conversation. She agreed with that assessment. Rather, she used
to. These days, she wasn't all that sure. Her son Rahul was a good
photographer. In fact, he'd seriously considered going professional.
He often took her pictures, especially when she was dressed to go
out. "Man, you look ravishing tonight. Let me click you," he'd say
and rush to get his Nikon.

But of late her pictures hadn't pleased her. Maybe she needed
to change her make-up. Tone down the black in her eyes. Or go
easy with the blusher. She had begun to look slightly hard. Harsh.
Besides, she felt the fineness of her features was getting blunted
with the years. Her face was beginning to look fuller and plumper.
Simran didn't like that. She'd suck her cheeks in and look in the
mirror hastily — yes, that was better. Just like those old photographs
in which she resembled a dark haired Grace Kelly — the same
serene expression and noble brow. The same symmetry of features,
the same long neck and well-defined jawline.

Simran often thought about Grace — what a tragic death hers
had been. What a waste of such beauty. At other times, she'd think
differently — what a fortunate woman — dead before she could
grow old, haggard and fat. Simran concluded that it was all right—
less painful — for not-so-beautiful women to age. It didn't seem
half as cruel. But for legendary beauties like herself, it was living
death. She'd mentally decided to end it all at fifty-five. By then,

the boys would be settled — married and with children of their own. She'd be a gracious grandmother, she knew that. But after fifty-five, life just wouldn't be worth living. In an empty house — just her with her creams. No. She'd be graceful about it and go. Her sons would understand. They knew how much beauty meant to her. They also knew it wasn't mere vanity — that stupid, superficial preoccupation with beauty. It was the beauty born of good health.

Of late, though, Simran herself had been preoccupied with her body. Her health had begun to worry her too. Her menstrual cycle, to be more specific. It wasn't as regular as it had once been. It had turned wildly erratic — sometimes she bled just eighteen days after her last period. And sometimes, she remained dry for two months running. Of course she knew it was the onset of "the change". And on one level, it rather relieved her. Simran was averse to bodily odours — her own included. While a Lanvin deo stick took care of her armpits during muggy summer months, and Guerlain talcs kept the rest of her body fresh-smelling and dry, there was nothing Simran could do to combat the stickiness of menstrual blood, or the stale, dead odour accompanying it. She'd tried deodorised napkins and imported tampons, but nothing effectively eliminated that slight whiff that penetrated through every kind of sanitary protection. No. Simran didn't mind at all if she stopped bleeding permanently. It was the other symptoms that made her anxious — the sudden shortness of breath, the excessive sweating, the vague fears, the notorious hot flushes, and above all, the fine growth of hair that had begun to sprout all over her face, combined with the faintly discoloured patches over her high, taut cheekbones. Simran had tried eating curds mixed with fenugreek seeds, soaked overnight; she'd started massaging warm olive oil over the darkened areas of her skin, and she'd tried to camouflage the new shadows under translucent powders or lighter-toned foundations. She knew a visit to her gynaecologist was overdue, but how she hated it when anybody — even another woman-probed her insides. She recoiled at the memory of the gloved, lubricated finger, the smell of antiseptic, the indignity of spreadeagled thighs. But Simran knew she couldn't put it off much longer. As it is, she hadn't been for her pap smears even though most of her friends had kept yearly appointments, after they turned thirty-five. She'd resisted going, thinking it was yet another fad, a new paranoia imported from the West. But her insides were clearly flashing her a signal. She'd be a fool to ignore it. She'd heard someone say at a bridge party that regular sex delayed menopause. And that women who had a healthy sexual appetite rarely suffered from gynaecological problems. That was it, then. She knew the answer. Obviously, her systems had gone awry because...well...because she hadn't had sex in years.

Not that she minded not having it. Simran had always found intercourse both painful and disgusting. When her husband died, at the age of forty-two, her first thought had been, "Thank God I won't have to sleep with that man again." But later, Simran had realised it wasn't 'that man' alone (though he'd been the 'only' man till that point) who offended her delicate sensibilities. It was all men. They were we so...so... brutish, so smelly and ugly with their funnily shaped genitals that grew and shrank awkwardly. She often wondered whether that piece of meat hanging constantly between their legs didn't in some ways affect their concentration. She often imagined herself to be a man in the privacy of her bedroom. Sometimes, she'd suspend a small object from a belt between her legs. She'd walk towards the mirror and laugh at the ridiculous sight. When her husband had been alive, she'd often observed his penis without letting him know she was staring. How grotesque it had looked — like a shrivelled up old tube flopping helplessly this way and that, with the testicles hanging at different levels like tiny, carelessly filled sacks. Sometimes when he'd been sleeping on his side, she'd sneaked up close for a better look and gazed up the small blind eye on the its head — the opening that discharged both semen and urine. It looked evil and all-knowing to her. She'd hated the way, pubic hair clotted with discharge stuck to her husband's fleshy thighs. She'd hated the chalky smell. The glutinous consistency. She'd hated the way her husband's testicles looked at a certain angle as they dangled between her legs while he thrust into her energetically. Most times she'd squeezed her eyes shut, opening them occasionally to silently ridicule the sight of a grown man behaving like a mad pig — grunting and rooting hungrily inside her.

After he died, Simran tried three other man. Tried. Tried them for size, as it were. It hadn't worked. She'd told herself that when Jeet, her husband, had been alive, sex with him had been a little like being stuck with a shoe that pinched permanently. Perhaps if she made love to someone else — someone more in tune with her needs —it would be different. At any rate, less uncomfortable. It hadn't turned out like that, though. Her first lover had been her dead husband's best friend. A man she'd known well from the time she'd married. A man she'd been strongly attracted to because he was so different from the man who'd been chosen for her by her parents. And yet, their encounter in bed had been a disaster. Simran, tense and rigid, had offered her body like a priceless gift, thinking Anand would be grateful. She'd hoped for worship; what she'd got was conquest. The look in his eyes when he entered her was that of a hunter gloating over his quarry. Simran had saved her tears for later, too proud to shed them in his presence and humiliate herself further.

She consoled herself about the "failure", putting it down to wrong timing. She ought to have played the grieving widow a little longer. It was decidedly bad form to climb into bed with the dead man's buddy a mere ten days after the funeral. So, she tried again six months later with a man she met at a quiet dinner.

Simran's social life, which had been totally controlled by her husband's whims, had begun to flower after his death. Invitations had started to pour in a month after the tragedy. Discreetly at first, and then in a flood. Matchmakers put out feelers to find out her views on remarriage. Simran was immensely eligible after all — wealthy, beautiful and a celebrity of sorts. She'd resisted initially, even though the few girl-friends she had, urged her to come out of her self-imposed exile and "circulate". Without too much enthusiasm, Simran had finally begun to do just that.

When she met Satya, she rather liked his old world courteousness. He was charming without being fake. Attentive without being obvious. She noticed his hands and liked them. His eyes too. They didn't devour her hungrily. Neither did they bore holes into her with curiosity. Satya was visiting from Delhi. Before she knew it, Simran knew he'd be gone. She decided, within ten minutes of meeting him, that she wanted to go to bed with him. Not because she was wildly attracted to him physically, but only to find out if her earlier experiences had been unfortunate ones. She was giving men as a sub-group, another chance.

She was also testing herself. The experiment was a failure but through no fault of hers — at least, that was how she saw it. Satya was far too overwhelmed by her beauty to get going. All he wanted to do was caress her naked body with his eyes, feast on her face, regard her as the ultimate treat. As Simran lay there langourously against the ivory-coloured satin sheets, she felt slightly nauseated. That was also the time she discovered it wasn't really worship she wanted from a lover but passion. And Satya didn't have any to offer.

Simran decided to give her body one last chance and this time, she plotted for it carefully. Maybe, she decided, it was time to play seductress. Maybe it would be more exciting if she enticed a man, lured him into her bed...even chased him a little. But the problem was, which man? There didn't seem to be a single worthy candidate around. But just when she thought she'd have to abandon her quest, she found him.

It happened in the first class lounge of an airport. Simran was off to London — her first trip without her husband. She was nervous and uncertain, never having had to negotiate the small details that international travel entails. Jeet had always taken care of those. As she sat on a sofa, flipping through copies of *The Economist* without really reading it, she suddenly noticed him as he helped himself to a drink. It was hard to figure out where he came from — his colouring was so strange. His clothes were even stranger — black jeans, black T-shirt, black work-boots and a prominent silver bracelet on his right wrist. His hair was light, almost blond, and he carried himself with the sort of nonchalance that either money or great talent breeds. Maybe he was in the entertainment business, she concluded, as she continued to steal quick glances in his direction. He noticed her looking and smiled. She looked away hastily and once again pretended to be reading.

They met while boarding the aircraft. He smiled again — warmly — held out his hand and introduced himself. The name was Indian enough. Though he looked like a foreigner. She liked the texture of his palm. Later, when she settled into her seat, she sniffed at her hand. What residue had he left behind? It wasn't tobacco, it wasn't leather, it wasn't an after-shave she could recognise, it wasn't sweat and mercifully it wasn't urine. Whatever it was, it smelt good. She sniffed again, more surreptitiously this time. It was a distinctly male smell, though she couldn't quite place it. Twenty minutes later, he walked over and asked if he could sit in the empty seat next to hers.

There were no preliminaries with this man. He looked into her eyes directly and said, "You are the most perfect creature I have ever seen — the most beautiful woman in the world. Are you travelling alone or joining someone in London? If it's the former, I'd like you to have dinner with me tonight."

His name was Amitava and his mother was Swedish. His parents had divorced when he was sixteen. He had opted to live with his father in India. Now, he travelled between London, New York and Bangalore as a partner in his father's business. "We are into exports in a big way — leather, garments, fashion jewellery," he explained. Simran could barley concentrate on his words, mesmerised as she was by the unusual colour of his eyes. He laughed at her open curiosity and said, "Look, one is greenish-grey and the other, golden-brown. I must have been a cat in my last life"! Simran blushed and looked away. She noticed the curling golden hairs on his forearms and the way in which his heavy eyebrows met over his eyes. His hands were large and heavy. She concluded he was a passionate man — the kind who would finally be able to light the dying fires within her.

It didn't happen.

Amitava, as it turned out, was far too much in love with himself to be concerned about his partner. It was he who was making a gift of his body to her and he expected her to be thankful. Thankful and proud that he, Amitava, had chosen her, when he could have had any woman. A far younger woman at that. If there was any passion in his love-making, it was reserved for himself. Amitava liked making love to specific music in a room fitted with mirrors. His turn-on was not the woman in his bed, but his reflection in those mirrors. He watched his own body, as it moved to the rhythm of the music, his eyes rarely leaving the multiple images of his muscular buttocks, his rippling arms or his taut shoulders as he balanced himself on his palms and ground into Simran.

It was after this disastrous experience with Amitava that Simran renounced sex forever, deciding it just wasn't worth the effort. She was glad in retrospect that she hadn't invested too much in it either. Simran knew women who lived from one orgasm to the next, dreaming, planning, scheming. Well, she concluded tiredly, she just wasn't one of them. Instead of wasting further time and energy in finding out what exactly the glories of sex were, Simran started to concentrate on herself. Occasionally, she felt a nebulous urge somewhere within her, which she thought might be sexual longing, but it was easy to ignore; to push aside and get on with the next beauty routine. At least that was something she could count on. Creams didn't let her down. And lotions soothed away her worry-lines like no man ever could.

Simran surveyed her dressing table fondly. She opened a few jars at random and checked their contents. Some needed replenishing. Some were untouched. She ran her fingers lightly over her sparkling collection of crystal perfume flacons. She picked up a piece of suede and started to clean their facets slowly. It was an act so sensual, she felt her body begin to tingle. She looked up

and saw herself in the dressing table mirror. She touched her face...
her mouth... she parted her lips... she ran her tongue over her teeth.
Her eyes were half-closed, her breathing became heavier as her
hand moved lower... she scratched her neck lightly with her perfectly
painted nails — it was a pleasant sensation. She continued the
downward movement till her index finger encircled a nipple. Simran
wet her lips and slipped out of her silken robe. The bed with its
lacy fluffy pillows strewn over it, looked inviting — like an
undemanding but perfectly attentive lover. Simran slid over its
smoothness, revelling in the sensation. Her skin was glowing, her
eyes shining. She wasn't alone either, she thought, staring
mesmerised at several softly-lit images of herself reflected in the
mirrors of her cool, perfumed room. Such beauty. Such perfection.
Such bliss.

Ten

REPEAT PERFORMANCE

THE DAY he turned eight, Ashish knew he was made for the movies. And the movies were made for him. It was the cameraman hired by his enthusiastic mother to shoot his birthday party who'd told him so. "You should join films. Has anybody told you what a good actor you are? Too good. You'll see when I show you the film."

That night Ashish had gone into his well-furnished room and locked the door. He'd stood in front of the mirror and scrutinised his face critically. Could he? Could he really? And what would his parents say? Their oft-repeated refrain flashed through his mind. "You are our only son. We want you to finish your studies and join papa's business. After all, he's doing all this for you."

Even at that young age, those words had driven a chilled spike into his heart. He hated the thought of selling automobile spare parts or sitting in one of the three shops his father owned in the city. He didn't want to spend his life dealing with corrupt mechanics and shifty-eyed garage owners looking for inflated bills or unrealistic discounts. How lucky his older sister was! Everybody left her alone. Soon she'd finish college, get married and make her own life. She already had a boy-friend and her future was as good as decided. With her gone, Ashish knew his parents would concentrate still further on him — push him, push him, push him. "Study hard, beta," his father would exhort at the breakfast table, and that was about as far as their communication went. Study hard.

His mother was quite sweet, really, but so silly. Ashish liked her a lot, though there was nothing he could talk to her about. It bothered him a great deal that she had nothing to say to him but she seemed happy enough feeding him round-the-clock and buying him fancy imported clothes. He'd often hear her telling her equally silly friends, "Ashish is not like other boys. I don't know...he's different. Quiet and secretive. Does your son talk to you? Tell you everything? Ashish never tells me anything."

The remark would bring a smile to Ashish's lips. He didn't tell her — or anybody at home — anything, because he had nothing to tell them. Besides, he found his father strange. And for that matter, a stranger. A moody, distracted man who took very little interest in his small family. Not that he was ill-tempered or anything, just boring. Besides, Ashish got the feeling his father didn't like him. He often wondered about it. What was it that he'd done to put him off? Got born? Was that it?

Ashish looked at his image in the mirror. He had very little of his father in him, at least physically. He was shades darker to begin with. Darker than both his parents as a matter of fact. And he lacked his father's fineness of features. Even at eight, Ashish could spot the obvious discrepancies. Was that the reason his father rejected him? His sister Soni was fair, light-haired and light-eyed. She bore a strong resemblance to their father, besides having her mother's winning smile. She was the one who could've joined films — she was certainly pretty enough. Ashish wondered what had made the cameraman come up with the comment he'd made at the party. He had certainly guessed Ashish's secret desire, peeped into his heart and uttered those frightening words: "You should join films." Instinctively Ashish had known he wasn't poking fun at him or treating him like a child. The man had sensed something the others had refused to see. Something that Ashish cherished and had dreamt about though never yet dared to articulate. Yes, he wanted to become an actor. An actor? Most people would've laughed. Not with those strange looks and that colouring. No way. And yet it was when Ashish participated in his weekly dramatics classes that he truly flowered...opened up...came out of himself and became another person. His teacher recognised his talent not his passion. At least she encouraged him by including him in all the small productions — that was enough for the time being. A small consolation. Ashish's mother had laughed seeing her son with make-up on. But Ashish himself had never felt as wonderful, as motivated. He'd come home in a euphoric state and said to himself as he stared into the bathroom mirror, "I'm an actor. I'm an actor."

And now, exactly twenty-two years later he was still saying the same thing. It was a part of his morning ritual. Each day, before brushing his teeth, he'd stare at his image in the large, bevelled mirror over the black wash-basin and announce, "I'm an actor. I'm an actor."

These days he said it out loud. He could afford to. He was an actor. An established successful actor. Not the hero he'd hoped to be, but a character actor without whom no commercial Hindi film was complete. His wife (the second one) was used to his morning monologue and had stopped reacting to it. His first wife, Sunila, had hated the words. "Oh stop that nonsense!" she'd snap, "it sounds so stupid. We all know you're an actor...you know you're an actor. Why do you have to repeat it everyday? Besides, it disturbs my sleep."

Now Ashish would joke about her irritation to his present wife, Ambika, "That's why I left her," he'd say. "She made fun of my mantra." And a mantra it had become. Ashish sincerely believed that if he ever forgot to utter those magical words first thing in the morning, he'd fluff his shots.

Ambika would explain to close friends, "I remind him to utter his magic formula each time he forgets...I'm the one who suffers otherwise. He has to give retake after retake the day he doesn't say it. And then he gets home even later than usual."

Ashish was one of the busiest actors in the business. His secretary had a hard time keeping up with his schedules. "No dates for two years," Kiran would tell interested producers. Or "Call me after a month — in case there are any cancellations."

Ashish liked the pace he'd set for himself. It had taken him five years of struggle to break into the circuit, but he'd done it. And without compromising too much. Sometimes he wondered how his parents felt about his success. Proud, he hoped, though he couldn't be sure. They'd retired a few years earlier — gone off to a secluded bungalow in the hills after his father had suffered a third heart attack, the one that nearly killed him. His mother had changed beyond recognition. She'd withdrawn into herself and all but switched off from life around her. The two of them had found solace in an ashram close to their wooded home. They regularly visited a swami who held discourses on the *Gita*, and drew hundreds of devotees to his door.

Ashish had met him several times, but remained entirely unmoved. He could see, though, what his parents sought in him — the peace of mind that had eluded them ever since the death of Soni in a tragic car accident days before her planned wedding. So now, Mr. and Mrs. Anand spent their days in prayer and meditation. Their needs were few and simple. They asked nothing of Ashish and gave nothing in return except impersonal blessings each time he went to visit. They rarely came to see him in Bombay pleading they couldn't take the harsh life of the city any longer. Besides, the car exhausts aggravated Mrs. Anand's accelerating asthmatic condition and the noises from the street drove Mr. Anand berserk, bringing on an instant anxiety attack.

In a way, this arrangement suited Ashish and Ambika perfectly. Their lives were structured so precariously — she with her thriving clothes and interiors business, he with his film commitments, that they really had no time or space for the senior Anands in their functional star home. Ambika kept promising to do it up in a manner that reflected Ashish's success, but her own contracts kept her completely occupied. For Ashish, however, this was a matter of little consequence. He hardly spent any time at home anyway and as long as he had a bed to lie down on, a telephone that worked and a bathroom mirror to talk to each morning, he was satisfied enough.

It also suited him to have an ambitious, busy wife. One of the reasons his first marriage had collapsed was because Anu had become a typical film cow — over-dressed, over made-up, fat and lazy. Once Ashish had started to make sufficient money, Anu had given up her hotel job, preferring to lie around at home eating, gossiping, shopping and watching video films. Ambika had shrewdly realised that in order to hook and hold someone as restless and intense as Ashish, she'd have to do more than make her body available to him. And wisely, she'd stuck to her resolve. Besides, Ashish was different, as she frequently reminded herself. He took his acting seriously. It meant a lot to him. It meant everything, in fact. Which was why they'd mutually adopted a "no children" clause. This again had been fine by her. The thought of a bloated belly, sleepless nights and endless diapers hadn't ever charmed her and she didn't care what people read into it. She enjoyed her work and the money it brought in. And unlike in her first marriage to a stockbroker, Ashish never asked her how much she made or what she did with it. Which was just as well for if Ashish knew, Ambika was sure, he'd be jealous and resentful.

They both had their secrets and it was mutually understood that they wouldn't pry into each other's lives. "We're a modern couple," Ambika would reveal in interviews. "He has his priorities and I have mine. We share a certain togetherness — but it's not the oppressive sort. We believe in giving each other plenty of space." Smart reporters knew just how to interpret that statement. "Space" had become a convenient euphemism for affairs in the film industry. The moment that word was dropped, the obvious conclusions were promptly reached. And in the case of Ashish and Ambika, the film press was not wrong. The only difference was that the two of them had decided early on in their marriage that discretion was to be the watchword. "If you don't tell me, I don't know," Ashish would tease Ambika, who'd smile a slow smile and maintain an enigmatic silence.

It wasn't his "affairs" that she minded. It was the lackeys. The hangers-on. Theirs was a constant, overbearing presence. They were there when Ambika opened her eyes and walked out into the kitchen in search of coffee and they were there when she tiredly went to bed, leaving Ashish to finish his "last peg" (the longest peg known to man). It was an aspect of Ashish's life she found very difficult to understand. Why did he need them? Why did he underwrite their expenses? Why did he carry them around like excess baggage on his outstation stints? Why did she have to put up with them? It was worse than having a live-in mother-in-law. A mother-in-law who laughed a lot, drank a lot and ate a lot. A very expensive mother-in-law, who never went to sleep, didn't take a single day off and if she possibly could have, would've happily got into bed with the two of them. It was one topic Ashish was reluctant to discuss, and one they always got into an ugly fight over each time Ambika raised it. "I need these guys," he'd say exasperatedly, "they are useful. And loyal."

Ambika had yet to figure out the why's and how's of that assessment. "What exactly do you need them for? What is it that they do for you?' she'd tried asking, making sure to keep the obvious irritation out of her voice.

Ashish had looked vague, reached for a cigarette and mumbled, "Things. I need them for stuff like...like...you know keeping a track of my dates...appointments...handling the riff-raff that comes around. Keeping me amused...massaging my neck...fetching me a drink... organising cigarettes."

"And girls?" she'd thought to herself. There were enough stories about Ashish's quick trysts in the make-up van — with extras picked out of the chorus line. But even that angle baffled her. He could get those girls on his own. He didn't need satellites for that. As for keeping him amused — wasn't that supposed to be her role?

"No, darling," a senior movie wife had explained to her, "your role is to maintain a facade. You pretend to be blissfully married, he pretends to be faithful. And everybody is happy. Besides, these days, if I were you I wouldn't let him touch me without a condom on...something crazy is happening in the industry. The heroes are sleeping with each other!"

Ambika had been far too stunned by the casualness of the revelation to react initially. Two days later, she'd phoned the same woman on the pretext of getting the address of a "divine wicker-work craftsman". And then, cautiously, she'd asked, "Remember your comment the other day? The one about heroes with heroes? Who told you?"

The woman cackled, "Darling, these things get around, you know...it's the latest-latest. A craze. Maybe they're just sick of us women. They need variety. But not with all that AIDS stuff floating about."

Ambika had replaced the receiver worriedly. Not that Ashish and she had a particularly passionate relationship, but they did go to bed on the odd Sunday when he wasn't shooting. The rest of the time both of them were too exhausted to make the effort — and it suited her fine. But now suddenly, she began to see the lackeys in a new role. Maybe they did more than merely fetch drinks and girls. Maybe their massage didn't stop at the neck. Maybe Ashish reserved all his energies for them. She started looking at them afresh. Suspiciously. Each little gesture, each exchanged glance acquired new meaning. She concentrated on Ashish's body language when he was with them. The way he used his hands, mouth, eyebrows — the jokes he cracked with their hidden layers of truths. The light touches. The shared cigarettes and drinks. Small intimacies she'd previously ignored and dismissed with a "men will be men" attitude.

She waited for the right moment to bring it up with Ashish. What happens to this confrontation? The moment never arrived or may be she didn't really want to know. It was one of those rare nights that he had come home early, thanks to a cancelled shift. He'd even abandoned his lackeys en route. Perhaps they were expected later, bearing plastic containers of take-away Chinese food. Ashish seemed reasonably relaxed as he hummed a popular hit and peeled off his sweaty clothes. Ambika stared at his naked body. Not bad, she mused. Not bad at all. If only it excited her. It had once, during those early days when she longed to touch him, lie with him, talk to him. But now she could look objectively, dispassionately at him and wonder where all that lust had gone.

Ashish had wanted her too, often desperately. She remembered that first heady encounter they'd had at a producer's gaudy home. He'd walked up to her with two drinks in his hand and gallantly offered her one. She'd shaken her head and whispered, "I'll pass." Ashish had then tried what he later confessed was his standard "hero tactic". He'd cornered her literally by placing the flats of his large hands against the wall behind her, thereby blocking her way. He'd also given her the full "eye treatment", head cocked to one side, lids half-closed and a moony expression on his face that generally drove recipients berserk. She'd stared at him coolly, half-amused, half-flattered and concluded that he was nauseatingly attractive. After ten minutes or so, he'd got to the point abruptly, "Let's stop wasting time being formal...I want you. I think you want me. Your place or mine?"

Ambika had laughed out loud, "You're pretty direct, aren't you? But I guess you're right. Why play games? My place. It's closer."

They'd driven along in silence with Ashish staring at the wet roads, Ambika, at the wheel, feeling strangely relaxed. This wasn't the first time she'd been picked up by someone. But on every previous occasion, she'd experienced a certain dread, an apprehension...panic too. Not now. For the first time she felt sure and ready. As she negotiated the slippery streets deftly, Ashish had searched for music in the glove compartment and settled for romantic ghazals. He'd asked her permission before lighting a cigarette, and later, in her small, neat flat, he had undressed carefully with his back to her while she had brazenly lain naked on the small bed and surveyed him clinically.

It had been a dramatic night. Ashish had switched off the lights, pulled up the sheets and looked at the spectacular celestial son-et-lumiere outside the curtained window. Ambika had been surprised and pleased by Ashish's considerate love-making. Rumours in the film press had made him out to be some sort of a sexual brute — all raw energy and rapid pumping. Enough women had been grateful for even that and Ambika had been prepared for worse. After making love, Ashish had told Ambika about his first wife....his parents....his dead sister...his childhood. She'd asked him wonderingly, "Why are you telling me all this? You hardly know me."

Ashish had leaned over, kissed her gently and said, "I know you. I know you all right. It's just that I want you to know me."

Now that the two of them led such depressingly insulated lives, filled with exaggerated civility and forced politeness, Ambika missed the earlier passion of the relationship, the storms and rages. "There is just emptiness in my heart for him," she'd recently confessed to her only friend, Minal. "A void — that's all that's left. It's so sad that these days he doesn't affect me at all... in fact, I often wish he'd die."

When those last few words had escaped her lips, she'd been as startled by their harshness as Minal, who'd repeated, "Die? You want Ashish to die? God! I didn't realise it had come to this."

Ambika had got up and walked to the window guiltily and whispered, "Frankly...I hadn't either...till now. It just seems like such a sham — our so-called "open marriage", our "understanding" of one another's "needs". I'm sick of the pretense".

Minal had joined her quietly and said, "Do something about it, in that case. You don't have to stay in a meaningless marriage. What's stopping you from walking out?"

Ambika, her eyes filling with unexpected tears had whispered, "Hope."

Ashish came back from the airport to find Ambika still awake. She was writing in her diary — the one she guarded so jealously. She looked up with a start. "Shooting cancelled? I thought you were coming back tomorrow."

Ashish had a strange look in his eyes and his voice sounded uncharacteristically high-pitched. Ambika went back to writing her entries, assuming he'd taken one of those air-taxis that served gallons of beer on flight. Ashish hovered around wordlessly. She waited, her body rigid with tension. She was hoping he'd go away and leave her alone — it was getting harder and harder to deal with his sulks and silences, especially when he chose to communicate in broken, incoherent sentences. She looked up with an expression that conveyed her impatience.

Ashish came and sat down on the bed, close to her. He'd broken out into a sweat and his forehead was covered with beads of perspiration. He stammered, "I don't know how to tell you this, Ambika."

She continued to write mechanically, refusing to look up. When she spoke her voice was flat, indifferent. "Another woman? Or is it a man?"

Ashish remained silent. She could feel his breath on her bare arm. Why was she making this so hard for both of them, she wondered. She decided to shut her diary and turned to him. "All right, let's hear it. I'm paying full attention now. Give it to me on the chin — whatever it is. I can take it."

Ashish reached out for her tentatively, his hands shaking, his fingers moving. She saw the despair in his eyes...and for a brief moment, felt the old stirrings of love...of affection...of caring...But almost as a reflex, she pulled away and reminded herself that she shouldn't weaken...shouldn't allow herself to feel vulnerable...he was manipulating her again...playing on her sentiments. As he had done dozens of times in the past. She'd been such a fool then...always succumbing to his pleas...buying his bullshit...pushing away her own hostility. Not this time. Her eyes were hard, almost cruel, as she faced him. Ashish was holding his head between his hands. She watched as tears poured out of his eyes and were absorbed by the rough denim of his jeans. She wanted to hold his hand, hug him, console him. But she couldn't. Memories of countless previous occasions surfaced as she watched her husband break down and thought cynically, "Probably, the new whore has walked out on him. Maybe a hanger-on has defected...or perhaps he has lost the next big banner film to a rival. Well, none of that concerns me. Besides, I don't want to play tranquilizer tonight."

She sat back on her bed, with Ashish's head in her lap. She couldn't unclench her fists to stroke his hair. She resented the weight of his head in her lap. Her legs were getting numb. She wanted to shove him off roughly and run out of the house, never to return. She felt the level of hate rising within her. Her knuckles were dead white against the pale blue of her nightgown as she waited for her husband to finish his outburst and leave her to write in peace. His body was shuddering uncontrollably now. "She or he must have meant a lot to him," she concluded.

Ashish looked up at her imploringly, "Please, Ambika, please...I have something important to tell you. Will you listen to me? Just listen?"

The contempt in her voice had a particularly hard edge to it, "Go ahead, Ashish, I'm listening. All ears, in fact."

He croaked hoarsely. "I'm dying, Ambika, dying. Do you understand?"

She threw back her head and laughed, "Really? Of what? A broken heart, a broken back, a broken prick — what?"

Ashish looked at his wife's exposed throat, as she continued to laugh. "It isn't what you're thinking, Ambika. It's terminal...I just got the confirmation. It's...it's..."

"Cancer? Or is it AIDS!" she asked mockingly, "Tell me another. She pushed him away and stood up. The laughter refused to stop "Cancer! AIDS! Ha!" she said to her reflection in the long mirror. "He has cancer. Believe that? God, the extent this man will go to just to attract attention."

Wearily, Ashish got to his feet. He stood up unsteadily, holding on to Ambika's dresser for support. His eyes were dry as he watched his wife dancing around the room chanting "Cancer, cancer, cancer".

Wordlessly, he walked out and went into his own bedroom. He reached for the phone. It was nearly 3 a.m. Too late to call one of his fellows. Too late even for them. Ashish reached for something in the lower drawer of his bedside table. He groped around till his hand found what he was seeking. He checked. It was loaded. Ambika's shrill laughter was echoing in his ears as he raised the gun to his mouth. He'd done it in the movies dozens of times. He knew how to shoot himself. He knew how to die. It was said nobody could beat him in a death scene. Nobody could die more convincingly. He'd won several awards for his death-bed performances. It was really so simple. Pull the trigger and bang! Imagine. He'd do it this time without a director telling him how. Nobody to say "cut". No retakes. Bang! He'd get it right in the first take itself. Bang! And he'd be dead. No applause. No "wah wahs". No plastic blood. Bang! As easy as that...as easy. Ambika could always pick up his award later. How effortlessly her wish had come true. Perhaps, too effortlessly for even her to value it as much as it deserved to be valued.

Eleven

DIWALI

IT WAS going to be a bleak Diwali for Kalindi. A week before the festivities, she was waiting in a darkened home for her husband Suresh to come back. Back to her and their two children, a boy and a girl. She sat by the window of her sea-side flat, gazing at the setting sun and feeling intensely sorry for herself. Kalindi hated to feel this way — yet another martyred woman, cribbing about the raw deal handed out to her by a man. It was an alien emotion to her. Kalindi preferred to see herself as someone strong and self-sufficient, not a pathetic, weepy creature with a tired, defeated look in her eyes and a permanent catch in her throat. She wasn't that kind of a drowning-in-self-pity woman at all. Anything but. People who knew her regarded her as a role-model — the woman who had it all — a gorgeous husband, the perfect family, a career — yes, that too — a super apartment, a great lifestyle, well-trained servants (a boon in a city like Bombay) holidays on a bi-annual basis, supportive in-laws in Ahmedabad to leave the kids with, a wardrobe filled with pricey "designer" clothes, plastic money and reasonable looks.

Kalindi wasn't a great beauty, but she knew how to make the most of herself. And her "outward presentation" (as Suresh put it) was as important to him as it was to her. "You are someone," he'd remind her on days she wasn't up to dressing up, "you aren't just an anonymous housewife with a nice hobby. If you don't think of yourself as an entrepreneur, if you don't behave and dress like one, nobody will take you seriously. Remember, as a marketing man, I can tell you this — package yourself correctly and you'll score points over the competition."

Kalindi's mouth twisted into a wry smile at the memory of his words. "Packaging", "Positioning", "Added advantage". Buzz words, jargon, she'd been hearing at breakfast, lunch and dinner for fifteen long years now. Words she'd stopped responding to. Overworked cliches, the lot of them, like most of Suresh's talk. It was only recently that Kalindi had begun to listen carefully to his daily lectures — not because they had changed but because she herself had. Now, each time Suresh opened his mouth to deliver his borrowed words of wisdom, Kalindi groaned inwardly. It was the predictability of his thoughts and actions that had started to get on her nerves and more recently, to get her down. The question of indulging in "conversation" did not arise with Suresh. He was the original "monologuist" given to sounding off on subjects dearest to his heart — politics and marketing.

During the first five years, Kalindi had listened dutifully, assuming her best, alert and involved expression. Maybe, she had been genuinely interested in her husband's thoughts at that point. No longer though. He bored her intensely, so much so that even her children's comics seemed more interesting. For the last couple of years in fact Kalindi had begun to switch off completely while he droned on. She'd mastered the art of giving the appearance of listening while her mind was elsewhere — on a different plane and in a different land. If Suresh sensed her gradual withdrawal, he didn't indicate it. He'd walk in cheerily and without a pause, break into a discourse on the "competitive edge". Kalindi's eyes would glaze over, though she still took the trouble to nod her head from time to time and say "uhh-uhh." "Really?" "Is that right?" Sometimes, the dryness of her tone surprised her and she stopped short, checked herself. What was she turning into?

Kalindi was careful to regularly switch the light of self-examination on herself. It would have been so easy to rephrase the question and ask, "What was Suresh turning her into?" That would've been grossly unfair to her husband though, and even in her darkest moments, Kalindi couldn't get herself to do it. There was a strong sense of inherent fairness in her character that stopped her from passing hasty judgements about others. And Suresh, after all, was her husband, not some stranger boring her at a dull cocktail party. A real stranger would have been easier to handle. All Kalindi would've had to do was wait for a pause in the conversation and then glide away with a soft, "Excuse me". She was often tempted to do just that with Suresh, especially when he got into one of his more bombastic moods. Suresh had all the answers. Whether it was world issues, complicated political crises, marketing snarl-ups, acquisitions and mergers, multinationals, Clinton's dilemmas, Narasimha Rao's myriad problems, Suresh could be counted on to come up with solutions. Only these days, Kalindi found his attitude laughable. Almost pathetic. And she hated herself for it especially since Suresh seemed to be totally oblivious of her scorn. Or else, would he have continued to inflict his infantile views on her knowing what a low opinion she had of them?

Suresh wasn't a dope. In fact, he was considered quite a whiz. As the head of his company, colleagues respected him and even his critics acknowledged that Suresh was amongst the top marketing men in India. Why then couldn't he interest Kalindi or impress her as he once had? She thought it had something to do with the rather unfortunate fact that they'd both grown in separate directions. But that was the lot of most working couples these days, especially when the wife's career registered a meteoric upswing along with her husband's. Kalindi believed she had handled that aspect of their relationship deftly by playing down her own priorities. She had made sure to place Suresh's career ahead of almost everything else in their life. Strangely enough, it was Suresh who was keener on her "making it", than she herself was. "Why waste your education, your talent? Work hard and get there," he'd tell her, pointing skywards. Now that Kalindi was "there" she didn't know what to do with her success, since success hadn't mattered to her in the first place.

"I like the idea of what I'm doing. I like the process...it doesn't matter where it gets me so long as I don't lose money on it", she'd explained patiently to Suresh.

He'd shaken his head dismissively and scolded, "Don't say that. Don't undersell yourself. Don't throw it all away. The top — that's where I want you to be."

The top! Kalindi laughed at the ridiculous import of those words. Where was this mysterious "top"? Who decided when a person got there? And what happened later, once you were through with the view? These were questions — abstract, silly ones, perhaps, that she longed to ask Suresh, or anyone, for that matter. She'd tried to, once, only to be snubbed by Suresh. "Don't lose focus," he'd exhorted. "The momentum is important. You are riding the crest now, make sure you stay there." With that he'd left the room to answer the phone. When he'd returned, the subject was already scratched off his agenda and there was no way Kalindi could pull him back to it. Not that she'd have got anywhere, anyway. Suresh wasn't the kind of man to indulge in this sort of "pointless" conversation. He called it an "irritating female trait". Once or twice he'd interrupted her rudely and switched topics while she was still in mid-sentence. After that Kalindi had taught herself to practise "internal dialogues"—long, extended conversations with herself. It was a monotonous and unchallenging habit but there wasn't anybody she felt close enough to, whom she could call over or phone. Besides, much as she hated to admit this even to herself, Kalindi was sharply conscious of the "image" the two of them projected in their circle. The image of a well-adjusted, happy couple. It was important to her. And it was certainly very important to Suresh.

But today, as she sat in her tastefully furnished flat, going over their last big fight, Kalindi felt miserable. Where had she gone wrong in "handling" her husband? Handling. The very word was offensive. He wasn't a pet at an obedience school. Or a wild horse that had to be broken in. Suresh was a pleasant enough chap, a mild-mannered sort of fellow who avoided confrontations as far as he could help them. This was basically Kalindi's view of marriage too. She detested scenes and angry words. When the children were very young, Suresh and she had had an unspoken pact that they'd settle their differences calmly and quietly, preferably not in the children's presence. Now that the two kids were away at boarding school, they didn't have to be all that careful. About servants, yes, but theirs were discreet and well-trained. At the first sign of an impending argument, they'd melt away quietly into the distant recesses of their own quarters and stay there till the call-bell, indicating the storm had blown over, was rung.

But this time their argument had reached a different plane altogether. It had turned ugly and vicious, with Suresh raising his voice (and his hand, at one point). "You are driving me to violence," he had shouted, his eyes wild with rage, his nostrils flared, his lips curled above those large, square teeth Kalindi had once found so attractive. When she thought back on the fight, the ferocity of the fall-out puzzled her—after all, it had been triggered off by something trivial, something so minor—a silly joke, really.

Suresh had come back at his usual hour and demanded tea. Normally, Kalindi would've dropped whatever she was doing and rushed into the neat kitchen, if not to actually make it then at least to supervise the laying of the tray and to make sure everything on it was as it should be—the starched napkin, the chilled glass of water, the knife and fork to tackle the snack of the day, the tea—not too dark, not too light and at just the right temperature. That evening, Kalindi had continued talking on the phone. It hadn't been just a chatty call, but an important one and work-related at that. The newly-appointed servant-boy had made the mistake—a monumental one in Suresh's book—of forgetting the napkin. Minutes later, Kalindi heard a crash and she knew without having to look up, that Suresh had hurled the entire tray onto the floor. Sure enough, the young servant had come running out of their bedroom, ashen-faced and quaking with fear. Calmly, she'd replaced the receiver, saying, "Listen, there's a small emergency, nothing major. I'll ring you back." She'd taken her time to go back into the room. Keep calm. Stay composed, she'd told herself as she'd opened the door and walked in. Suresh had been seated on the bed, staring fixedly ahead of him. The samosas were lying on the carpet and tea stains had ruined the new quilted bedspread irrevocably.

"What happened?" she'd asked. Her voice had sounded long-suffering, even though she hadn't intended it to. He swung around to face her. "What happened?" he'd thundered. "I'll tell you what happened. That monkey you've employed forgot the napkin."

Kalindi had been tempted to say, "So, bloody what if he did?" Instead, she'd busied herself picking up the plates and samosas. "I'll get you a fresh cup." She'd said as she had started to leave the room. "I don't want it. I don't want tea. This is the sort of rotten service I get in my own home. Do you know I haven't even eaten any lunch today — nothing at all. I bust my ass working, working, working — and I can't get a decent cup of tea when I get back. Do you know why? Because you are too involved in your own life, with your own priorities. You've become a big career woman...earning a lot of money." Suresh spat out the words "Career woman" like another man would've said, "two-timing bitch".

Kalindi had walked out, her eyes stinging with tears but her head held high. She hadn't been surprised by Suresh's words. The accusation had become familiar to her over the past year—ever since she'd got further involved in her job and taken on extra commitments. Yes, her income had doubled but what did Suresh expect her to do with the extra time she now had? The children were away at school, the house eerily empty. Suresh's timings were more or less predictable and Kalindi could afford to invest more of herself in her business venture — the one she'd started to impress Suresh with in the first place.

Besides, she liked the extra income it generated. She liked having her own money and more importantly, she enjoyed the absolute control she had over it. Unlike other wives she knew, there was no question of her asking Suresh for "pocket money".

How childish and humiliating that concept was — and yet so many of her friends revelled in it. Revelled in the daily pride-stripping exercise, when they stretched out their palms and asked their husbands for money. Some men were gracious about it. And generous too. But 'mostly they used the opportunity to taunt and lecture their wives. Or worse, ask them for detailed accounts and justifications as if their homes harboured petty thieves hell-bent on stealing and looting the mighty bread winner. Kalindi often asked her friends how they put up with this without feeling diminished. One of the women had explained, "One develops a thick skin after a point. Besides, what choice do we have? We don't make our own money—where are we supposed to turn to for expenses?" It was a topic she'd often discussed with Suresh. "Women must be self-sufficient," he'd say absently. And yet, when Kalindi's small business took off and she began spending more time outside the house, Suresh's resentment had become vocal and obvious. "It would be a different matter altogether if I expected you to pick up the bills, pay for household expenes or if I asked you for money," he'd begun to say. "But now you carry on as if you're some tycoon. Constant phone-calls, constant tensions. And all of us are getting neglected. Look at the state of the house."

And Kalindi had looked. Really looked. Without prejudice. The house looked like it had always looked — reasonably neat and reasonably well-run. She didn't count herself amongst the model housewives of the world. But she wasn't a sloppy, indifferent one either. She took pride in her environment — at work and at her residence. But where Kalindi saw an ordered sort of place, complete with fresh flowers and stores that didn't run out, Suresh only saw shortcomings and short-cuts. He'd arrive from work and pick on the first servant to cross his path — anything could trigger off an instant tantrum — an ashtray slightly askew, a window left open, a drape not pulled properly. At first Kalindi would try and anticipate what was likely to upset her husband, then it had become a kind of game. Sometimes, she'd deliberately leave something around — a wet towel, a hair brush in the living room, a chair carelessly pulled out — just to see his reaction. She experienced a perverse sort of thrill, almost an innocent sense of power. How predictable her husband had become! The fuse was getting shorter and shorter. The big explosion had to come. Yet when it did, Kalindi found herself totally unprepared for it.

She'd taken the tea tray back to the kitchen, her hands trembling, her mouth refusing to listen to her brain, which kept telling it to stop sliding around uncontrollably. The servants had lowered their eyes so as not to embarrass her further by staring at her visible distress. The new servant had been lurking in the shadows, expecting to be shouted at, fired instantly. Kalindi had left the kitchen and gone into the children's room. She often took refuge there these days. There was something oddly comforting about being surrounded by their things — photographs, books, abandoned keds, clothes, Garfields and Trolls. She'd switched on the fan and lain down on her daughter's narrow bed. It still smelt of her Primrose Bath Gel. She'd tried to rationalise where she was going wrong, where they were going wrong. Was there any truth at all in Suresh's bitterly articulated charges? Was she switching off? Turning away from her home? Her husband? Concentrating selfishly on herself, her needs, her career? Her achievements?

She'd started as she'd heard the door opening. It was Suresh. She could tell without looking.

"There's no Dettol in the bathroom," he'd snarled, "And no fresh towels, either. What's going on in this house, I'd like to know. I pay a lot of money to run it. Nobody has as many servants as we do. And I can't have a decent cup of tea after all this?"

Kalindi had gotten up and said, "I'm sorry." It was a tactic that generally worked. She'd assumed a humble stance, head lowered, back bent.

Suresh hadn't been prepared for meekness. He'd stared at her suspiciously. "No you aren't," he'd said.

She'd looked into his eyes — a direct unblinking look and repeated, "I am, Suresh. I truly am."

He'd shaken his head disbelievingly. "What about? What the

hell are you sorry about?"

Kalindi had said blandly. "The Dettol. I'm sorry it isn't there. I can send out for some right now, if you like. Or if it can wait, I'll get it tomorrow." She'd tried to leave the room, but he'd pushed her back in roughly.

"I see you've stopped smiling these days. Or talking properly. I get the feeling you avoid me—avoid being in the same room. What's the problem? Are you unhappy? Suffering? I don't like unpleasant faces around me. A man comes home tired after working all day...he expects a smile. Relaxation. Not this nonsense."

Kalindi had reminded herself to keep mum. Experience had told her it didn't do any good to argue or even to put forth her point of view when Suresh was in this mood.

He'd prodded her shoulder. "Tell me, what's your problem. Go on..."

It was something about his manner — the way he challenged her to dare speak her mind, that goaded Kalindi to burst out, "Everything's the problem. I'm sick of your bullying, sick of your rudeness, sick of your threats, sick of your accusations."

He'd stood there with his arms stretched against the door frame, his left foot tapping. Before Kalindi could get her breath back, he'd leaned menacingly towards her, "I see," he'd hissed, "It's obvious you don't like things around here any more. Well, the option is yours. You are free to go where you feel happier. I wish you well." With that he'd whirled around and stalked back into his room. Their room. At least what had once been theirs. Though Kalindi had never really felt a part of it. Never really belonged.

That had been five days ago. In the past, scenes like these would have blown over fairly soon. By breakfast. Suresh would have shut his eyes and willed himself to sleep by 10 p.m. The next morning he would have been fine. And Kalindi would've pretended to be fine too. He'd have rushed off after delivering a string of instructions and she'd have immersed herself in organising the household. But

145

this time was different. Major. Suresh had refused to look at her.
Or even acknowledge her presence. She had gone about her routine
like a robot. Coldly. Mechanically. Rage had gradually been
replaced by indifference. Kalindi had scribbled, "Marriage is the
ugliest compromise in the world", in her planner.

She'd written long and loving letters to her children. She'd
made the usual pre-Diwali preparations — cleaned the house
thoroughly, got rid of unwanted household articles, bought new
clothes for the servants, ordered sweets from the lady who
specialised in them. She'd bought an embroidered kurta for Suresh,
a saree for herself, and presents for the children. To be given to
them when they arrived for their X'Mas break.

She was sure Suresh had noticed all this — he generally didn't
miss the smallest detail. But since the cold war was still on, he'd
refrained from commenting. Which was just as well. He would've
found fault with practically everything — pointed out Brasso stains
on the large plant holders, cobwebs dangling from remote corners,
fine layers of dust on hard-to-reach cupboard tops, unpolished
silverware in the cabinet, undusted picture frames on the walls. At
one level, Kalindi was relieved. And yet, paradoxically enough,
she missed his nagging, his pushing, his taunts. For the first time
in their marriage it was Suresh who had switched off. There was
a dead indifference in his eyes when he was home. It affected
Kalindi deeply — more than she had thought it would. She'd
imagined she'd become immune to his frequent jibes. She'd thought
she was tougher, stronger and therefore the victor in their undeclared
war. If earlier on she'd harboured dark, murderous thoughts about
Suresh — about men — now she felt helpless, almost vulnerable.
It was an alien feeling. And yet she recognised it only too well.
Stripped off all defences, Kalindi felt exposed and weak. But far
from denying it to herself, she'd started to wallow in these new
feelings, believing that for the first time since her childhood, she
was allowing herself the luxury of being true to the messages her
heart, not her mind, was sending. Kalindi had unconsciously tuned
into the emotional side of herself. A side that had been suppressed

146

for such a long time. It felt good. It felt real. She was tired of being cerebral. Rational. In-charge. Invincible. Yes, Diwali would be lonely this year. And dark. But there was a light shining within her — the flame steady and strong. And Kalindi was no longer afraid. Not even of herself.

Twelve

FLOWERS

"DON'T FORGET to bring a veni for me tomorrow," the dying woman rasped from the hospital bed. Her wizened old mother exchanged glances with the rest of the family. Vandana raised her eyes to gauge their expressions, "and also my diamond earrings...mangalsutra and bangles...it's my wedding anniversary and I want to dress up...as I always do on this day."

Nobody had the heart to tell her that she'd be wasting the monumental effort involved in getting dressed up for the occasion. The man she was doing all this for, her husband Vasant, wouldn't be there to see her. Finally, her mother spoke, adopting a tone of voice that was entirely out of character for her. "You rest now Vandana...come on, close your eyes. Try and sleep. We'll worry about all these things tomorrow."

Vandana held out her frail arm and gestured weakly for her mother to come closer to her. Mrs. Gokhale leaned over the emaciated body of her once beautiful daughter. The stench from the bandages was unbearable. Mrs. Gokhale had already smelt death. Vandana grasped her mother's shoulder and beseeched her with tear-filled eyes. "Please ma...please...do it for me. It's important..."

Mrs. Gokhale pulled away quickly before her daughter could detect the pain in her own eyes, the pain she was trying so hard to camouflage. "All right, I'll do it," she said reluctantly. She turned her back on the shabby, steel cot with its lumpy mattress

149

and soiled sheets. Her daughter deserved better than this...this...
unspeakably cruel fate. Her precious daughter and favourite child
was dying and nobody could help now. But was this the way to
die? She bit her lip, suddenly unable to contain the bitterness.
Even stray dogs had a more dignified death, she thought. They
don't have their bodies invaded and punctured with tubes, needles,
probes. And to see Vandana, with her milk-white, flawless skin
which she had once been so vain about, reduced to a grimy heap...a
collection of bones loosely held together in a wrinkled, bruised,
dehydrated, abused sheath of tissues. God had been so harsh, so
unfair to this innocent, young woman, a mother of two. So very
merciless. Why? What had her poor child ever done to deserve
this? If He had wished to take away her life, at least He could have
done so with more grace, more pity. Mrs. Gokhale couldn't bear
to see her daughter's suffering any more. In fact she had actively
begun to pray for an early, swift death. If Vandana knew she
hardly had any time left, she didn't show it. But then, for these
past few days, she'd hardly been lucid enough for any length of
time for Mrs. Gokhale to even talk to her...not about her sickness,
but other matters. Important matters. Like Vasant and the future
of her children.

Vasant. Even the mention of her son-in-law's name brought
frown to Mrs. Gokhale's broad, unlined brow. Vasant, in her eyes,
was beneath contempt. He was despicable and low. To call him a
villain was an understatement. He was a blackguard. A two-timing
blackguard whom she hoped she would never have to see once
Vandana was gone. Tomorrow was her daughter's wedding
anniversary. The twelfth one. It was a day Vandana had always
treated on par with a religious festival. A day when she would
awake at dawn to offer prayers at the little shrine she had had
especially installed in her room.

Fifteen years ago, Vandana had met a man in the corridors of
her suburban college and fallen in love with him instantly. Perhaps
Vasant too had been sincere in his affection for her then. But
unfortunately for Vandana, his love had vanished within the first

year itself, while hers had only grown stronger. Mrs. Gokhale had often wondered about her daughter's unshakeable faith in that faithless man — Vandana was not a stupid woman. An immature one, perhaps, but not stupid. She was perceptive enough about other people, then what was this special power Vasant wielded over her that prevented her from recognising him for what he was? A third-rate manipulator, who had married her for her inheritance and beauty.

Mrs. Gokhale shuddered at the memory of their elopement. It had shocked their family (though not Mrs. Gokhale herself) and provided enough gossip within their conservative community to keep tongues wagging even five years later. Vandana's sisters ("moralists", she'd sniffed dismissively) had taken it as a personal affront that she, the baby in the family, had run off and married a man of her choice, thereby ruining their chances of finding a good match. Vandana had brought immense disrepute to the family. For years, they'd stopped talking to her and strongly disapproved of Mrs. Gokhale's decision not to disinherit her or cut her off permanently from the family's fold.

Today, as Mrs. Gokhale walked towards her parked car wearily, unable to forget the spectre of her daughter's shrunken body lying listlessly on that ugly cot, she thanked the Almighty for that decision. Vandana needed her. Vandana had always needed her. On one level, Vandana had remained a child even after she'd had two of her own. Mrs. Gokhale firmly held back the tears of rage that were threatening to stream down her cheeks. "I will not cry — not now. Not later. Not even when the flames from her pyre touch the sky," she told herself. That would be conceding defeat. She didn't want God to think he had triumphed by snatching away her beloved child.

She climbed into her car tiredly as she had been doing each evening after Vandana's hospitalisation. She'd known the day she'd accompanied her in the ambulance that this was going to be a one-way journey for her terminally ill daughter. Nobody else in the family had been willing to confront the horrible truth. Only a mother recognised death in her child's eyes, Mrs. Gokhale had thought grimly to herself. And Vandana was definitely dying.

Mrs. Gokhale had virtually given up eating after Vandana had fallen ill. Even the few morsels she forced into her reluctant mouth were hard to swallow. How could any mother relish food when her child's sustenance came via an intravenous drip? How could she even think of a regular meal, knowing her daughter would never eat one again. No. Mrs. Gokhale had made up her mind about one thing — once Vandana died, she herself planned to give up all cooked food. If it meant sacking the cook and closing down the kitchen, so be it. Her system wouldn't allow it. The revolt had already begun. Mrs. Gokhale was barely existing on a diet of curds and fruit and only because she knew she needed strength to face the ordeal that lay ahead. She certainly couldn't afford to fall ill now — not when Vandana needed her so desperately.

She sat at the large mahogany dining table and pushed a few blanched almonds around the plate. She tasted the curds set especially for her and wrinkled up her nose. Her reaction was identical each night. They were either "too sour" or "too sweet". She'd forbidden the cook to bring any of Vandana's favourite fruits into the house. She couldn't bear to look at pomegranates, even as she drove past crowded street-side bazaars. Vandana loved the gem-like, ruby-red juicy seeds of the fruit which looked as beautiful unopened as it did once split. And she'd stopped eating guavas which also happened to be her own favourite fruit. Mrs. Gokhale stuck to a rigid, self-punishing diet restricted to over-ripe bananas and oranges with two cups of milk twice a day. She would've skipped dinner altogether had it not been for the sleeplessness that an empty stomach induced. And nothing was as unbearable in the present circumstances as a night spent wide awake, tossing restlessly on her large bed, haunted by memories of Vandana, the child she had had the greatest difficulty bearing and delivering. The child everybody said had brought bad luck to her father.

Mrs. Gokhale winced at the stigma which had stuck to Vandana, at least in the eyes of her late husband's family. To begin with, the fact that she was a girl-child had seemed an unfortunate omen to them. "Did you really need another daughter?" they'd asked, as if she had had a choice in the matter. Within six months of her birth, Mr. Gokhale had suffered a huge loss at the stock exchange. It had been a clear error of judgement on his part, combined with greed and poor advice from brokers. But his misfortune had been blamed on Vandana, whose birth-chart had been pulled out and closely examined by astrologers. They'd filled pages with strange diagrams and configurations before concluding that the little girl had a major flaw in her horoscope. A flaw that affected her father's destiny adversely. Mrs. Gokhale's mother-in-law had glared at her accusingly, fixing her with a look that made it very clear that she knew just who was to blame for this tragedy. Strangely, Vandana's "defective" stars had endeared her to her mother. Mrs. Gokhale had become fiercely protective of the bright-eyed, beautiful, perfectly featured baby who gurgled contentedly in her crib and demanded nothing.

A year later, Mr. Gokhale was found dead in his bed. It was never clearly established what had killed him — heart failure or the will to live. It was whispered that he had taken his own life, unable to cope with the failure of his business as a trader in commodities. Others blamed it again on the little girl's stars. It was she who had brought a curse on the family. Mrs. Gokhale's in-laws had shunned her and her children since that day. But each insult and each taunt had made her mother's resolve to defend her youngest and most vulnerable child stronger. In any case, it was difficult for anyone but the most prejudiced person to dislike Vandana. She had a charming quality that endeared her to people. There was a certain innocence, a touching guilelessness about her that succeeded in breaking down the staunchest and most critical resistance.

When the time came for Vandana to choose — Vasant or her family — an inexplicable chill had gripped her mother's heart. It wasn't so much that she disapproved of Vandana's impulsive decision to run away, it was the man she'd foolishly selected to spend the rest of her life with that made Mrs. Gokhale deeply unhappy. Sure enough, Vasant had betrayed his young, trusting wife over and over again during the fifteen years of their marriage. And Vandana had foolishly covered up for her weak, avaricious husband — even to her furious mother. In the face of hard, irrefutable evidence, Vandana had refused to believe that Vasant had been regularly two-timing her.

In the beginning, it had been casual affairs — one-night stands with available women. Mrs. Gokhale had been amazed by the number of such women in the city. And Vasant obviously had a way with them — a particularly seductive modus operandi few could resist. It wasn't as if Vasant was a particularly handsome man. Tall, yes, well-built in a paunchy way, it was more his attitude than his physique that made him stand apart from other men in a group. Mrs. Gokhale tried to find the right words to describe it. Lazy arrogance? Complete self-assuredness? Contrived charm? Or the oldest and most difficult-to-resist trick in the book of all seducers — shameless flattery? That was it. Vasant looked at each woman through half-closed eyes, as if he wanted to bed her there and then. He paid her extravagant compliments in a deliberate and searching way, his hungry eyes travelling up and down the entire length of her body. The compliments weren't the standard ones either. He'd say to a woman with a mousy facade, "Did you know you have a beautiful mole at the nape of your neck?" Or to another diffident creature, "The slope of your shoulders is extraordinary. I have never seen such a graceful angle." Vasant was also shrewd enough to prey on women with low self-worth — those who hadn't ever been paid a compliment by a man — not even their own, generally uninspiring, husbands.

Vandana had trained herself to laugh Vasant's social flirtations away. Questioned by her mother during the early years of her marriage, she'd said lightly, "That's how Vasant is...he can't help it if women throw themselves at him. He charms them, that's all." His "charm", however, soon began to extend itself beyond the

154

paying of mere compliments. Vasant had started straying — going off on mysterious business trips without leaving contact numbers. Vandana had also started receiving strange phone calls at even stranger hours. She'd tried confronting Vasant in the initial stages, but he had invariably succeeded in defusing (and finally, dispelling) her anger by holding her close and murmuring soothing words into her hair. Finally, Vandana had stopped asking inconvenient questions. She'd told her mother, "I accept him the way he is. I cannot change him. I'm not sure I even want to." After that, Mrs. Gokhale had decided not to interfere in her daughter's private matters. It was better that way. And certainly far more peaceful.

But Vandana's fragile marriage did suffer a serious shock just before her first bout of illness. It was the time Vasant disappeared for more than a week without a trace, as it were.

"No news?" Mrs. Gokhale would phone thrice a day to enquire.

"No news," Vandana would confirm tonelessly.

"Shall we inform the police?" the older woman had asked after the fifth day.

"Let's wait a little longer. I'm sure he has been held up somewhere. And you know how these phones are — ours has been giving us trouble for a month now."

Mrs. Gokhale had then decided to take matters in her own hands. She had begun by making enquiries at the club her son-in-law frequented. After the first few peculiar looks and evasive answers, she'd gotten the answers she was seeking. The receptionist at the counter had reluctantly admitted that Vasant had taken off for Ooty with a "friend". He'd made the bookings from the club itself since it had a reciprocal arrangement with an Ooty club. Mrs. Gokhale had come straight to the point and asked the receptionist bluntly, "What's the friend's name? I want to know."

The man had pretended he didn't know. "So many of our members request us for bookings. How do you expect me to remember the details?"

She'd passed him a crisp — 500-rupee note and said sternly, "Try. I'm sure your memory will serve you well if you try hard enough."

He'd pretended to be shocked, then offended. Another note passed over the polished wooden counter. The man had slipped both into his pocket and scribbled something hastily on a small slip of paper. Snatching it up Mrs. Gokhale had marched triumphantly off to her waiting car.

Florence D'souza. Florence? Florence? She'd heard that name somewhere. Where? Of course, she'd heard it from Vandana. Wasn't she the woman who Vandana played badminton with at the other, suburban club? The one who came to their parties dressed very flashily? Mrs. Gokhale tried to recall some more details. Florence worked as an executive assistant to the managing director of a pharmaceutical company. She was separated from her husband and the mother of two. She was brassy, loud and excessively made-up. She was also very clever. Or maybe cunning was the right word. Vandana considered her a friend, Mrs. Gokhale thought bitterly. A friend. That's how trusting her poor daughter was. When was she ever going to learn? When would she see through that no-good husband of hers?

Mrs. Gokhale decided to keep the information from Vandana. In any case, her foolish daughter would only cover up for Vasant and come up with some cock-and-bull story full of the most incredible coincidences. Instead, Mrs. Gokhale decided to take her trusted accountant into confidence. She bought him a ticket to Ooty and briefed him thoroughly on what he was to say to her son-in-law when he reached. "Be calm. But be firm," she told Godbole, "Give him this letter from me and wait there while he reads it. Enclosed inside the envelope are return tickets to Bombay. Tell him I expect him back immediately. Do not make a scene. Do not get into an argument. Do not wait for explanations. And most important of all, do not speak to the woman, under any circumstances. She means nothing to us. He, unfortunately, is married to my daughter. Do you understand what I'm saying?"

Godbole had nodded his head. He was Mrs. Gokhale's sole "inheritance" from her late husband's family — and a priceless one. He handled all her affairs loyally and well. Mrs. Gokhale valued Godbole, but she also made sure he knew his place. He was her employee and that was his only role in their lives. Involving him in the present crisis had unfortunately become unavoidable because there was nobody else she could depend on. Even so, she wanted Godbole to realise that this was an exceptional situation. She reminded him once again to follow instructions as usual, nothing more.

According to Godbole's version (on his return from Ooty), Vasant had received him cordially and without the slightest embarrassment. Why, the man had even offered him a drink. He had read his mother-in-law's letter...and...and laughed. The woman sitting by his side, smoking nonchalantly, had asked for the letter and read it through quickly. With one efficient flick of her wrist, she'd crumpled it up and thrown it into the nearest waste paper basket. Godbole said she'd otherwise remained silent throughout.

Vasant had got up from the cane chair in the verandah where he'd been having tea with the woman and walked up to Godbole. Putting an affectionate arm around his shoulders (which Godbole insisted he'd tried to shrug off), he'd told him in the friendliest possible way to "bugger off". At this point in the narrative, Godbole had refused to repeat Vasant's exact words, conceding only after Mrs. Gokhale had tapped her cane imperiously on the marble floor and snapped impatiently, "Exact words. I want his exact words. What did he say to you? Tell me — it's important." Godbole's ears had twitched with embarrassment as he had repeated Vasant's dismissal. Mrs. Gokhale's eyes had blazed, her hand holding the cane, trembled, as she'd thanked Godbole politely before dismissing him.

Vasant had rolled up a few days later. With no explanations. Not even for his demoralised hysterical wife. He'd had the nerve to show up at Mrs. Gokhale's house for the traditional Sunday lunch at which the whole family got together for a feast of sorts. Mrs. Gokhale had been surprised to see him and enraged by his brazenness. But she'd kept silent, her eyes glowing like coals, her voice thin and high-pitched with suppressed rage. She'd looked pityingly at her daughter's ravaged face and wondered at her strange destiny. To be stuck with a man so callous, so cruel, so heartless...and yet have it within her to keep her lips sealed. Why?

Mrs. Gokhale often wondered about it. Why did Vandana force herself to put up with it? It couldn't have been out of desperation — there was always a home waiting for her. She didn't depend on Vasant financially — Mrs. Gokhale had seen to that by providing her with a comfortable income of her own through early and shrewd investments. If it was truly love what kind of love was it? Lopsided, unjust...almost perverse in its intensity. Mrs. Gokhale could barely get herself to look in the direction of the scoundrel sprawled across her favourite armchair, reading the Sunday papers, pretending nothing had happened. He'd even had the gall to ask her casually if she'd ordered his favourite jalebis for dessert. Since Vandana had been watching her face closely, Mrs. Gokhale had forced herself to nod so as not to upset her daughter. Besides, the grandchildren were present, and they might have asked awkward questions. Mrs. Gokhale couldn't do that to the young ones. She couldn't snub their father in public.

A week after that lunch, Vandana had been hospitalised for the first time with a severe pain in the abdomen. Vasant hadn't been around. This time he'd been traced to Pune — with the same woman. Godbole had "done the needful" (as he put it), with his usual discretion. Mrs. Gokhale had then phoned Vasant in some seedy hotel room and given him the news of his wife's precarious health. He'd feigned great concern and promised to start back for Bombay immediately. Obviously, he'd got diverted on the way. It had taken Vasant sixteen hours to make the four-hour trip home. When he'd reached the hospital (after a leisurely bath and nap), Vandana had just about regained consciousness. Her eyes had lighted up with undisguised joy at the sight of her husband and tears had streamed down her pale cheeks. Vasant had laughed and joked, telling her with absolute assurance that it was nothing to worry about — probably just indigestion. "What did you eat last night? Prawns? Come on, confess — it was prawns, wasn't it?

How many times have I told you to avoid prawns — you know they disagree with you!" he'd mock scolded.

Vandana had looked shame-faced and contrite. She'd clung on to his hand and admitted sheepishly that yes, she had indeed eaten a bowlful of badly cleaned prawns. Later, Mrs. Gokhale had found out from the cook that Vandana had been fasting the previous day — one of her religious fasts — one of those that she periodically undertook for the continuing prosperity and health of her flagrantly infidel husband. Mrs. Gokhale had hastily altered the venomous look she had shot in her son-in-law's direction to a less hostile one as Vandana intercepted it. After a few minutes of meaningless conversation and a jaunty farewell, Vasant had taken off for yet another tryst, leaving the old lady visibly agitated.

Vandana had reached feebly for her mother's arm, her eyes pleading mutely as she'd asked in a small and stricken voice, "Why do you hate him so much? What has he done to you?" Mrs. Gokhale had choked back her rage and restrained the impulse to articulate what her true feelings were. She'd known just how fragile Vandana's condition was, even at that early stage. Besides, what was the point in enlightening her foolish daughter now when it was already too late? In any case, Mrs. Gokhale half-suspected that Vandana knew the truth about Vasant — and had always known it. She had only chosen to be blind to it. Marriage was such a complicated business. Countless veils screened its ugly realities and protected the partners by making them accomplices.

Mrs. Gokhale had known that aspect of it in her own marriage. And she'd preferred to live with the daily deceptions that husbands and wives train themselves to endure. It was now her turn to respect Vandana's prerogative — after all, it was her marriage and her husband. But, as Mrs. Gokhale snorted in anger, Vandana was her child, her flesh and blood, her legacy. It was she, Mrs. Gokhale who had a greater right over her, particularly since Vandana's husband was a worthless bounder who couldn't be counted on for anything, least of all to render help in the crisis that was threatening his wife's life.

It was no use pretending, even to herself, that Vandana was going to live. Mrs. Gokhale had come to terms with that fact remarkably fast — she'd seen it in her daughter's half-closed eyes during the "blood-letting", as Mrs. Gokhale called the simple procedure of drawing a sample from the prominent vein in Vandana's limp arm. In a way she was almost relieved. It would be a good thing for Vandana to slip away into another — possibly better — life, away from the daily perfidy of her no-good husband. Abruptly, she'd said, "No...I don't hate Vasant. Why should you say such a thing?" She'd immediately regretted the remark — it demanded some sort of a response from a woman who was barely in a position to breathe without that simple act causing her acute discomfort.

Vandana's pale eyelids had fluttered pathetically, as she'd struggled to keep them from closing. Her voice, barely a hoarse whisper, had reached her mother's ears, "You've always hated my husband...I've known that all along. From the time I told you I wanted to marry him, your mind was made up. But...he's not a bad man...as you seem to think. He's...he's different."

Mrs. Gokhale had ssshed her daughter and patted her hand. "Be quiet...quiet now...don't say anything."

But Vandana obviously had been keen to carry on the conversation. Mrs Gokhale could sense how deeply disturbed she was by the rapid movement of her eyeballs and the shallow heaving of her shrunken rib-cage. Vandana's voice, a little stronger now, had insisted in a firm tone. "Please...it's important...I know you think Vasant is a selfish man, a no-gooder...that's not true. There is another side to him that only I know. He is loving and kind...and...funny. He makes me laugh. He tells me jokes. Do you know, he even washes my hair sometimes? Can you imagine that? Do you know of any other husband who does so much for his wife? He cares for me. I know you don't believe it...but he does." That little outburst had cost Vandana a lot. The strain had been too much for her. Mrs. Gokhale had watched her small face disappear into the slightly discoloured pillows. The exhaustion had drained her of the little colour she had left in her system. Vandana had already begun to resemble a corpse, Mrs. Gokhale thought, grimly. She had a vision of her daughter on the bier — yes — this is how she would look when her body was prepared for its final journey. Of course, there'd be lots of flowers surrounding that well-loved face. And garlands would cover her disease-wracked body. There'd be a strong smell of Tata's Eau-de-cologne everywhere. (Hospital staff tended to sprinkle it generously — especially when the "deceased" exuded a stench from rotting insides.) There'd be attar too...and rose water. Jasmine agarbattis on four sides of the body. Melting ice. White poplin sheets. Ropes to anchor the body onto the bamboo bier. An earthen-pot with burning, smoking coals. Spider-lilies and tulsi leaves. A priest mechanically chanting mantras. And Vandana...her beloved Vandana. What would she be dressed in? Her red-and-gold wedding saree? The one in which she'd made such a radiant bride? The one that suited her fair complexion and brought out the brown in her eyes so beautifully? Well...why not? It would be important to Vandana to look her best...for Vasant. And, Mrs. Gokhale decided, she'd comb her daughter's tresses...oil them with care. Adorn her forehead with a bright red bindi. Fill her wrists with green bangles. Attend to her narrow, pretty feet. Camouflage the blue-black marks of countless pin-pricks puncturing her arms. Plug her well-shaped nostrils with cotton-wool to prevent fluids from trickling over her mouth. And...her mouth...bruised and tragic-looking. Mrs. Gokhale hoped fervently that the doctors would leave at least that alone...not stuff a wad of gauze in. Vandana's lips were far too delicate for such an act of disfigurement. It was her prettiest feature — perfectly bowed and naturally rosy.

Mrs. Gokhale watched her daughter sleeping. She summoned a nurse and instructed her to make sure Vandana was kept free of pain. "Sedate her if necessary...I've spoken to the doctors. Give her extra pain-killers if you have to...but I don't want her to suffer. She has suffered enough already ."

She pondered over Vandana's remark, "he washed my hair

sometimes." In the past, Mrs. Gokhale would have been tempted to shoot back acidly, "Oh yes, I'm sure he does, dear. And if you are foolish enough to be content with empty gestures like that, you deserve nothing better." But now, as she pondered more deeply over Vandana's gratitude towards and love for Vasant, she thought she could understand — just a little — the sort of attraction he held for a woman like Vandana. And other equally foolish women like her. Women willing to throw their lives away for a rake ready to flatter their small egos with even smaller gestures that cost him nothing more than a tiny investment of time.

Yes, Vasant seemed to have enough of that precious commodity on his hands to lavish on his slavish female companions. How clever he was! How cunning! Perhaps he even powdered their backs...changed their clothes...crooned them to sleep. There were enough gullible women in the world just dying to be treated like helpless infants. Her daughter was one of them too. Just another child-like, trusting creature looking for a father she'd never known. And Vasant preyed on precisely that specific need — capitalised on her juvenile insecurity. Made her dependent; made her regress, in fact, convinced her that he and he alone could baby her, pamper her, love her, take care of her. What a monumental fool she really was. An adult woman totally contented with the simple pleasure of a hair-wash from her husband. No, Mrs. Gokhale corrected herself. It was more than just a hair-wash — it was the act of nurturing. An act Vasant had obviously perfected. No wonder Vandana worshipped this worthless man. Worthless in Mrs. Gokhale's eyes. But if a shampoo was all it took to please her immature daughter, who was she to quarrel about that? With a sigh of deep resignation, Mrs. Gokhale admitted to herself that she'd lost the battle. She stood defeated. Even after all these years, she had not been able to vanquish Vasant. And now, in any case, it was too late.

Had she been a brutal woman, she could have won the last round with ease. All she would have had to do to knock that blackguard off his pedestal was to reveal his frequent infidelities to her daughter with irrefutable proof. That was it. Just confront Vandana with the horrible truth. And ask her then if she still loved such a man. If she still found it within herself to regard him as her cherished mate, her lord and master, her adored husband. But of course, she wasn't going to do anything of the sort. She wanted her daughter to go in peace, clinging on to her illusions, loving the man who had brought her nothing but sorrow. But...had he? Had he really? Or was it Mrs. Gokhale alone who was unhappy? Maybe Vandana, foolish, ignorant Vandana didn't know better. And didn't want to. Perhaps her daughter's definition of happiness was vastly different from her own.

Vandana was willing to settle for very little — a pittance, really. And who was Mrs. Gokhale to disagree? No, she would spare her daughter the final humiliation of facing the truth about her husband. She herself would deal with Vasant later. Oh! yes, she would. She'd teach him a lesson or two all right. He was probably planning his own future even now as his wife lay dying. Mrs. Gokhale was certain he was banking on whatever money Vandana would leave behind coming his way. The new woman — whichever one — would move in before her daughter's ashes were cold. And grab everything in sight — Vandana's jewellery, Vandana's sarees, Vandana's perfumes. And Vandana's bed of course. Well, Mrs. Gokhale would see to it that that would never happen. She owed her daughter that much. She'd instruct her lawyers accordingly. Seal everything off. Prevent Vasant from looting what was rightfully Vandana's alone. Mrs. Gokhale straightened her shoulders and resolved that she wasn't going to let Vasant get away with what he'd done to her daughter. Even if it meant a prolonged court battle. Even if it killed her.

Vandana's eyes were unnaturally bright on the day of her wedding anniversary. The nurses reported that she'd been talking animatedly since dawn. Her excitement was apparent to Mrs. Gokhale the moment she entered the room. "Have you brought all my things?" Vandana demanded, "My saree...bangles...flowers for the hair...I must look my best today."

Mrs. Gokhale choked back her tears and nodded silently. Flowers for the hair. What hair? There was hardly any of it left now. The wisps that were sticking to her daughter's scalp would not be able to withstand the weight of the heavy flowers, so Mrs. Gokhale had instructed the flower-woman outside the small Ganpati temple to make the lightest possible veni — one that wouldn't tug painfully at Vandana's straggly strands. "Use aboli flowers and less thread," Mrs. Gokhale had told the toothless woman. Aboli — the delicate pale orange blossoms that Vandana so loved. No fragrance but a fine fragile beauty of their own. Mrs. Gokhale had selected a matching saree with orange motifs. It was a colour that only women with a certain complexion could carry off well. Orange needed just a hint of yellow under a fair skin to offset its hidden flames. Vandana looked wonderful in orange. Why, even her wedding saree — the one she'd be wear at the funeral — had more orange in it than red.

Vandana seemed far stronger and brighter than her mother had seen her in a long time. "What time is he coming?" she asked excitedly. The "he" of course, was Vasant. Vandana never addressed her husband by name as a sign of respect for him. Or awe, as Mrs. Gokhale put it.

"Soon," her mother told her shortly. "Soon". But even as she uttered that word. Mrs. Gokhale knew she'd lied. Vasant was missing again. He'd left town the previous evening, without leaving any message as to where he was going. Not even his mother-in-law's best efforts had succeeded in locating him this time. Mrs.Gokhale had hoped that Vandana would forget — she did suffer occasional memory lapses these days and wasn't always lucid. Now, after seeing her excitement, she prayed that Vandana would collapse into a fatigued sleep and forget the significance of the day. But for now, Vandana was like a child at a party. She couldn't wait to get out of her hospital gown and into her freshly pressed beautiful saree. "He likes me in this," she sighed contentedly, fingering its fine texture. The nurse came in to help change her. The sight of her ravaged body shocked her mother.

Besides, this was the first time since Vandana was a little girl that Mrs. Gokhale was seeing her practically naked. With tears stinging her eyes, she watched the emaciated figure of her child as the nurse sponged her impersonally. The skin had a yellowish pallor to it, the sharp angles of her hip bones were practically tearing through the wafer-like layer of flesh covering them, Vandana's once beautiful, firm breasts now lay pathetically over her rib-cage like empty plastic bags. Only her stomach looked unhealthily bloated. Mrs. Gokhale cast a quick glance at her pubes, the hairs looked scanty and had turned prematurely grey. She looked away quickly, not wanting to shame her daughter — the woman who had once taken such pride in looking after her figure, her body, her skin, her hair. Now even her legs (reduced to a stick-like appearance) which lay lifelessly on the sheets were covered with long, unruly hair. And those once graceful arms now moved with a strange, marionette-like jerkiness. Despite that, Vandana's ethereal radiance still managed to shine through as she instructed the nurse to groom her with care. Mrs. Gokhale sprayed her favourite cologne on Vandana's wrists and over her temples. Then she excused herself, saying she had something urgent to attend to.

The public phone on the same floor was not working. Mrs. Gokhale tiredly climbed up to the next floor and dialled Vasant's number, to check whether he was back from his trip. A strange voice answered — a woman's. She asked who it was and then covered the mouthpiece. Mrs. Gokhale heard a muffled conversation before Vasant finally came on the line. "I'll be there, I'll be there," he said, sounding edgy and irritable.

Mrs. Gokhale asked quietly, "Do you remember what day it is?"

There was a moment's silence, before Vasant said uncertainly, "Of course, I know...it's, it's Vandana's birthday. I'm aware of it...What did you think, that I'd forget? I've...I've...even got her a present. Tell her. She'll be happy."

Mrs. Gokhale gritted her teeth and counted to ten. It wouldn't do to lose her temper now. Besides, two or three impatient callers were already waiting to use the phone. Coldly but politely, she said, "It isn't Vandana's birthday — that's two months from now. And I don't think she'll be around to see it. However, it is her wedding anniversary...rather, your wedding anniversary — yours and hers. She is waiting for you...please try and come as soon as possible." She didn't give him a chance to respond before hanging up. Had she given Vasant even a few seconds more, he would have utilised that short period to invent a quick excuse. Mrs. Gokhale didn't want to give him the option — not today of all days. If Vasant let her down now, it would kill Vandana almost immediately. She wouldn't survive the night. And it wouldn't be cancer that would kill her, but a broken heart.

Wearily, Mrs. Gokhale went back to maintain her vigil by Vandana's side. She didn't really expect Vasant to show up before an hour or so. Vandana had fallen into a light, restless sleep. The excitement of dressing up had obviously been too much for her. Mrs. Gokhale herself dozed off on the cold, hard aluminium chair next to the cot. When she awoke, dusk was falling. She felt disoriented and confused. How long had it been anyway? An hour? Two hours? She looked at Vandana quickly. She was still asleep — very soundly asleep. Maybe the nurse had given her a sedative to calm her down. Mrs. Gokhale reached out to touch her daughter's forehead. It wad cold and slightly damp. She hastily switched on the dim beside lamp. Vandana's face was unusually calm and peaceful. Mrs. Gokhale hadn't seen her daughter look tranquil in a long time. She leaned over her with a 'kerchief to mop her brow and adjust the pillows. That's when she noticed Vandana had stopped breathing. Mrs. Gokhale put her face close to her daughter's to make doubly sure. She picked up one of her wrists simultaneously to look for a pulse. There wasn't one. Frantically, she pressed the call button, buzzing repeatedly. The nurse appeared, looking slightly annoyed. Mrs. Gokhale said agitatedly, "My daughter has stopped breathing...look...feel her pulse...no pulse...do something...call a doctor, get someone quickly. Don't waste time."

The nurse glanced briefly at Vandana's still figure and announced flatly, "She's dead."

166

"Mrs. Gokhale dug her claw-like nails into the nurse's plump arm. "No, she isn't. She is definitely not dead. It's probably the effect of the sedative. Call the doctor...he'll know what to do."

The nurse repeated in the same tone, "She's dead. I'm sorry. But nothing more can be done." With that she began unhooking the saline drip and expressionlessly putting things away. Mrs. Gokhale rushed out of the room shouting, "Doctor, doctor...where's the doctor? My daughter needs a doctor immediately. Will someone fetch the doctor urgently? It's an emergency..."

As she reached the staircase, still asking hoarsely for a doctor, she ran straight into Vasant, dressed in a dark suit, freshly bathed, heavily perfumed, obviously ready for an evening on the town. Seeing his mother-in-law rushing around hysterically, he took two steps back and ducked out of her way. She passed him without displaying the slightest signs of recognition. He saw her rushing down a long corridor.

Vasant strode purposefully towards his wife's room. He didn't have to ask the nurse a single question. He knew. He stared at Vandana's face for a minute and asked shortly, "When did it happen? When did she go?"

The nurse shrugged, not looking up from a sheaf of case papers she was putting together. "Don't know. I wasn't on duty. My shift has just started."

Vasant looked quickly around the room. He noticed his mother-in-law's handbag and a few of Vandana's small belongings — the little shrine she'd set up by her bedside which now had stale, withered flowers adorning it. He noticed his framed photograph, taken in younger and happier days. He picked it up idly and turned it over. The inscription read, "To my adorable Vandana. You are always in my heart, darling." He remembered the day she'd asked for it and the flourish with which he'd signed behind it, before giving it to her. He replaced the frame slowly and smiled at the memory. The nurse was filling in something in an untidy scrawl. "Excuse me," he said, "but where is the other lady — the one who is always here."

The nurse looked up crossly, obviously annoyed at being interrupted. "Oh, that one — she has gone in search of a doctor. I told her nicely 'Madam — it is too late. The patient is dead'. But she refused to listen. What to do? Some people don't understand simple English. Doctor! What can the doctor do? Bring the patient back to life? Besides, she was going to die anyway...maybe not today...but ten days from now...four weeks from now...soon. Better to go quickly, no? Why suffer unnecessarily?"

Vasant smiled at the woman. She wasn't all that bad-looking. And so young. How young? Twenty? He lit a cigarette and stood near the window. No point in hanging around...besides, Mrs. Gokhale would be back any minute. No point in meeting her either. She was sure to create a scene. Yes, he had come too late. But he'd got held up at home. Women! He shuddered involuntarily. Their demands never seemed to end. Anyway, the point was, he'd come as soon as he could get away without causing too much of a scene. How was he supposed to know Vandana would die today of all days? The least the old bat could've done was to tell him it was serious; that Vandana was critical. Just like her to have kept it from him. Spiteful bitch. She must have done it deliberately, just so she would be able to accuse him later of neglect and indifference.

He threw out his half-finished cigarette and gazed at the nurse's figure as she bent down to retrieve some unused tablets from the bottom drawer of the medicine cabinet. Nice legs, he concluded absently. He glanced once more at Vandana. Poor thing, he thought. Poor foolish thing. Sweet woman. But not his kind. Never had been. It was a mistake to have married her. A big mistake. Marriage itself was a mistake. After a point, every woman became a bore. A clinging, possessive, whining bore. He wasn't going to make that mistake. Ever again. Definitely not. No second marriage. Of course, Florence would be furious. But he knew how to handle women like her. It was the Vandanas of the world who made him edgy, nervous and uncomfortable.

Vasant quickly checked his image in a small mirror on the wall,

opposite the cot on which his wife's corpse lay. He smoothened
his thick hair into place, and adjusted his silk tie — a recent
present from Florence. He checked the time in his watch. Oh hell!
He was running late as usual. He patted his jacket pocket to make
sure he'd remembered to carry his wallet. And then he paused...as
if he'd forgotten something. "Sister," he called out, "Here's some
money...for...whatever...you know...expenses and things...just take
care of it...of everything...will you?"

The nurse took the money from his hands wordlessly. And
winked. She knew the old woman would pay her too. By why tell
this nice man that? Quickly, she stuffed her pockets with the extra
strips of tablets that wouldn't be required now. She looked around
for other things to pinch before the ward boys got their hands on
them. She even took the extra veni — she'd wear it later when she
went out for a movie with her boy-friend. The nurse walked out
of the room leaving Vandana alone...the pale orange of the Aboli
flowers creating a glowing halo around her small face.

Thirteen

LATE ARRIVAL

MADHURI, AMLA'S mother, was in her mid-forties when Amla was born. The monsoons in Bombay had lingered on and on that year. It was late September but the rains continued to lash against the broken windowpanes of a modest nursing home in a distant suburb as Amla emerged from her mother's tired, over-worked womb. She was the eighth child and seventh daughter. Her mother, lay back against the shabby pillows (smelling of other women's hair oils) and moaned softly, "Why another girl? In what way did I displease the goddess this time? I fasted...I prayed ...I sacrificed...I even offered my remaining gold bangles. Another son...that's all I asked for. One more boy...."

Madhuri was sure her husband, a school-teacher at the local municipal school, would be enraged. After all, it had been she who had insisted on "one more try". She was the one who'd been obstinate....superstitious. Madhuri had convinced the father of her earlier seven children that he'd bless her for the decision. She'd placed her bony hands over the loose folds of her lax belly and said fervently, "I know my womb by now. I can tell it's going to be a boy. The signs are different. I feel exactly as I did when Hiten was inside me." And she'd turned dramatically to the little altar in the room and folded her hands. "Amba Devi has heard my prayers."

Suresh had looked at his wife pityingly and asked, "Boy or girl...who will feed this child now? We can barely manage the other seven."

Madhuri had smiled mysteriously, "I will. Why do you worry? I still have a few gold ornaments left. I've made arrangements with the pawn-shop owner. Besides, you know my breasts always overflow with milk. I will feed my son for two...three...four..years. After that we shall see. There'll be less mouths to feed, anyway, by then. Kunali will be married soon...maybe she'll become a mother herself. She is over twenty now."

Suresh had nodded impatiently. "I am glad you remember that! It is time for us to become grandparents and you insist on delivering a child. What will our neighbours think? I won't know how to show my face in school. They laugh at me as it is. Even the children point and jeer. Have you no shame left?"

Madhuri'd sat up in bed, her eyes flashing. "Shame? Shame?? What for? Has some stranger placed his seed in my womb? Was it not you with your hungers who came into my bed? Did I force you to cohabit with me? Why didn't you ask yourself whether you felt any shame when you spread open my legs? Why didn't you think of those school teachers and neighbours at that moment?"

Suresh had left the room. He knew he was wasting his time arguing with such a wilful woman. Madhuri always managed to have her way. Besides, she was really and truly obsessed with the idea of producing another son. She claimed an astrologer had told her she would be the proud mother of two handsome, rich, strapping sons one day. It was there in her horoscope. "How can I fight destiny?" she'd asked Suresh, challenging him to contradict her. And now, here she was, patting her wrinkled, lined belly and dreaming of her eighth child — her unborn son.

Amla weighed barely five pounds at birth. The nurse said, "This time you've produced a mouse. And a dark, hairy one at that. Poor girl — who will marry her?" Madhuri hadn't noticed either her newborn's size or appearance. She'd only been concerned with what lay between those tiny little thighs (which weren't much thicker than a grown-up's index finger). Amla was born with exaggerated large labia. For a brief moment, even the young doctor who'd delivered her had been confused. "It's a boy!" he'd announced triumphantly almost as if he himself was personally responsible for the fortunate event, Madhuri's heart had all but leapt out of her mouth as a shrill exultant scream had escaped her lips, "See! I knew it, I knew it," she'd gloated without bothering to look for herself. It had been left to the slightly more observant nurse to point out that the "boy" didn't seem to have a penis. A quick, rough examination by the doctor had confirmed the horrible truth. But nobody had been daring enough to break Madhuri's trance and bring her down to earth. The doctor had finally ordered the nurse to tell her. And everybody had all but forgotten, the wiggly, hairy, little Amla squirming and shivering on the weighing scales near the basin. She could have died that very night. And perhaps it would have been better if she had. But Amla's horoscope foreclosed such a possibility. Death would have been far too kind an option.

Amla grew up a lonely, intense child in her large, noisy family. It was only the time she spent with her father that brought big smiles to her solemn, small face. Suresh liked his youngest child, now that she was teenager. She was the only one he could talk to, the only one who seemed to genuinely enjoy the company of a retired old man. The older children had long gone to their own homes. Except for his son — his vagabond son, who still stayed in the house because he had no other place to go to. Besides, the boy's mother had threatened Suresh often enough that if he drove his son away, she would leave with him. Suresh knew this was a foolish, empty threat. His son Hiten was nothing more than a scrounger, incapable of looking after himself. The little money he earned when he could hold down a job as a reporter, he'd promptly gamble and drink away. "Free lodging," Suresh would frequently shout, "that's all that keeps this no good fellow here."

Madhuri would rush out of the kitchen, nostrils flared, to retort, "Your only son. Flesh of your flesh. Blood of your blood. And this is how you treat him."

Only little Amla understood Suresh's rages. He knew she did. Not that they ever spoke about her brother, but Suresh could tell from the expression in her dark, deep eyes as she witnessed their confrontations. Nobody ever seemed to notice Amla as she sat in a corner, absorbed in her school books. Madhuri had lost interest in her youngest daughter the moment she'd been forced to accept the shape of her genitals. At that instant, the milk in her breasts had dried up and she'd refused to suckle the sickly infant. The others in the family had reacted with irritation and indifference. A new baby wailing in one of the two rooms of their small tenement flat meant a serious disruption in their crowded lives. The older girls, compelled to baby-sit Amla, while their mother concentrated on feeding Hiten, felt resentful towards the undernourished, unattractive infant mewing like an ill kitten all day and practically, all night. The older two soon moved to different towns — one to Pune, the other to Surat, soon after their respective marriages. That made a little more room in their cramped home though far from enough.

As Amla grews, her looks improved, though she failed to grow normally in physical terms. She remained a sparrow-like creature under five feet in height and frail of body. It was only the strange luminosity of her large, dark eyes, which seemed to jump out of her small face that made people notice her. Amla was almost unnaturally still most of the time. Her movements were so economical, one almost missed them. And yet, it was her stillness that allowed her to observe the most minute objects around her. And feel passionately about inanimate things that other people didn't even care to notice. She could stare for hours at a pedestal fan and large tears would pour out of her eyes watching the untiring rotation of its blades. When asked why she was weeping, she'd sob, "Look at the fan. How tired it must be. Poor thing...does nobody feel sorry for it?" Her sisters would laugh maliciously at her remarks and mock her sensitivity. Amla would feel equally sorry for the wheels of cars, buses, and bullock-carts and find herself crying while on her way to school. She began to write poetry when she was eight. Even though the construction was sometimes weak, the thoughts expressed were mature beyond her years. Only Suresh seemed to understand his daughter's intensity and responded to it with respect and kindness.

Amla's mother's health had begun to deteriorate soon after the delivery. It had as much to do with the collapse of her spirit as with her body being unable to cope with the strain of raising so many children on such restricted resources. Amla's association with her mother remained distant and wary. She'd watch while the older children hovered around her sick bed, fussing endlessly, bringing her fruit and milk to soothe the painful ulcer corroding her insides. Madhuri never asked for Amla and in a way, Amla was grateful to be left alone — she really had nothing to say to her mother. Even if she occasionally did, her mother was not interested in hearing it.

Brought up wearing her sister's altered hand-me-downs and eating Hiten's leftovers, Amla grew up feeling second-hand and stale. Her birthdays went by unnoticed and before the family knew it, it was time for Amla to appear for her school leaving exam. There was just a month left to go for Amla's finals when her sister Devi's engagement was announced. Madhuri bossily told the family at dinner, "Devi is lucky to have found such a good match. We must put up a good show." Amla shrank still further into the one corner of the room that received extra light from the bulb hanging nakedly in the common passage outside their home. Madhuri carried on a long monologue about Devi's fortuitous stars. "I'd always known she'd find a good home. My astrologer had told me so when she was born. Besides, Devi is fair and clever — she could have got anybody."

Amla was finding it next to impossible to concentrate on her books with her mother's excited voice ringing through the room. She tried blocking her ears with bits of cotton wool pinched from her sister's toilet-box. It didn't help. She could still hear her mother's monologue. "After Devi's marriage, I'll be able to relax. All my responsibilities will be over. Devi has an excellent combination of stars in her marriage house....unlike Amla."

Hearing her name, Amla stopped reading her notes on *A Midsummer Night's Dream*, and listened to her mother's strident voice without looking up from her book. From the corner of her eyes she noticed her father signalling to her mother to lower her voice. But Madhuri was exulting in her triumph, her eyes bright with excitement, her voice even harsher than usual. "Devi is the luckiest out of all the girls. Not only is her future husband rich, he's also good-looking. And almost as fair as she is. And her new home has to be seen to be believed. Grand. It's absolutely grand. Filled with luxuries. I saw a fridge, a toaster, telephone. And the boy's mother told me they'd soon be getting a washing machine — with a little help from us. I've always said, Devi is a real Devi — she is Lakshmi herself. Goddess of wealth. Just see...after her marriage into that family, she'll bring still more prosperity to them. Mark my words. Poor Amla has nothing in her stars — nothing to look forward to. No marriage, nothing. What can I do? That is her destiny."

Amla sat stiller than usual. So still in fact, that she forgot even to breathe. It was only when she spluttered and coughed that Madhuri turned and saw her. Slapping her own forehead dramatically, Madhuri snarled, "Oh God! She has begun that coughing-nonsense of hers again. I hope she doesn't fall ill now and spoil everything. There's so much to do before the function...and this girl will ruin it all for everyone by falling ill just at that time."

Amla looked up beseechingly at her mother and pleaded, "Please...please...I am only trying to study...you know my exams are just a month away. I can't concentrate with all this noise around me."

Madhuri exploded "Noise? Did you hear that? She calls it noise. We are discussing a happy occasion — a celebration. This child has always been abshakuni. She says inauspicious things deliberately. Now look at how she has upset me...and Devi. Sheer jealousy. That's what I call it. Nothing else."

Suresh went up to his youngest daughter and gently told her to take her books and go elsewhere. "But where?" Amla asked him, "Hiten is in the next room with his friends watching TV. Where can I go?"

The father went out into the common passage they shared with their neighbours and suggested she study in the far corner...or in the shared toilet. Amla sighed deeply and shut her books. "There is no bulb in that bathroom," she said, "besides, I feel scared there. It's so far. And now it's dark. Rats run over my feet and cockroaches fall off the walls."

"Don't make such a fuss," her father insisted, giving Amla a gentle push. He wanted her out of the way only so her mother would spare her further torment. But Amla misunderstood his gruffness and began to cry, further enraging Madhuri.

"See that — the girl weeps when her sister's engagement is announced. She cries as if there's a death in the family. Well....one day soon there will be a death in this family....my death. But only after Devi's wedding." She swooped down on Amla and pushed her into the passage snorting, "Exams! We know how brilliant you are. What will you get by studying so much? A first class first, huh? Will you top the school? Win all the awards? And even if you do, will those awards get you a husband?"

Amla placed her hands over her ears and fled to the farthest corner of the long corridor, more afraid of her mother's wrath than the rats that would soon be scampering over her bare toes.

It was while she was still in college that Amla's father died. And with him, any hope that Amla had harboured of things getting better for her at home. There were just the two of them left now. Mother and daughter. Hiten had extracted a flat from his in-laws and moved out with his pretty bride. Amla had taken up a part-time job in her friend's mother's boutique. Her salary took care of college fees and sundry expenses. Madhuri jealously controlled the paltry bank interest earned on Suresh's life-savings. She was old and weak in body, but her spirit was feistier than ever. All day long she lay on her bed moaning and complaining about the latest servant-girl. No domestic was willing to stay in their house, such was the reputation Madhuri had earned in the neighbourhood. Each week saw a fresh person — generally an underage girl from a nearby slum. Without exception, they left Madhuri's employment abruptly, preferring starvation to abuse.

Amla longed for help around the place, especially at night when Madhuri moaned the loudest and needed assistance to go to the distant toilet. Some nights, she woke up Amla as many as five times, often cursing loudly if she didn't spring out of bed at the first command. "Lazy...no good girl. You are fit for nothing. I carried you in my limp, exhausted womb for nine long months. Why? Because I wanted another son — I'm not lying to you. Instead, I got you. The least you can do in return is to look after me now that I'm old." Amla didn't mind these "duties" as much as she minded her mother's stream of barbs. And now that her father was no longer there to cushion them Amla had no one to comfort her as she lay stiffly on a worn-out mattress spread on the hard, cold, stone floor and listened keenly to the uneven pattern of her mother's breathing. She felt more desolate than she ever had in her life.

Once a year, her sisters would descend on them, bringing their noisy, badly brought up children along. Madhuri would enthusiastically talk about the visit weeks in advance. But once the house was filled with uncontrollable kids, she'd take to her bed and start reciting God's name at a volume that would drown the collective sounds in the two rooms. It was left to Amla to play the attentive lady of the house and wait on her sisters. It was also left to her to find the resources to feed them all. Simple meals, no doubt, but where was even that much money to come from? She'd watch her sisters sitting on the one bed in the house, close to Madhuri, chatting animatedly about their lives while the children chased each other down the passage and demanded biscuits, aerated drinks and milk. Amla would strive to cope, struggling with the supplies in the kitchen, often being forced to dilute the milk with water and scrimp on the sugar. The sisters would sometimes catch her at it and complain to Madhuri. "We come her because we love you. It is our right to visit our maternal home. But look at Amla's attitude, she behaves as if we are outsiders. Or worse, enemies. Our children go hungry. We spend so much on train-fares to bring them here for their holidays. They look forward to the Bombay visits. And what do they get in return? Watered down milk and stale food served by their mean aunt."

In all the years, Amla had never got into arguments with her sisters, preferring to keep her distance and remain silent. But this time it was different. It was crucial for Amla to do well — she was aiming for a scholarship. The scholarship meant a lot to her. It was the one thing that would allow her to escape. She hadn't dared to consider the consequences of abandoning her sick mother in case she actually succeeded in winning it. All she knew was that if she did, she'd grab the opportunity and flee. As far away from the hell that was her home as was possible. Besides, Amla had also met someone who had promised to help her. He was her sociology professor — a scholarly, serious, married man.

Amla's crush on Srinivasan was as intense as everything else in her life. If he knew about her feelings, he didn't let on. He gave the impression that his interest in her was purely academic. She was the brightest student in his class, and he had decided to appoint himself her mentor. But Amla instinctively knew that Srinivasan did harbour emotions that went beyond his involvement in her grades. She knew, for instance, that he noticed when she wore her hair differently or if she ever forgot to adorn her forehead with a bindi. Srinivasan would make an oblique reference that would bring an instant rush of blood to Amla's pinched unhappy face.

College had become her haven and refuge. Each morning, when she awoke after a restless, light sleep interrupted by Madhuri's demands, Amla would dress with care, often sticking flowers into her long braid and filling her wrists with cheap, colourful bangles. Just the thought of sitting through Srinivasan's class would bring a spring to her step and a song to her lips. These were changes that didn't go unnoticed by Madhuri. She'd taken to making cutting remarks about Amla's appearance each morning. During her sister's visits, Amla would often overhear them gossipping with Madhuri about Amla's transformation.

"She's looking different these days," one would say questioningly.

"Yes...something seems to be up. Maybe she has a boy-friend in college," the other would add.

"Boy-friend? And Amla? Huh. Who'd look at her? If you ask me, all those bright colours make her look even darker," her mother would contribute witheringly.

Strangely enough, their hurtful remarks no longer bothered Amla. Just the thought of meeting Srinivasan would keep her going and raise her spirits. The main problem in her life was time. She had even less of it to herself now that the house was full. She'd tried studying in the library after college only to find her concentration wavering. What if she was needed at home for something? What if her mother wanted her to run an urgent errand? Finally Amla decided that it was better to head for home and try and steal a few minutes of study between chores rather than waste precious minutes staring distractedly at her books in the musty library.

She thought she hadn't heard right. Were they really discussing what she thought they were? Could it be possible that her eldest sister had made this particular trip especially to scout around for a bridegroom for her daughter — Amla's young niece? No. It couldn't be true. Neeta was, what? Amla quickly counted and soon ran out of fingers. Yes...it was true. Neeta was all of eighteen — just two-and-a-half years younger than Amla herself. They'd practically grown up together even while belonging to different

180

generations. She heard Devi asking her mother worriedly, "But...but...shouldn't we at least try and get Amla married first? Don't you think it will look very bad if Neeta's marriage precedes hers?"

Madhuri retorted, "Are we going to hang around forever for that to happen? If we all wait for Amla to find someone, Neeta's chances will disappear. I tell you, if you find a good match for the girl, go ahead and finalise it. Don't delay matters."

Neeta's mother sounded hesitant as she added, "People in the community might find it shameful. What will we tell them if they ask? Imagine having an unmarried aunt in the house."

Madhuri declared firmly, "You leave all that to me. I will give them a fitting reply. We will say Amla is going abroad for further studies and is not interested in marriage right now. These days many girls do that — go to England, America. People will believe us."

Devi's voice was lowered as she asked her mother, "But....what will we tell Amla? She's sure to feel bad if she hears about Neeta's marriage."

Madhuri answered without bothering to keep her voice down, "What is there to tell Amla? Is anybody committing a crime? It is in some fortunate girls' destiny to marry at the proper time and start a family. Others are born unlucky. That is their fate. Don't worry about Amla. She is not as soft as you think. It won't affect her. I'm certain."

But affect her, it did. Amla felt humiliated and small. An unmarried aunt...that would be the label attached to her at the forthcoming wedding. Disgraceful. She could already visualise the strange looks and whispered comments she'd be subjected to. There'd be taunts and insults directed at Madhuri as well — but that wasn't really Amla's concern. Within their narrow-minded community, it was her wretched position that would attract the maximum attention. And after this significant event, her chances of finding a bridegroom would be doomed forever. Amla would stay on the shelf permanently, condemned by the elders and looked down by her contemporaries. Amla could anticipate the cruel remarks and ugly comments. Poor Amla. Spinster. Dark-complexioned. Bad horoscope. No future. No luck.

She sat on a small stool in the passage trying to concentrate on her studies. She could hear excited voices from within. She sensed the deliberate exclusion — nobody wished to include her in this conversation. She was not wanted there. Her sisters were pretending they couldn't really see her tiny form sitting desolately outside. Her mother had entirely forgotten she was there, so wrapped up was she in the wedding plans. But Amla heard every word, even as she tried to blank out their voices. She knew they were going jewellery shopping the next afternoon. Not to buy anything just yet. It was to be a preliminary expedition to check on the prices and latest designs. She longed to join them, to be accepted as one of the group. Even her sister-in-law had been asked to come just because she belonged to the "Marrieds Club". Not that anybody liked the uppity woman who'd snatched away their only brother. But then, she was the daughter-in-law of the family and as such, enjoyed a unique status.

Amla sat on a small stool miserably waiting for the summit to end. She needed a few things from her trunk, but didn't dare intrude. She knew the sight of her would upset the others and make them self-conscious. They'd clam up and look uncomfortable. They'd wait with ill-concealed impatience for her to leave the room before resuming their interrupted conversation. Amla began to weep silently, her small body shaking with unexpressed grief. Her trembling was making the stool rattle. She held on to the railing of the balcony to steady herself. She wished she could speak to Srinivasan — pour out her heart to him. Surely he would understand her sorrow. He was the only person on earth who would. She had to talk to him immediately. Amla decided to take a bus to his residence. She had memorised his address from the college register. It would take her approximately forty-five minutes to get there. One look at her distraught condition and he'd recognise everything — her feelings for him, her desperation, her anguish.

And he'd surely offer a solution — an instant salve. Often, she'd been tempted to talk to him about her private hell but had resisted the impulse. But just the kindness of his searching glance had assured her that he somehow recognised her pain.

Amla rushed down the rickety wooden staircase and into the street. It was as if she'd been blinded and her other senses dulled. She walked to the bus stop without really seeing anything.

She found his home after searching wildly in a dark, narrow lane. Her heart was soaring when she rang the bell. Srinivasan would know why she was there. The door was opened by a slim, fair woman with flowers in her hair. "Is Sir in?" Amla asked confidently.

"No. He has gone for a walk. But...who are you and what work do you have with him now — after college hours? It's very late — he doesn't see students at home."

Amla hesitated, "I'm not just a student. I'm....I'm Amla. Hasn't he told you about me?"

The woman looked amused, "No....he hasn't. He doesn't tell me about every young girl in his class. What should he have told me about you, anyway?"

Amla was stumped for an answer. "Nothing. Nothing, I suppose. I just thought he might have mentioned my name. You see I'm in trouble. I really need to meet him. Do you mind if I wait here for a while? I don't want to go home."

The woman looked at her irritably. "Yes, I do mind. I'm busy cooking. My children are waiting. And, like I told you, we don't allow students into our home. After college hours, especially. My husband will get most upset if he sees you. Besides, what kind of trouble are you in anyway? No. Don't tell me. Just go....please go."

Amla had tears in her eyes as she appealed to Srinivasan's wife. "How can you be so cruel? Don't you see what he means to me? I am depending on him to...to...help me."

The woman asked impatiently, "Help you with what ? Money? He doesn't have any. Studies? He doesn't give tuitions. What sort of help do you need?"

Amla looked around her desperately, "I need a place to stay. Just for the night. I promise I'll leave tomorrow. By then I'll know what to do, where to go. I need a place to study — look, I've even brought my books along. I'm going to get a scholarship."

The woman laughed, "That's what they all think. Do you really believe it's all that easy? Even my husband thought he'd win a scholarship and go abroad for further studies. But look what happened. Here we are, stuck in this lousy college with a paltry salary. He is so frustrated and unhappy. But what can he do?"

Amla tried to hold her hand but the woman pulled away. "Don't touch me. I've seen girls like you...too many of them. Srinivasan has that effect on young, immature females. Do you know something? I was also his student once — just like you. I also believed he could solve all my problems. But look where I've landed — in this shabby house, stuck with noisy children, washing, cleaning, sweeping all day. And my husband? What does all this matter to him? He has girls like you in his classrooms to make him feel big, feel important. He doesn't even notice my existence, anymore. Anyway...that's another story. And do you know something? He didn't get a scholarship...but I did. And what did I do? I gave it up...sacrificed the golden opportunity...for him. So...just go away...go home. Study under a streetlight if you have to. Don't waste your time here."

Amla turned to leave. She started running unthinkingly out of the unlit gulley. She ran straight into Srinivasan. She knew him from his smell. He held her close to him and said, "Amla...Amla...don't cry. I'm here...and I'll help you."

She continued to sob, her body shaking violently. "I only wanted to study in peace," she said brokenly, "I didn't mean to disturb you." Holding her away from him he looked into her stricken eyes. "You don't have to explain anything. I understand."

Amla clung on to his hand. "I knew you would, Sir. I just But...but...your wife....."

He shook his head. "Don't worry about her..." And he led Amla away gently into an even darker corner of the narrow deserted

street. Amla felt his warm hands over her breast and stiffened.
"Trust me," said Srinivasan, as he unbuttoned her blouse. She
closed her eyes, her limbs rigid with fear and anticipation. He
pushed her gently against a stone bench as his hands continued to
explore the contours of her body. Amla could tell from the familiar
way in which he manoeuvred her frame against the curve of the
old bench that Srinivasan had been there, at that very spot, many
times. It was too late now. Amla lay back passively and examined
the overcast sky for stars... and wondered which one to blame for
her own rotten destiny.

Fourteen

THE BINDI

WHEN SUSHMA married Asif, the Bombay bomb blasts had yet to take place. Not that their courtship and subsequent wedding had been any the easier on account of that, but had the city been rocked six months earlier, it's entirely possible that Sushma's parents would not have allowed her to marry Asif. And Asif's would probably have left town, taking their son with them.

When information of the blasts first reached Sushma, she was busy teaching her regular class of restless eight-year-olds. The ancient-looking school peon walked in to give her the terrible news. He was a Muslim. She looked into his terror-stricken eyes and understood. Mushtaq was probably wondering whether he'd be able to leave the school premises at 4 p.m. and get home alive. He'd been working there for twelve years — this was like a second home to him. But after the riots, he'd been forced to return to his village or face the unspoken but clearly discernible wrath of his neighbours — and worse — his co-workers in the school.

Mushtaq had returned to his duties after twenty days, looking sheepish, unable to meet the eyes of his colleagues. He was told there had been talk in his absence of sacking him. "Some parents aren't comfortable with the thought of a Muslim being in charge of the bus-queue. What if trouble breaks out again? Who wants to take chances these days?" Mushtaq had hung his head down in pain. So this is what it had come down to. For Mushtaq, the school's children — especially the little ones, were a part of his

187

otherwise joyless life. He loved them, loved their laughter...even the pranks they played on him. And he took his duties seriously. He knew each and every "bus child" by name. It was his strong arm that pulled the kids up into the vehicle. And it was he who made sure the doors were properly bolted once everybody was safely inside. Parents — yes, these same people asked for Mushtaq by name when their child was sick and needed to be seated comfortably away from the bus bullies. And it had been Mushtaq whom the principal had deputed to the sportsfield to keep an eye on the young athletes competing there.

Mushtaq had known about Sushma's wedding even though it had been a very private affair. Like Sushma herself who was such a private person. Secretive, almost. Unlike other teachers who gossiped in the staff room during lunch break, Sushma kept to herself. But with Mushtaq, she'd established a rapport of sorts. She asked him for small favours from time to time and he obliged because he liked this neat, quiet, organised woman who took her job seriously. He'd watched her in class, earnestly going over the solar system for the sixteenth time with a dull student nobody else had patience with. He'd observed that she didn't waste a second between periods, hanging around giggling with the other teachers. She sat at her desk, head bent low, correcting homework or setting test papers. Sushma also hung around much longer after school. The sweeper women would find her in class when they came to tidy up. She'd be writing away with such concentration that only when the dust raised by their brooms triggered off a string of sneezes would she look up, gather her things and leave. A few minutes later, they'd see her at the school gate, waiting for someone. Only Mushtaq knew who that someone was — Asif. The others speculated but didn't dare ask. Teachers — the more gossipy ones — had drawn their conclusions long ago. They'd figured Sushma was in love with a married man. Why else would a young woman in this day and age go about her romance in such a clandestine fashion? Sushma obviously came from a "good" family. She stayed fairly close to the school. She needn't have worked at all. From the way she dressed, it was apparent that her wardrobe had nothing to do with her salary. "She's killing time," said Mrs. Pereira to the other teachers. "Instead of sitting at home, she comes and sits here." If Sushma sensed their resentment, she didn't reveal it. For her, it was only the children in her class who mattered. Nobody else.

Mushtaq found out about Asif when Sushma once requested him to phone Asif's office. It must have been something of great importance to her, Mushtaq figured, seeing how agitated she looked.

"Madam, are you all right? Anything wrong?" Mushtaq had asked.

She had stared at him unseeingly and said, "Yes. I mean no, no, nothing's wrong...but please, just call his number, ask for Mr. Asif Khan...and ...and tell him there has been an emergency. I can't keep our appointment this evening, o.k?"

Mushtaq had nodded and gone to a public phone. Sushma had given him the coins for use and specifically instructed him not to call from the school office. Mushtaq had thought to himself, *"kuch gadbad hai"* and gone to a nearby Irani restaurant to make the call. "Asifbhai," Mushtaq had asked softly.

"Yes. Who is that?" The voice was refined and sweet. He must be a proper gentleman, Mushtaq had thought.

"I have a message from....from....Madam Sushma."

After a short silence, Asif had asked, "Is she ....is she....all right?"

Mushtaq had hastened to say, "Yes, saab, she's all right. But she said to tell you she can't come today...because...because...of some emergency, saab."

Asif paused. "Who are you? And where are you speaking from?"

Mushtaq had said, "I'm the school peon, saab. My name is Mushtaq Ali...and...and...this is Madam's message...I don't know the reason, though."

"All right...thank you, Mushtaq," Asif had said before disconnecting.

Mushtaq had experienced a vague sense of unease. He'd hoped Sushma was not in some kind of trouble. Mushtaq wanted to help, though he also knew it was beyond his station in life to make such an offer to either Sushma or Asif. Mushtaq had asked himself why he felt so involved — almost protective about the two of them. Maybe it was because of the despair he had glimpsed in Sushma's eyes. Maybe it was a doomed romance in Mushtaq's assessment. These things never worked, not even if the girl converted. After all, you are what you are born into. That is what defines you for the rest of your life. Adopting another's religion was unnatural and...unconvincing. An artificial act. A superficial transformation. Sushma could never become a good Muslim. Mushtaq simply could not see her as one. And even if Asifbhai decided to renounce his own religion, would their marriage work?

People needed to believe. At least Mushtaq did. Without belief, there was no hope. Besides, Sushma looked a genuinely god-fearing person. A woman with values. It was always harder on people like that. People who lived with their self-respect wrapped around them like shawls. Mushtaq worried about her types. He hated to think she'd be hurt. Asif? Well, he was a man, after all. He'd be all right after the initial heartbreak. Marry another woman. Marry within the community. Procreate. Live, like most men—a life defined by the society they'd chosen to be a part of. Mushtaq was both right and wrong about the two of them.

Sushma and Asif's marriage was a registered one performed at a mutual friend's small flat and attended by the two families. It had been decided that Sushma would not convert to Islam or change her name. Asif's parents announced to the small congregation present that they wished to respect their daughter-in-law's religious sentiments, adding that they were confident that religion would not become an issue in this marriage.

"Sushma is free to follow her faith. We, as her in-laws, have no objections." Asif looked at his bride....searching his face for signs of embarrassment or discomfiture. There were none. After the signing ceremony a small dinner party was arranged at which Sushma and Asif moved around a little uncertainly — almost self-consciously — as if to gauge in that one evening what future responses were likely to be to them. The latest "Hindu-Muslim couple."

One woman whispered to Sushma, "Will they allow you to wear a bindi now?"

It was something Sushma hadn't thought about till that point. Her hand shot up to her forehead like a reflex action to check whether hers was in place right then. Bindi — strange question for that woman to be asking. Was a bindi *that* important? For Sushma it had always been a cosmetic option— more a fashion statement than a religious symbol. There were days when she went without wearing one and didn't notice its absence. But suddenly, by that one question, it had assumed an importance that hadn't existed previously.

She looked across the room at Asif. How handsome and composed he looked. Proud, too. Or was she imagining it? Did Asif *look like* a Muslim? Sushma wondered! He didn't sport a beard or anything. His nose wasn't hooked. And he didn't wear a cap. To her he looked like any other Indian. Any other Indian? She stopped herself. God! That was a strange thing to think. Asif *was* an Indian. Sushma's attention was diverted as an old aunt cornered her. "Tell me... will you start eating beef now?" she asked. Sushma shrugged, "I've been eating beef off and on for years anyway so it won't be something new to me."

The aunt's eyes widened, "Do your parents know this? You must be the first person in our family to have tasted beef. But then, you are also the first person to marry a...a...Muslim."

Sushma turned away quickly, stung by the crudity of her aunt's observation. But then she was known in their family for her directness. She was the one who rarely minced words. People were accustomed to her blunt dismissals and Sushma had often been at the receiving end of her harsh pronouncements She had wondered about it too. Unlike her cousins, Sushma was a quiet, withdrawn girl and most times, people left her alone. That included her parents. But something about her personality invariably provoked her aunt into giving her a mouthful. That evening she'd only just begun. "Is it true Muslim men make their wives have a hair bath after conjugal relations? Imagine shampooing in the middle of the night on your honeymoon. Rather inconsiderate, don't you think? Inconvenient and obvious too. And what if you make love more than once? In our time, twice or thrice a week was the minimum during the first few months. Poor you — think of what it will be like when you're in...where is it you two are going? Somewhere cold, right? Most Indians go to a cold climate for their honeymoon. Isn't that silly? Why go somewhere to shiver? But anyway — wherever it is that you'll be going, mark my words, he'll ask you to get out of your warm bed and wash your hair."

"Excuse me...I have to talk to someone else," Sushma said, moving away but her aunt gripped her arm.

"Show me what they've given you. Let me see everything. I'm sure they've passed on trifles, thinking we won't know the difference. Had you been one of them, they'd have had to give you a lot of bride-money — they call it mehr or something. Plus, at least five different sets of jewellery. Clothes too. Lots of clothes. My neighbours are "M's" you see so I know all their customs."

Sushma moved away from her quickly. She was beginning to feel slightly sick from all the sherbet she'd drunk, just to keerp her dry mouth moist. She caught her mother's eye and thought she looked sad but noticing Sushma, she recomposed her expression swiftly and shot her a kind glance. That was very brave of her, Sushma thought. She was beginning to feel rather miserable herself. The evening had been carefully orchestrated so that both sides maintained a cool distance. It resembled a cease-fire in Beirut, Sushma thought. All it needed was one stone to set things off. Or maybe she was overreacting as usual. Asif moved easily from one

small group to the next. Maitreyee, one of Sushma's competitive
cousins, came up to her and whispered, "He's quite sexy—your
Asif. I hear Muslim men are great in bed. True? Well-hung and
all that. Also very demanding. You'll probably be making love—
and babies—all the time. Look at Benazir Bhutto—she conceives
the minute that husband of hers gets out of jail. By the way, your
saree is nice. I don't know what I'd expected to see you in — some
sort of a 'Mughal-e-Azam' outfit maybe. A great big gharara or
something. And thank God your man is not in a silly sherwani.
Nice tie — bet you gave it to him."

Sushma smiled indulgently. Maitreyee was an impulsive girl
given to shooting her mouth off. Sushma quite liked her, even
though they'd shared an uneasy relationship throughout their school
days. Uneasy on account of Maitreyee's compulsive need to outshine
Sushma in every area of activity (which wasn't difficult at all).
Sushma had always been a diligent but average student. People
expected her to do well — but not brilliantly. While Maitreyee had
been the star — a super-achiever for whom winning meant
everything. And she'd left Sushma behind in the marriage race as
well. Sushma recalled Maitreyee's wedding day when her cousin
had triumphantly told her, "See, I did it before you. I'm a married
woman now."

Sushma had congratulated her warmly before saying, "Are we
running some kind of a race?" Today, as she listened to Maitreyee
all but gloating over her victory, Sushma felt slightly sorry for her
foolish cousin. She leaned forward and said conspiratorially. "Asif
is great in bed, just great. You can't imagine how terrific our sex
life is. I'm so lucky."

Maitreyee stared at Sushma incredulously. "Can't imagine this
is you talking. You were always such a bloody prude. I'm shocked,
really shocked. What's got into you?"

Sushma smiled. "That's what happens when you marry a Muslim,"
she said softly. And winked. Leaving Maitreyee with her jaw dropped
and eyes widened, disapproval written all over her face.

Later, back in their bridal suite, Sushma turned to Asif, "I'm a little confused," she said. "I hope we've both done the right thing."

Asif held her by the shoulders. "Don't tell me you're scared...or sceptical...after all that we've been through. What matters is that our parents have confidence in us. Who cares about the others? Remember the number of times they tried to break it up? The boys they showed you? The girls I was asked to meet? Listen Sushma, we are in this together and forever. There is no room for doubt. Not now."

Sushma looked way from the flower-bedecked bed. For a minute she felt nauseous — the clinging, over-sweet fragrance of the blossoms was too heady. "What will happen to our children? How will they cope? What will they be — Hindu or Muslim?"

Asif smiled indulgently and kissed his wife. "Let's first make them, shall we? I don't mind starting right now."

While they rested on bolsters much later, Sushma thought of the first time she'd met Asif at a friend's home. He'd volunteered to drop her back and she'd promptly agreed, attracted by his quiet confidence, his beige sports shirt and old-world manners. Two days later, he'd phoned and hesitantly suggested a meeting. Sushma had accepted promptly, her mind racing ahead, thinking of a suitable outfit for their date. It was only months after they'd been seeing each other regularly (and exclusively) that Sushma was jolted by her mother's abrupt question. "Asif is a Muslim boy...do you know what you're doing?"

Sushma had stared at her mother disbelievingly, "I know he's Muslim — so what?"

Her mother had sighed. "Don't dismiss it with a 'so what'? If you are serious about this relationship, there are going to be problems. Your father has been asking me questions. What shall I tell him?"

Sushma had sat down on her narrow bed before saying, "There's nothing to tell him right now. But, suppose some time in the future, if we do decide something..." Before she could complete her sentence, her mother interrupted her brusquely, "Decide *what*?

If you are thinking of marrying that man, forget it. We will never accept this marriage. Think of the family sometimes. These sort of marriages never really work....you'll be miserable. Besides, nobody will marry your sister. People from our community will shun us. Don't be so utterly foolish. Normally you are a sensible girl. Sushma had laughed a little bitterly at that. "I'm sick of being sensible. For the first time in my life I'm feeling happy, really happy... and I don't want to spoil it all by being sensible."

Her mother hadn't allowed her to finish. She had rushed out of the room, her face flushed and angry. Sushma had experienced deep shame at her mother's reaction. She'd always thought theirs was a "progressive" family. Her father often lectured the children at the table on how lucky they were to be growing up in a free India — an India free of prejudice. He'd talk to them about the great virtues of secularism and quote passages from Iqbal and Tagore during the course of the evening. He had Muslim colleagues at his office who were invited home for parties. Often, the families spent weekends together, relishing handi biryani and gushing over phirni. During Ramzan, it was the done thing to go to the crowded Bhendi Bazaar and eat at the food stalls lining the majestic green Masjid. Sushma herself had gone to school where students thought more about shopping trips to Hong Kong than of each other's religions. Damn it, theirs was a modern family. Devoid of hang-ups. Sushma had been shocked at her mother's words. And far too embarrassed to repeat them to Asif.

When the time came for the families to finally meet, after several stormy sessions between the respective children, Asif had been the calmer of the two. "Let me handle this," he'd told Sushma, "I've done a good job with my own people. It wasn't easy...but some sort of a breakthrough has been made. I'll talk to yours."

The chosen setting had been "neutral" — an impersonal five-star coffee shop. Behind the surface politeness, both sets of parents had been ill-at-ease and watchful. It had needed Sushma's mother to get the agenda for the evening off the ground. "We are not happy with this at all, I'm sorry to say," she had declared in an unnaturally loud voice. Sushma had tried to stop her at that point by placing a restraining hand over her arm.

Asif had intervened quietly to say, "It has been a difficult decision for Sushma and me as well. We are here to seek your blessings and guidance on how best to formalise our relationship without causing additional awkwardness to anyone."

Asif's father has then spoken up to say, "This has been a shock to our people too. But now that Asif had made up his mind we have no choice but to accept his decision. Your daughter will henceforth be considered a part of our family...our only son's wife. We will try our best to make her happy."

When Sushma reached her home, located in a leafy, shaded bylane off Carmichael Road in the early afternoon of Marth 6th, she found her father-in-law waiting for her in the small foyer of their building. She was surprised to see him. He was a frail man with a nagging heart condition who rarely ventured out of his booklined study on the fourth-floor of an old building which did not have a lift. Sushma's first thought was that something had happened to Asif. Afzalbhai, her father-in-law, shook his head and waved his hands to indicate all was well with her husband.

"Why are you waiting downstairs in that case?" she asked him. He answered her slowly and carefully. "What has happened to our city is terrible — just terrible. I was afraid whether you'd be able to reach home safely. There is trouble on the streets—or so the servants were saying."

Sushma walked slowly up the four flights with him. "I haven't got the news...the full news...how bad is it? What does the BBC say?"

Afzalbhai wheezed as they continued climbing. "What can they say? They've been giving numbers...details of deaths...what else? Such a horrible thing...who could have done it? A demon, only a demon."

Sushma asked gently, "Is Asif home?"

He shook his head, "I have told him to stay at his colleague's house at Churchgate. I wasn't sure what to do...not after what happened last time."

The house was still and quiet as the two of them went inside. Local TV reports about the bomb blasts had just started to trickle in.

Sushma shuddered at the memory of the "last time"....it had been a month after her marriage, almost to the date. The smell of something burning had woken her up. Something fairly close to her. She'd shaken her husband awake and whispered, "I think there's a fire in the house....I can smell it."

Asif had sniffed sleepily and then stirred himself awake. "Maybe the watchmen have lit a fire to keep themselves warm. They do that at this time of the year. Go back to sleep...it's nothing."

Sushma had tried to, but minutes later she'd heard the shouts. And then the cries. "*Maro, maro.*" This time she'd grabbed Asif's shoulders urgently and said, "Wake up....something's wrong...Asif...I can hear screams."

Just then there had been an insistent knocking on their bedroom door and Sushma had heard her mother-in-law calling out to them in a terror-filled voice. They'd opened the door and the two old people had rushed in, their faces pale and strained. "Riots," they had whispered in lowered voices as if afraid someone would overhear them. "They've broken out again. Don't go out into the balcony. Don't switch on the lights. Let's all pretend to be asleep."

Asif had stared at Sushma. "Riots? In this area? Impossible. How can that happen?" He left the three of them in the bedroom, and went out into the open balcony that looked out onto the main street.

Sushma had tried to keep her in-laws calm by saying, "Don't worry, whatever it is, the police will be here soon...someone must have telephoned."

Asif came in minutes later and the expression on his face was clearly read by all of them. "It looks serious. There are hundreds

197

of slum dwellers downstairs. I can see flames beyond our compound walls — obviously their huts have been set on fire. These are the people from that small hill — women, children. I'm going downstairs to see what can be done."

Afzalbhai had grabbed his son. "Don't be crazy. Have you lost your mind? They'll kill you. Think of Sushma. Think of us....someone is sure to tell them you're a Muslim. And then?"

Asif was swiftly changing into his jeans. "They won't kill me. I have to go. Don't worry...nothing's going to happen."

Seeing how determined Asif was, Sushma had decided to join him and went into the bathroom to change. Her mother-in-law was seated on the bed when she emerged in a salwar-kameez. "Don't leave us alone...stay here please," she had pleaded, her eyes wide with fear.

Sushma put an arm around her reassuringly. "Asif may need me downstairs too...I'll be back quickly."

She had run down rapidly, scraping her arm against the rough banisters. She saw Asif in the centre of a large crowd of wailing women. Other residents from their building were beginning to emerge from their flats gradually. "Watchman, watchman — call the police. Throw all these people out. Lock the gates? What are you fellows doing? Sleeping? Why have you allowed this crowd in?"

Sushma watched as an armed mob gathered outside the compound shouting, "Hand over these people to us...kill them. Kill the traitors...send them back to Pakistan. Bastards. Whores. Bitches."

Asif was trying to pacify the maddened crowd at the entrance by holding up his hands and pleading with them. Someone from the third floor yelled out to him, "Asifbhai, forget your histrionics. Go home, go home. These people are trouble-makers. Goondas. We don't want them here. Throw them out, watchmen."

Asif appealed to his neighbours to keep calm by folding his hands and saying, "These are unarmed women, helpless children. Let's keep them here in safety, at least till the police arrive."

Suddenly, a voice from the fifth floor boomed, "Arrey you miya... why don't you shut up. Bloody Pakistani spy. If your heart is bleeding for these filthy slumwallahs, you can join them in their huts yourself. We don't want to get involved."

Obviously encouraged by the man on the fifth floor, another neighbour shouted, "These bloody mullahs think they can get away with murder. Pampered, fucking bastards. Asif, are you protecting these people because they are Katuas? Watchmen, ask them if they're Hindus or Muslims." The watchmen shouted back, "Muslims, saab. It's a Muslim slum."

The crowd outside roared. "Traitors. Kill them. Rapists. Thieves. Taking over our country....we won't let them get out of here alive. They've just killed two of our people. We'll make them pay for it."

Sushma went up to the gate and dragged Asif back. "Go upstairs," she urged him, "It's no use...our neighbours are beyond reason. Nobody will be able to control them if the slum people succeed in jumping over. I'll talk to the neighbours..." She hesitated before adding softly, "They'll listen to me...because...because...I'm a Hindu. I'm like them".

"You are such a fool," Sushma's mother told her over the phone the next morning, "as if in such a situation anybody cares who or what you are. You could have been killed. Taking such a risk to save that man — that husband of yours — I still can't accept him as one of us. I'm sorry."

Sushma tried to tell herself that her mother was probably overwrought. It had been a trying, traumatic night for the entire city. Sushma hadn't yet summoned up the courage to read the newspapers. But from what the servants were saying, she knew it had been a horrendous night. She could hear her mother-in-law talking to relatives in Baroda. "Who could have thought something like this would happen in Bombay — in this area at that? Nobody is safe anymore. Bombay is finished. If it hadn't been for Sushma, we don't know what those Hindus would've done to us. They are butchering our people all over the city. I told Asif to stay home — but would he listen? Anyway, he has reached his office safely, that much I know."

Sushma trembled at the memory of being jostled, pushed and tripped the previous night. At one point she had been sure the mob would trample over her. She'd overheard one of the watchmen telling the leader of the Hindu mob that had arrived to deal with the slum dwellers, "She says she is a Hindu. But she is married to a miya. They must have converted her. As if they leave our women alone. Now she is calling herself a Hindu because it suits her. But what is her surname? Ask her?" It was the same watchman who had come to her seeking help for getting his young daughter admitted into a primary school.

Her mother-in-law was droning on. "Soon we'll be starving here. The mutton man hasn't come. Nor the egg-and-bread fellow. Who knows? Maybe they were stabbed on their way to our house. Maybe they've fled to their village. Everything is so uncertain. We are thinking of leaving this building...after all, we are surrounded on all sides by Hindus. They could break down our doors and kill us any time — nobody would come to our help, I can tell you."

Sushma felt intensely sorry listening to her. Yes, she was over-reacting. But the times were such. Everybody was on edge and suspicious. Some of the Parsee teachers at school had declared their "neutral" status by issuing a statement that read, "While we condemn what's going on in Bombay, we would like to state that, we Parsees are not involved and must not be forced to take sides". The class teacher of Standard VB had come up to Sushma during the tea-break to say, "It must be so difficult for you. Whose side are you really on — your husband's or your father's?" Sushma had repeated the comment to Asif later and promptly regretted it. Now, overhearing her mother-in-law's garbled conversation, she was beginning to wonder. People had always said mixed marriages rarely worked. And Sushma would smile knowingly to herself. After all, she knew better. Look at hers. She had integrated so easily, taken to their ways. Asif had told her repeatedly she was free to keep an altar with Hindu gods in her room if she wanted to. He'd encouraged her to celebrate Diwali...bought mithai home...burst crackers in the balcony, till Sushma had protested mildly. "I'm not a child to enjoy crackers. Diwali has nothing to do with noise. Let's just enjoy the lights around us and be happy." The relief on his face had been obvious enough.

As soon as her mother-in-law disconnected the phone, it rang again. The call was for Sushma. It was a college friend who worked for a city eveninger. "Sushma, are you. o.k? I heard there was trouble in your area last night. In your compound itself — right? Want to talk about it? I can send a reporter over. And a photographer too, of course."

Sushma took a deep breath before saying, "Look...I don't want to talk about it. It was a harrowing experience...terrible...I still haven't recovered....so please don't send anyone." But the woman had continued, "Would you prefer to talk over the phone? I can take down your quotes — no problem. We are looking for a human-interest story...you know....one of those 'I was there' type of things."

Sushma interrupted her, "I said I don't want to discuss this, o.k?"

The woman had refused to give up. "I can always call later...when you're calmer...it will be an exclusive. I'll play it up on the front page...trust me."

Sushma had failed to keep the contempt out of her voice as she snapped, "I don't think you've understood....or perhaps I haven't made myself clear — leave me out of this. I've been through enough."

The woman cut in, "Wait, wait, wait....don't hang up. This is just my point — my angle — people are fed up. But if everyone says, 'leave me out of it', how will the truth emerge?"

Sushma said tiredly, "That's your job. Get it out of someone else, not me."

The woman sneered, "What a cowardly attitude. Must say I didn't expect this from you. Don't you understand your being married to a Muslim makes you different? A first-person account of what you went through — all the contradictions and confusions of your position would make a great story. A scoop."

Sushma said firmly, "Look, I'm hanging up now. Try some other victim."

The woman hissed, "I can still run the story, you know—based on this very conversation. Let people know what a chicken-heart you are. Afraid to stick your neck out. Why? Because of your husband. Scared, aren't you? Scared they'll come for you if you say something. Well, they'll come for you anyway. Let me tell you one thing — you are screwed. Fucked. Whichever way you look at it." And she rang off.

Sushma was shaking — a combination of rage and fear. Her first thought was 'How dare this woman ring me up out of the blue and talk to her like that. Threaten me'. The fear was equally real. Maybe there *was* some truth in what she'd said. Maybe they would come for her — whosoever "they" were. And maybe her marriage had been a horrible mistake. She recalled an old uncle telling her father, "You people in the name of liberalism are letting Hinduism down. What nonsense is this? Why didn't you stop your daughter from committing this madness? Remember, this absurd decision will cost her dearly. It is sheer obstinacy on her part, nothing else. And lack of firmness on your part." His wife had added maliceously. "This is what happens when you allow girls to have too much freedom. Look at my Nisha — how happy she is! And who found the boy for her? We did. This Sushma of yours was always stubborn — even as a child. Quiet and stubborn — fooling everybody into thinking her silence was meekness. But I always knew. Now see what she's done. Disgraceful, I tell you." Sushma had agitatedly asked her parents later why they'd listened to such talk without objecting or protesting. She'd cried, "You could at least have defended me...protected me. I'm not marrying a villain....a murderer...a convict. So what if he's a Muslim?"

So what if he's a Muslim? The irony of those words sank into her as the journalist's cruel taunts continued to ring in her ears.

What had happened to the city? Had everybody gone mad? People were beginning to sound like raving lunatics. There had been riots before. Communal riots. People had been killed. But life had also gone on without ordinary citizens being forced to take sides. Choose. This was new. And Sushma was certain this was only the beginning. But there was nobody she could tell that to. Not even Asif.

The following weeks were nightmarish for Sushma. One of the teachers at school asked her solicitously, "So...will you be joining one of the Peace Groups in your area? I believe things are still tense there." Sushma pretended she hadn't heard her and tried to change the subject. The woman wouldn't give up, "Have they started house-to-house searches in your neighbourhood? They have in our complex. Just yesterday some men had come to ask questions about the residents — how many Muslim families? Which floors? Thank God we don't have any 'M's in our building. But the next block is full of them—dirty people. We told them to go there."

Sushma whirled around. "You actually directed them to the place?"

The teacher smiled. "What else? We're sick of them anyway. Can't keep a track of their wives and children. The way those people multiply...soon there'll be more of them than us."

Sushma was aghast but decided to keep quiet. The teacher looked at her pityingly. "But for you, it's different...you don't know what or who you are."

Sushma flared up and said, "I beg your pardon. I know very well who I am. I am a Hindu woman married to a Muslim. Does that make me some sort of a freak? I'm sick of talk like this. It is because of people like you that Bombay is getting ruined."

The woman said impassively, "I'm sorry....I don't agree. It's because of people like you....people with a mixed identity and no loyalty that not just our city but our country is getting finished. In your place, I would go to the slums and do something. Look at other citizens from posh areas — they are holding fasts and demonstrations."

Sushma snorted derisively, "Don't equate me with those

hypocrites. They are doing it for themselves. To save their own precious skins. Go to their homes and find out how they treat their servants—worse than slaves. Underpaid, underfed slaves with no time off. It has become fashionable to join all these groups. Well...I don't care what you people think, I'm staying away."

The teacher responded smugly, "At least I'm doing something here — right here in school. In my own small way, I'm contributing. Ask the children in my class. Today we discussed what's going on in Bombay openly. I encouraged them to talk. You should have heard some of the comments...Even the children are blaming the 'M's. Mind you I didn't prompt them or anything. They came out with all this stuff themselves. Children these days are smart. They know what's going on."

Sushma sighed and packed up her red plastic snack box. She hadn't touched her sandwiches. "Children only repeat parrot-fashion what they've been hearing at home. Don't forget, our kids are primarily from Hindu backgrounds."

The teacher bristled. "And why not? After all, we are a primarily Hindu country, Mrs. Khan, in case you'd forgotten. It's time we stopped feeling so apologetic about it. I've put up a sticker on my door at home. I'm sure you know the one I'm talking about: *'Gaurav se kaho hum Hindu hain.'* I'm very proud of it, too. So is my husband. And my children. We celebrate all our festivals. Wait till you have to celebrate yours husband's — then the fun will begin."

As Sushma walked back wearily to her class, she thought about that word — fun. How could her colleague have used it, even as a barb? There was nothing "funny" about the situation. It was tragic. And pathetic.

She sensed hostility each time she walked into her building these days. Sushma's mother-in-law overheard the bai who scrubbed vessels in four of the flats gossiping with the other servants. "This family is not wanted here by the neighbours. I'm not saying it — after all, I have to feed my children. A job is a job, whether it's in a Hindu or a Muslim home. But the lady on the third floor was telling me to leave the job. She said my life could also be in danger if I continued to work for Muslims. Last night some goondas had come to the compound. They were doing dadagiri downstairs and asking the watchman about Asifbhai. These people should shift somewhere else, at least till everything settles down."

The other servant spoke in low tones, "I have been with them for ten years. No problem. But now I'm also thinking—after all, we are poor people. If anything happens, we'll be the first to be attacked. They'll kill them....sure...but only after they kill us. That's what the night watchman said."

The bai continued scrubbing vigorously. "The problem is the new daughter-in-law. Everybody asks me. 'How has she adjusted? Has she become a Muslim?' I don't know what to say. If the neighbours are keeping quiet, it's because of her. She's all right, I suppose. But what made her marry one of them?"

The old cook shook his head, "That is what I've also been wondering about. Modern girls are beyond anybody's control. In our village too, young people are behaving irresponsibly — marrying anyone, doing anything. Times are such...bad times. Two men were killed near the vegetable market yesterday. Stoned."

The bai stopped scrubbing. "Did you see it?'

"No," he said, "I went later."

"But were the bodies still there?"

The cook looked distinctly disappointed as he shook his head. "The police had taken them away...but the neighbour's cook saw them."

The bai lowered her voice, looked over her shoulder and asked, "Were these men one of us....or them?"

The cook placed his finger on his lips and whispered gleefully, "Them...them."

The bai looked relieved as she sent up a silent prayer heavenwards before saying, "Thank God."

Sushma's mother-in-law moved away swiftly. She wasn't at all surprised by the conversation. These people were all the same. They ate your food, took your money...and wished you dead. But it was difficult to get Muslim servants in this area. Unless you sent for them from Lucknow or Hyderabad. And then there was no guarantee they'd stay. Bombay did that to outsiders — intimidated them. It wasn't a friendly city. And now it had proved to be heartless too. Just last night, her husband had instructed the security man on duty to remove their nameboard from the lobby. Just in case, he'd said. The man had laughed, mocked her husband, and replied, "Those who want to know where you live will find you anyway, saab...from the voter registration rolls. It's no use removing this."

The daring of the fellow. It was amazing how his attitude had changed during the past few weeks. Earlier, he'd come begging for tips on any and every occasion. She'd give him all the leftover biryani. Her son's old trousers (not the frayed ones — those she'd kept for her bai's drunkard of a husband). She'd also loaned him money for his daughter's wedding two years ago. And now the same man was talking back to them like this. They were all the same, these ungrateful Hindus. And now they'd started behaving like bosses...as if every Muslim in Bombay was their underling? And there was nothing anybody could do about it. Her husband had warned her to keep her mouth shut. Not talk too much on the phone either. Who knew whether anybody was listening? In addition, it was awkward to talk freely even within the family now that Sushma was in the house.

Whatever it was, she was still one of them. Everybody had to be extra careful not to hurt her feelings. Asif's expression was worth watching at the dining table. She felt sorry for her son. And she hardly got any time to speak to him privately. Certain decisions would have to be taken soon. Two of their cousins had made up their minds to emigrate. It would take a little time, but her mind too was made up. There was no future left for them in this country anymore. For any Muslim for that matter. That was certain. Asif could get a job anywhere with his qualifications — Canada, America, Australia, Singapore, Dubai. Of course with Sushma in the picture now, he'd have to consult her. Maybe she'd refuse.

After all, her people were all here.

Not that Asif hadn't known discrimination before all this nonsense started. Two or three companies to which he'd applied had told him frankly that he didn't stand a good chance because he was a Muslim. Just like that — straight to his face. At least they'd been honest, though unlike others who'd rejected him without any explanations and given the jobs to other candidates — inferior candidates, because they belonged to the right religion. Funny, but most people refused to face this problem. Refused to discuss it even pretending it didn't exist. So far Asif was doing well at the office. But who knew how his bosses would react when it came to a promotion? People had become so touchy and hypersensitive. Merit was no longer the issue. Or maybe, in the case of Muslims, it never had been. It was just that the double standards had now been thrown into the open. She walked back slowly to her bedroom. It felt more and more like a prison these days.

Sushma was visiting her parents to reassure them everything was fine at her home. Sushma's father was in a strange mood. She noticed anger in his otherwise gentle, faraway eyes.

"What's come over you these days, papa?" she asked, though she'd half guessed the answer.

He stared at the television set stonily, "I never approved of this marriage, Sushma. I'd felt it in my bones that you were making the wrong decision. And now, look at what's happened!"

Sushma exchanged glances with her mother. "Nothing has happened to my marriage, papa. What's happening in Bombay has little to do with me — or you. It's temporary madness. Things will settle down soon. Already, people are calmer. Life is definitely returing to normal."

Her father exploded. "Normal? What is normal? Who says things are normal? They can never be normal after this...this...terrible thing. The memory of the blasts will haunt generations. I will never trust a Muslim again. They're all anti-national, I tell you."

Sushma was shocked by the harshness of his words. He was a mild man...a man who rarely expressed such passionate opinions.

She noticed her mother's edginess and told herself not to engage either of them in an extended debate. This was one area she wasn't going to see from her parents' viewpoint ever again. Her father switched off the TV set and turned to her, saying, "I hadn't imagined that my daughter would turn into a hypocrite one day. You are talking without conviction. Your mother and I want you to know it's still not too late for you to reconsider your marriage."

Sushma felt the tears — hot tears — coursing down her face. "Reconsider? How can you say such a thing to me? I love my husband and I'm very happy with him. I came here to tell you that....not to discuss a future divorce. I'm shocked that any father could suggest such a thing to a newly married daughter. My in-laws are good people. They've been very nice to me."

Her mother looked across at her husband and said, "Let's not argue. She's here for such a short time. We hardly see her anymore."

Sushma could tell from her voice that her mother was trying very hard to defuse a potentially explosive situation. But Sushma's father's eyes were blazing as he stared at his daughter. "This is no time for political correctness. One must speak out. I'm not at a rally here...I'm in my own home. I'm free to say what I feel. Even if Asif is an exception, he will be bracketed with the rest. And so will you. What I'm saying is, come and stay with us till all this trouble blows over. We are concerned about your safety. We've heard people are going from flat-to-flat looking for Muslim surnames. Tomorrow they could come for you. I'll speak to your in-laws and tell them if you like..."

Sushma stood up abruptly. "I think I'd better go home. I'm sorry but I cannot — will not — leave my husband. I don't think anybody is going to harm us. But even if such a possibility exists, my life is now bound with him...with them."

Sushma left her mother crying pitifully as she picked up her bag and walked out.

Outside, in the cool evening air, she took several deep breaths and tried to compose herself. She'd never seen her father in such an excitable frame of mind — and it worried her. He was a calm sort of person, not given to overreaction. Her mother too was not the sort of woman who burst into tears when confronted by a crisis. What had come over them all? Or was she missing something significant? The twenty-minute drive to her home seemed interminable that day. She stared at people on the street without really seeing them. Busy people. Bombay was full of them — hundreds and thousands of anonymous little worker ants scurrying around, going from God-knows-where-to-God-knows-where, with anxious frowns and distracted expressions, on their faces. She noticed a sticker on the car right ahead of her. It repeated the "*gaurav se kaho*...." slogan. Sushma started looking for the same, orange-coloured sticker on other cars. Quite a few of them had it displayed prominently on the rear windshield or bumper. She wondered what Asif's old driver, Farouqbhai, thought of all this. Sushma would have liked to ask him, but knew better.

The previous afternoon, the bai had come to her room, ostensibly to borrow fifty rupees. She'd chosen the time wisely—Sushma's mother-in-law had left to visit her niece in the suburbs. After loitering around near the door of Sushma's room the bai had said in a low voice, "I don't like asking for loans, usually, but what to do? Times are difficult these days. There is curfew in our area. All the vegetable vendors have gone away. I have to walk two extra kilometres to look for scraps — rotten cabbage leaves and dried up pumpkin. My family lives on rice...gruel. We are too afraid to get out of our chawl. I am forced to come here. Because I must feed them."

Sushma didn't want to appear unconcerned or unsympathetic but she could sense the bai's mood and didn't want to encourage her. Withour being asked, the woman squatted companionably on the floor next to where Sushma was relaxing on the bed. She opened her paan pouch and busied herself with the dried tobacco leaves and lime. "I've been working here for eighteen years," she told Sushma, "I've seen Asifbhai as a child. Such a sweet boy. Very generous. Very kind. The parents too...good people...considering they're Muslims." Sushma pretended she

209

hadn't heard, refusing even to look up from the magazine she was flipping through. The bai carried on. 'They are my maa-baap. Like my parents. I have eaten their salt. Why should I lie? "They've treated me well. But now I'm thinking...should I look for another job?"

Sushma turned to her and exclaimed, "That's absurd. Why should you leave a place where you've been happy? There is no problem here for you — you get your pay, and it's a good one, two sarees, food, loans. What more do you want?"

The bai chewed her paan thoughtfully, "Life is more than just a good salary. My neighbours are telling me to quit. I've tried to convince them that these people are different. 'Look', I told them, 'they even have a Hindu daughter-in-law — one of us. Would they have agreed to the marriage if they'd been like the others?' But they don't. I can understand their anger....so many of our people have been killed by them. So many."

Sushma put down her magazine. "Why do you believe all these stories? Most of the reports are nothing but rumours. Do you know anyone who was killed? Has anybody from your chawl been directly attacked?"

The bai sighed and beat her forehead with her palm, "The things I've seen. The things I've heard...late in the night...I've seen with my own eyes...trucks and trucks with knives, guns, swords.... for those people. Muslims. People who we've grown up with all our lives. These same people will use the weapons to kill us in our beds...murder us in our sleep. They are treacherous...very treacherous."

Sushma said flatly, "I don't believe you. And if what you're saying is true, why didn't anybody tell the police?"

The bai laughed, "The police!" she said disdainfully, "Those impotent fellows. Those eunuchs. What will they do? And do you think they don't know about all this? People move around openly in our locality waving choppers in our face — challenging us to stop them, report them. Now our men too have begun arming themselves.

210

Sushma stood up. She was surprised to find herself breathing heavily. She glanced at her image in the mirror on the opposite wall — her pale skin was flushed, her nostrils flared. "Stop this nonsense," she told the bai angrily, "You have no right to talk rubbish like this — it's dangerous. You could land yourself in trouble — and land us in a mess along with you."

The bai got up and tucked her pouch into her saree. "We people — poor people — are simple. We don't understand politics. We react to what we see...feel...experience. Right now the men in my chawl take turns to sleep at night. Our children are kept locked up in the house. The same people we used to mingle with freely all these years have turned into killers. Should we just wait for their knives? No. We must fight back....save ourselves before they finish us. That is my advice to you even though I know it will make you angry. Save yourself... there's still time."

Sushma couldn't bear to read the newspapers any more. Asif told her she was being a coward. She felt embarrassed to watch "The News" on television along with the rest of the family. She knew her father-in-law was suppressing his comments in deference to her presence. Sometimes though, unable to contain himself, he'd mutter, "Hopeless. Hopeless. Biased reporting. Partisan propaganda." And then he'd look guiltily towards Sushma to see whether she'd heard....and reacted.

Asif had also become apologetic, especially late at night, when he found her restless and awake, her entire being focused on the sound of sirens shrieking down the main road, or the clang of bells as fire-engines speeded off to douse yet another conflagration somewhere—a cluster of shops, shanty town, a godown. Asif would stroke her face, her bare arms, the nape of her neck and say, "It will all be over soon...think of it as a nightmare."

Sushma knew that too. What he wasn't saying — not yet — was that he was thinking, planning, finding out discreetly if, as everybody said, there was no hope left for the likes of him in India, where should he relocate? Sushma had heard him talking to his parents at the dining table early one morning. She'd seen her husband walk to the phone and make a long-distance call to a cousin in Florida. "What's it like out there? Recession's pretty bad, we hear...how bad? How's the job market?" He hadn't said a word about it to her and she'd been too scared to ask. Asif was thinking about emigrating. And he hadn't thought of consulting his wife.

Sushma brought up the topic with her mother-in-law a few days later. She'd planned on her opening line. It had to be tangential and vague since she didn't want to reveal just how little she knew. And she didn't want to let Asif down. "America is a nice place," she said brightly. Her mother-in-law nodded and Sushma continued, "I've been there once with my parents. I liked it a lot. You must have gone too....Asif mentioned a holiday with a cousin in Florida." The other woman busied herself folding washed clothes and said nothing at all. It was her way of letting Sushma know that the subject was not open to discussion so far as she was concerned. Which only meant that Asif hadn't yet worked out the problem in his own mind and seen it through or else he would have included Sushma in the decision. It hurt her to think that was the reason — the only reason she alone had been left out of the family discussion. And once again a familiar doubt began to haunt Sushma — had they excluded her deliberately because she was a Hindu? An "outsider" in their midst? Didn't they trust her? Would they ever? Were they that suspicious?

At Asif's uncle's funeral, she heard her husband say to a distant cousin, "I'm convinced there is no future left for us in India...I've never been so depressed in my life. I can't concentrate at work. And even at home...well, things are just not the same."

The cousin nodded his head understandingly. "We are all in the same boat, friend. You know what happened to our neighbour's shop — the big one at the traffic lights? It was burnt down, burnt to cinders overnight. All his workers have left. He has not yet put a figure on his losses....lakhs...maybe crores. How will he have the heart or the energy to start again? It's hopeless."

Sushma saw the despair in Asif's eyes and she felt her own welling up. Was running away the answer? She'd begun to feel alienated from her own parents. Every topic led to just one subject. The atmosphere bristled each time she visited. At work too, she found it hard to answer questions posed by children in her class. A co-teacher commented, "You are being paranoid, Sushma. Forget it... after all, it isn't as if you've been affected directly or anything. Nobody you know got killed, right?" Sushma continued to correct test papers, unwilling to reopen the subject. But the words rang in her ears: "directly affected", "nobody killed". Was there nothing more to the present situation other than your own skin? That afternoon she resigned her job.

She'd been finding it increasingly difficult to cope of late. Plus, she couldn't concentrate on her classes. Even her loyal students had noticed how distracted she was. "My heart is just not in it," she'd told Asif the previous week.

"Then just fuck the job", he'd snapped irritably.

This wasn't Asif's usual language at all. But he'd started cursing a great deal—especially at her. Even as they lay together in the stillness of the night, he'd abruptly throw the covers off and stalk out of the room, cursing under his breath. She'd asked him, "Do you regret our marriage? Do you hate me for being a Hindu?" and he'd snarled, "Spare me the martyred tone... stop those cliches. It's too late for regrets in any case."

Sushma herself was changing. Changing faster than she realised. An edge of defiance had crept into small, everyday acts that had once been so unimportant to her. She'd started wearing large, elaborate bindis—especially when the family was going out together. She'd taken to displaying her simple mangalsutra prominently and stopped wearing salwar-kameezes in favour of traditional sarees. If her mother-in-law disapproved, she chose to keep quiet. It was Asif who asked her one evening, "What's all this....are you trying to tell me—us—something? I've never objected to your bindis— but I notice they're getting bigger and bigger? Stop rebelling in such a childish manner, Sushma. If you are deeply unhappy, there are ways to resolve that."

Sushma looked at him levelly, "Like how? Through your saying 'talaq' three times and declaring us divorced? Is that your grand solution?"

Asif sat down wearily. "I didn't think we'd reach this point so quickly. I didn't think I'd ever hear you utter those stupid, ignorant words."

Sushma broke down on hearing the anguish in his voice. She started to gulp rapidly in an attempt to hold back her sobs.

"Let the tears flow," he said, his voice barely a whisper, "If I could cry, I would too."

There was a flame-coloured sky outside their window and Sushma could hear the birds chirping as they returned to their nests before dusk darkened the horizon. It was that suspended time of day full of uncertainty and dread that had always scared her when she had been a child. She clung on to Asif, her slim body shaking with sorrow. "I've tried," she kept repeating, "but it isn't working. And I'm so tired". He stroked her hair and held her close. It was a familiar embrace. The only one she'd ever really known. And yet, the comfort she was seeking eluded her. Sushma didn't feel safe anymore. And Asif's strong arms felt like a cage as he tightened them around her. She felt as if she was choking, suffocating....but she didn't resist. She didn't try to free herself. She felt weak. Too weak to run. And in any case, there was nowhere left to go.

The birds had stopped chirping when Sushma turned tiredly to Asif and said, "I want to go to bed. Let's just sleep now....before the birds wake us up again."